WHAT IF WE WERE ...

AXELLE LENOIR

WHAT IF WE WERE... © 2020 AXELLE LENOIR

Published by Top Shelf Productions, an imprint of IDW Publishing, a division of Idea and Design Works, LLC. Offices: Top Shelf Productions, c/o Idea & Design Works, LLC, 2765 Truxtun Road, San Diego, CA 92106. Top Shelf Productions®, the Top Shelf logo, Idea and Design Works®, and the IDW logo are registered trademarks of Idea and Design Works, LLC. All Rights Reserved. With the exception of small excerpts of artwork used for review purposes, none of the contents of this publication may be reprinted without the permission of IDW Publishing.

IDW Publishing does not read or accept unsolicited submissions of ideas, stories, or artwork.

Editor-in-Chief: Chris Staros.
Design by Tara McCrillis.
Originally published by Curium Mag and by Front Froid.
Translation by Pablo Strauss and Aleshia Jensen.

ISBN: 978-1-60309-480-1   23 22 21 20   4 3 2 1

Visit our online catalog at topshelfcomix.com.

WHAT IF WE WERE ...

SINCE THE DAWN OF TIME (EIGHT YEARS AGO) MARIE AND NATHALIE HAVE BEEN KILLING TIME WITH THEIR FAVORITE GAME: "WHAT IF?" IT'S PRETTY SIMPLE: ONE PERSON PICKS A TOPIC – SAY, "FRUIT." THEN BOTH PLAYERS HAVE TO IMAGINE WHAT KIND OF FRUIT THEY WOULD BE. WHAT WOULD IT BE LIKE TO BE A FRUIT?

EASY TO PLAY; HARD TO MASTER. OBVIOUSLY, IF YOU GET A DEAD-END TOPIC – LIKE, SAY, "FRUIT" – OR IF THE PLAYERS ARE LACKING IN IMAGINATION, YOU'D PROBABLY HAVE MORE FUN STARING AT THE WALL. LUCKILY, MARIE AND NATHALIE ARE EXPERTS. EVEN AFTER ALL THESE YEARS, THEY NEVER FAIL TO COME UP WITH FRESH IDEAS.

LET'S MEET THE PLAYERS:

- ***NAME:*** MARIE
- ***HEIGHT:*** 5'5
- ***WEIGHT:*** SERIOUSLY? I DUNNO... LIKE A TON?
- ***FAVORITE ANIMAL:*** UHHHH... SKUNK? WHY DO YOU WANNA KNOW?
- ***ZODIAC SIGN:*** CANCER... I KNOW, IT'S THE WORST!
- ***FAVORITE TOPICS:*** HARRY POTTER, FANTASY, AND MUSHY LOVE STORIES.
- ***SPECIAL MOVE:*** CRUSHING MY OPPONENTS FOR THE WIN.
- ***ANYTHING ELSE?*** YEAH! MOM, IF YOU'RE READING THIS, I'M SLEEPING AT NAT'S TONIGHT. WE'VE GOT HOMEWORK, OR SOMETHING.

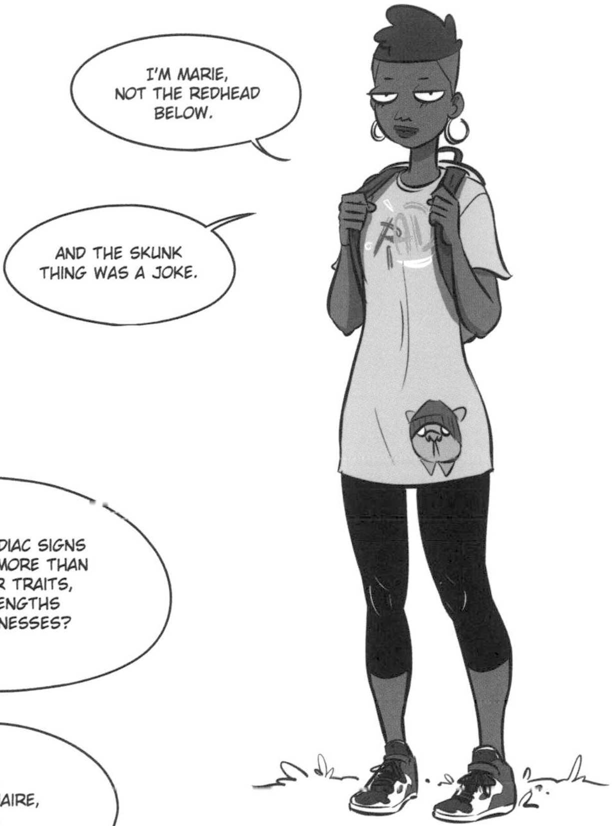
I'M MARIE, NOT THE REDHEAD BELOW.
AND THE SKUNK THING WAS A JOKE.

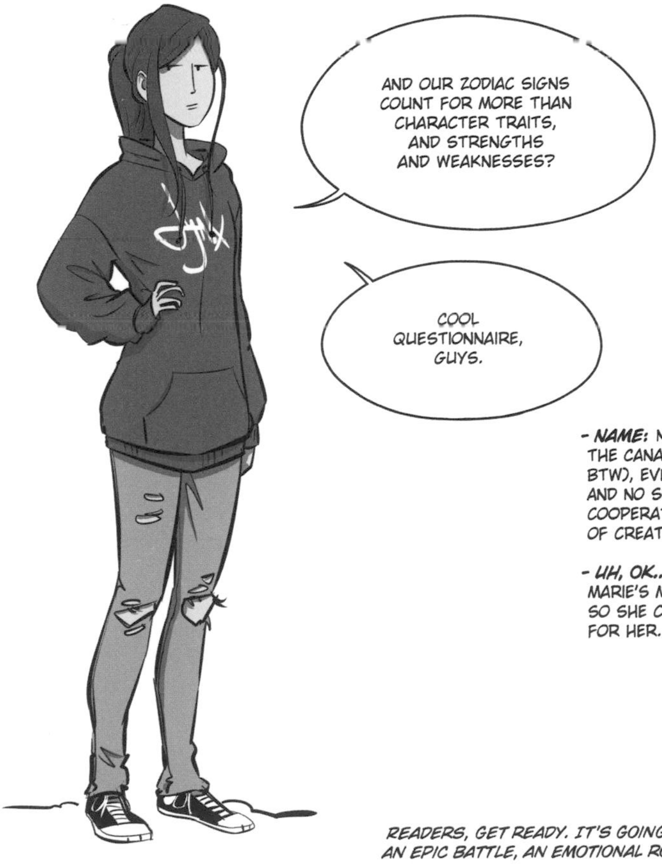
AND OUR ZODIAC SIGNS COUNT FOR MORE THAN CHARACTER TRAITS, AND STRENGTHS AND WEAKNESSES?
COOL QUESTIONNAIRE, GUYS.

- ***NAME:*** NATHALIE, 5'9, 160 LBS., AMBIVALENT CAPRICORN, THE CANADIAN LYNX (TOTALLY NOT RELEVANT TO THE GAME, BTW), EVERYTHING ASTROPHYSICS AND METAPHYSICS. AND NO SPECIAL MOVE, SINCE THE GAME IS BASED ON COOPERATION, NOT COMPETITION. (BUT SOMETIMES MY FEATS OF CREATIVITY GIVE ME GOOSEBUMPS).
- ***UH, OK... ANYTHING ELSE?*** AND BY THE WAY, MARIE'S MOM, YOUR DAUGHTER ***IS*** COMING OVER, SO SHE CAN TRY TO GET ME TO DO HER HOMEWORK FOR HER. BUT DON'T WORRY, IT'S NEVER WORKED YET.

READERS, GET READY. IT'S GOING TO BE AN EPIC BATTLE, AN EMOTIONAL ROLLER...

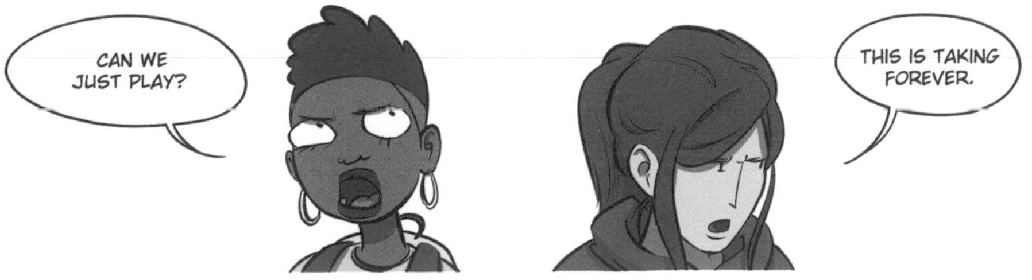
CAN WE JUST PLAY?
THIS IS TAKING FOREVER.

GAME ON!

WHAT IF WE WERE... VIKINGS

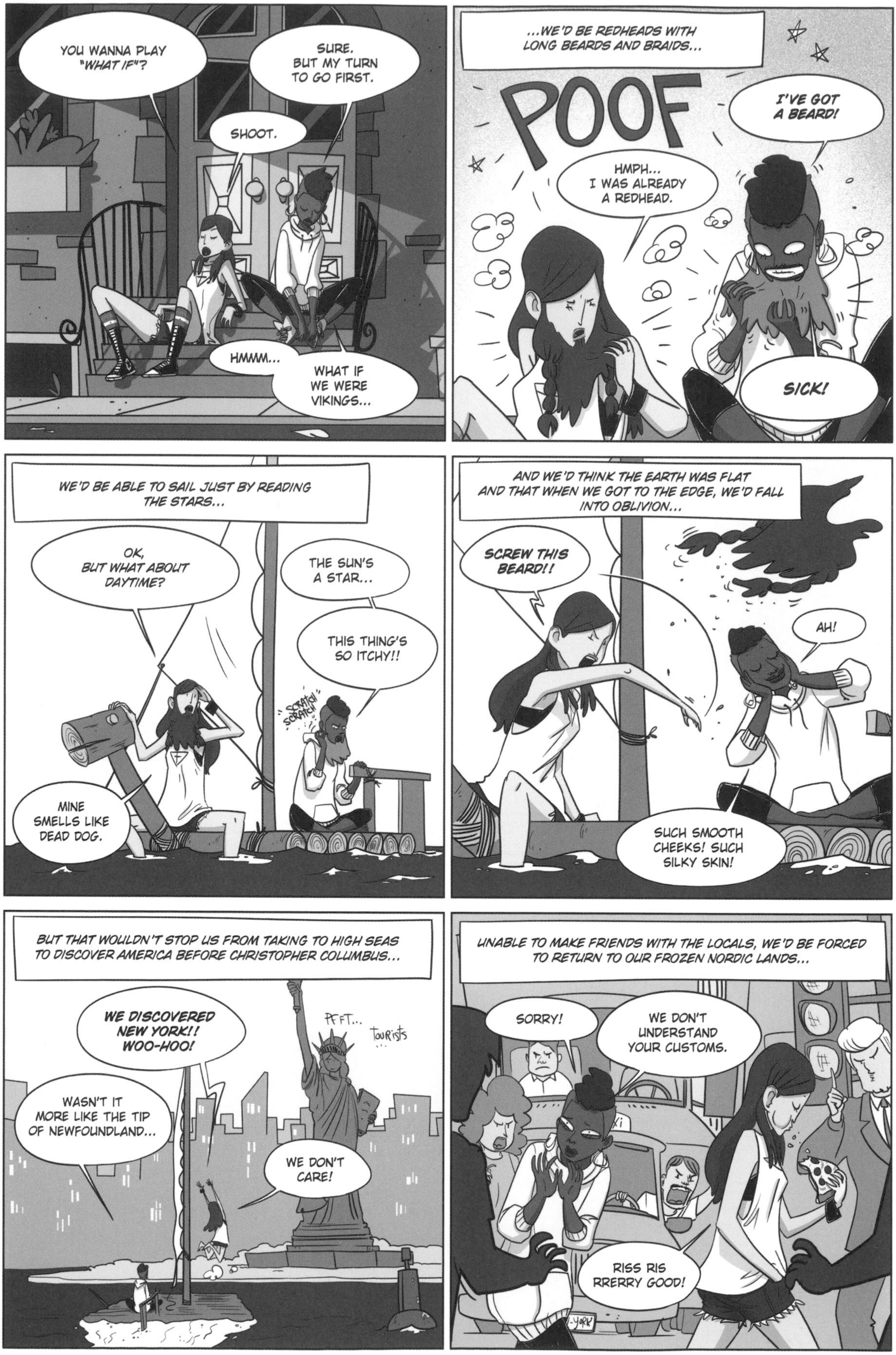

YOU WANNA PLAY "WHAT IF"?
SURE. BUT MY TURN TO GO FIRST.
SHOOT.
HMMM...
WHAT IF WE WERE VIKINGS...
...WE'D BE REDHEADS WITH LONG BEARDS AND BRAIDS...
POOF
I'VE GOT A BEARD!
HMPH... I WAS ALREADY A REDHEAD.
SICK!
WE'D BE ABLE TO SAIL JUST BY READING THE STARS...
OK, BUT WHAT ABOUT DAYTIME?
THE SUN'S A STAR...
THIS THING'S SO ITCHY!!
SCRATCH SCRATCH
MINE SMELLS LIKE DEAD DOG.
AND WE'D THINK THE EARTH WAS FLAT AND THAT WHEN WE GOT TO THE EDGE, WE'D FALL INTO OBLIVION...
SCREW THIS BEARD!!
AH!
SUCH SMOOTH CHEEKS! SUCH SILKY SKIN!
BUT THAT WOULDN'T STOP US FROM TAKING TO HIGH SEAS TO DISCOVER AMERICA BEFORE CHRISTOPHER COLUMBUS...
WE DISCOVERED NEW YORK!! WOO-HOO!
PFFT...
TOURISTS...
WASN'T IT MORE LIKE THE TIP OF NEWFOUNDLAND...
WE DON'T CARE!
UNABLE TO MAKE FRIENDS WITH THE LOCALS, WE'D BE FORCED TO RETURN TO OUR FROZEN NORDIC LANDS...
SORRY!
WE DON'T UNDERSTAND YOUR CUSTOMS.
RISS RIS RRERRY GOOD!

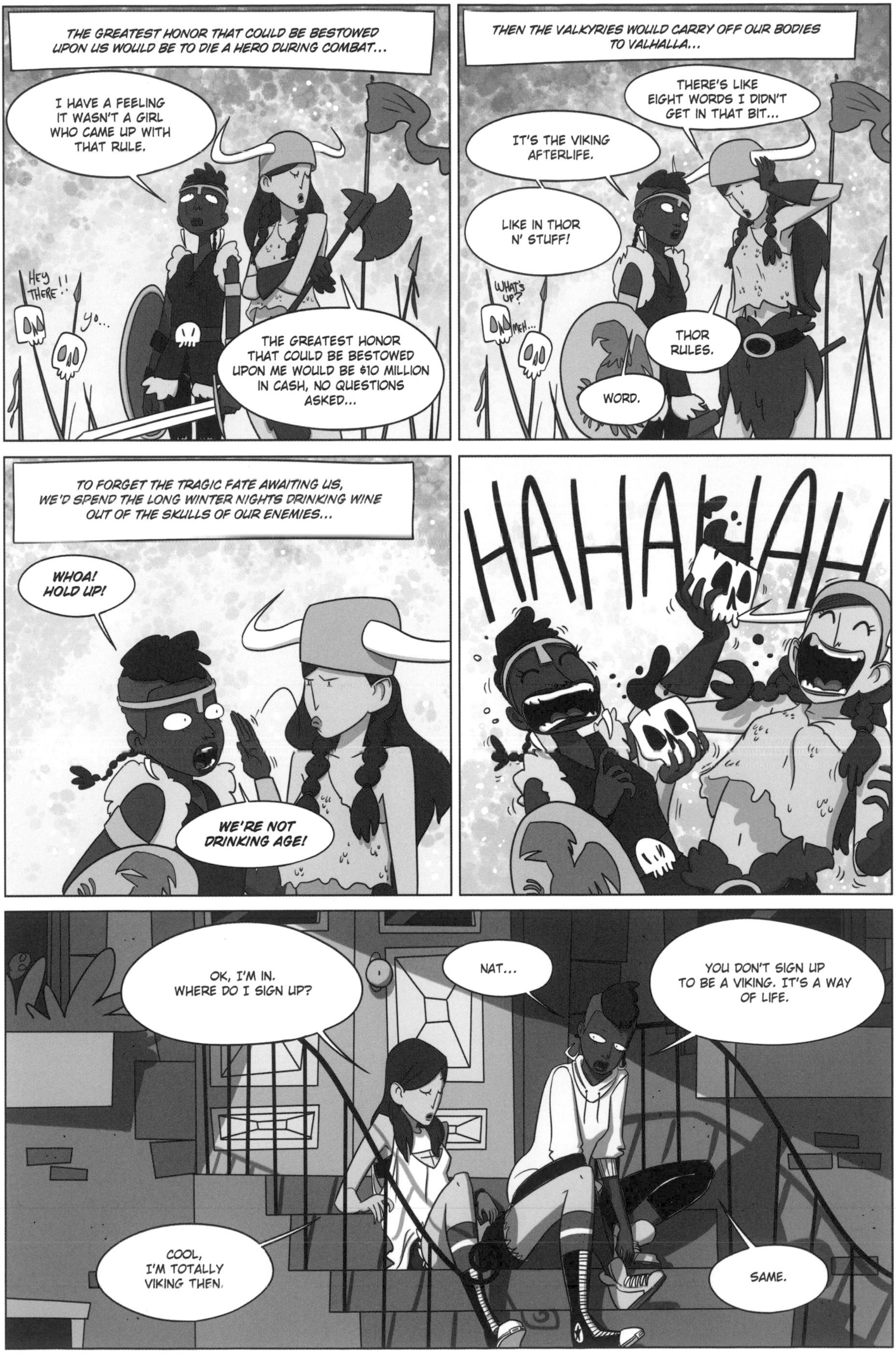
THE GREATEST HONOR THAT COULD BE BESTOWED UPON US WOULD BE TO DIE A HERO DURING COMBAT...
I HAVE A FEELING IT WASN'T A GIRL WHO CAME UP WITH THAT RULE.
HEY THERE!!
YO...
THE GREATEST HONOR THAT COULD BE BESTOWED UPON ME WOULD BE $10 MILLION IN CASH, NO QUESTIONS ASKED...
THEN THE VALKYRIES WOULD CARRY OFF OUR BODIES TO VALHALLA...
THERE'S LIKE EIGHT WORDS I DIDN'T GET IN THAT BIT...
IT'S THE VIKING AFTERLIFE.
LIKE IN THOR N' STUFF!
WHAT'S UP?
MEH...
THOR RULES.
WORD.
TO FORGET THE TRAGIC FATE AWAITING US, WE'D SPEND THE LONG WINTER NIGHTS DRINKING WINE OUT OF THE SKULLS OF OUR ENEMIES...
WHOA! HOLD UP!
WE'RE NOT DRINKING AGE!
HAHAHAH
OK, I'M IN. WHERE DO I SIGN UP?
NAT...
YOU DON'T SIGN UP TO BE A VIKING. IT'S A WAY OF LIFE.
COOL, I'M TOTALLY VIKING THEN.
SAME.

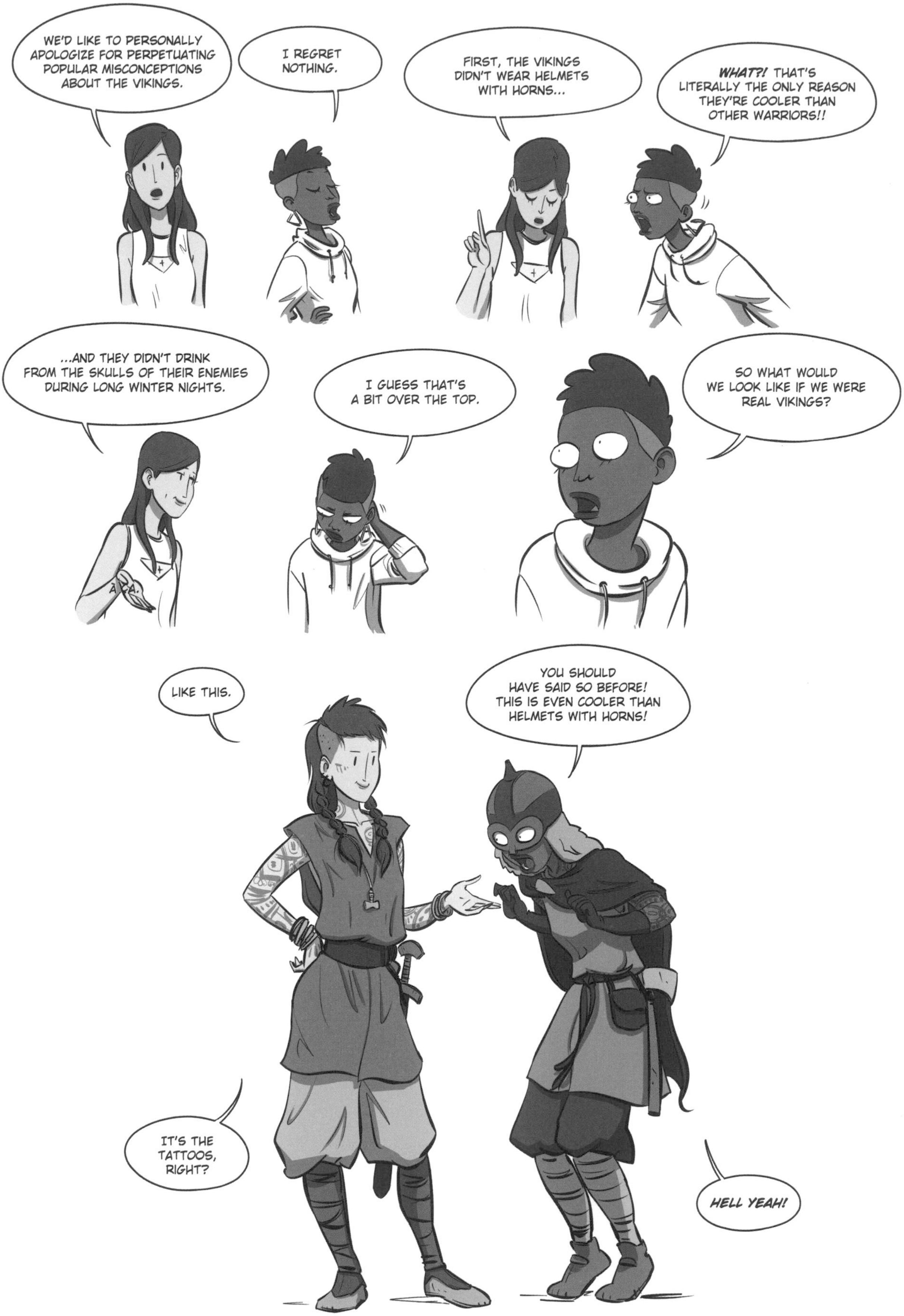
WE'D LIKE TO PERSONALLY APOLOGIZE FOR PERPETUATING POPULAR MISCONCEPTIONS ABOUT THE VIKINGS.
I REGRET NOTHING.
FIRST, THE VIKINGS DIDN'T WEAR HELMETS WITH HORNS...
WHAT?! THAT'S LITERALLY THE ONLY REASON THEY'RE COOLER THAN OTHER WARRIORS!!
...AND THEY DIDN'T DRINK FROM THE SKULLS OF THEIR ENEMIES DURING LONG WINTER NIGHTS.
I GUESS THAT'S A BIT OVER THE TOP.
SO WHAT WOULD WE LOOK LIKE IF WE WERE REAL VIKINGS?
LIKE THIS.
YOU SHOULD HAVE SAID SO BEFORE! THIS IS EVEN COOLER THAN HELMETS WITH HORNS!
IT'S THE TATTOOS, RIGHT?
HELL YEAH!

WHAT IF WE WERE... DOUBLE AGENTS

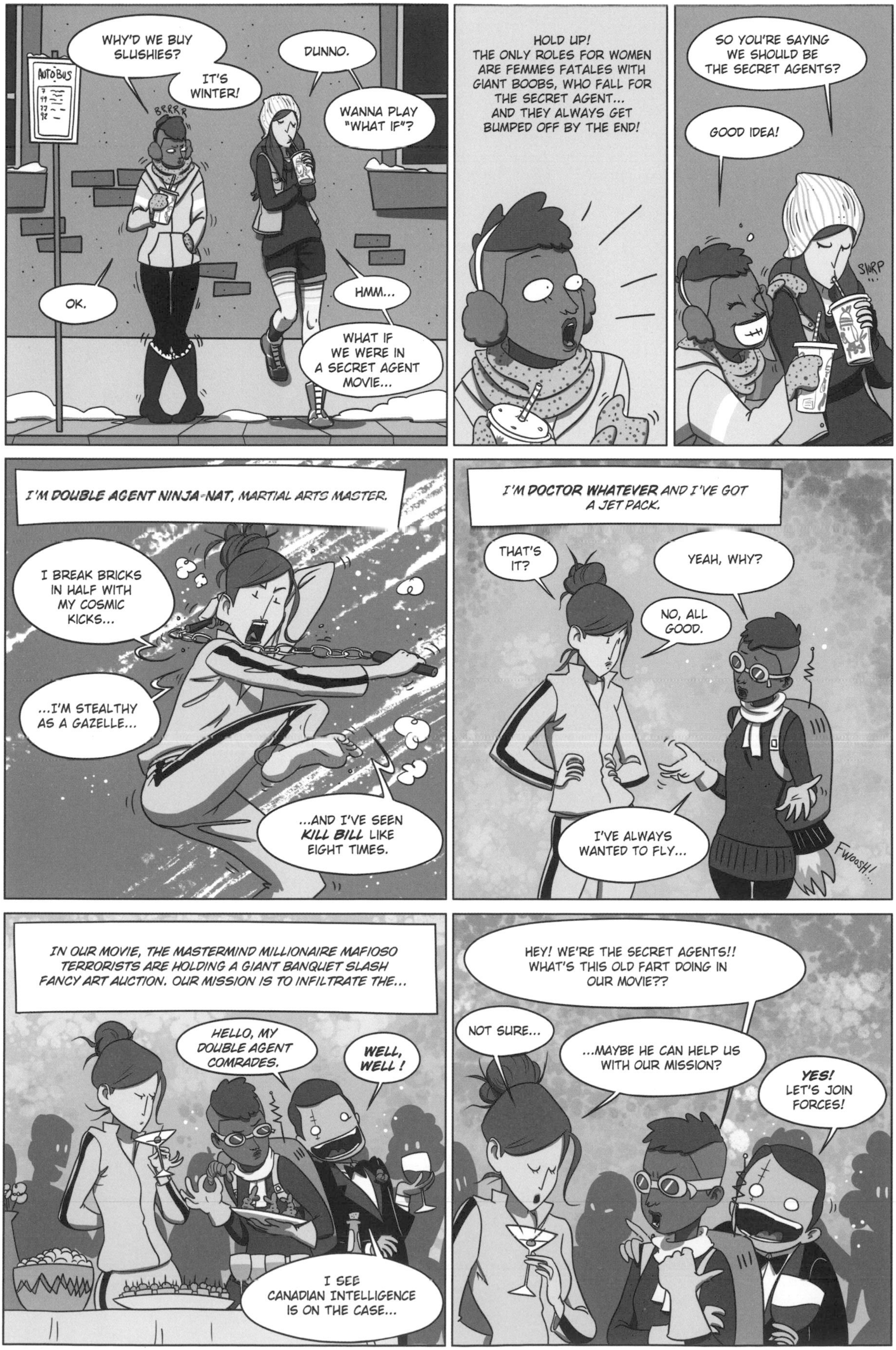

AUTOBUS
WHY'D WE BUY SLUSHIES?
IT'S WINTER!
DUNNO.
BRRRR
WANNA PLAY "WHAT IF"?
OK.
HMM...
WHAT IF WE WERE IN A SECRET AGENT MOVIE...
HOLD UP! THE ONLY ROLES FOR WOMEN ARE FEMMES FATALES WITH GIANT BOOBS, WHO FALL FOR THE SECRET AGENT... AND THEY ALWAYS GET BUMPED OFF BY THE END!
SO YOU'RE SAYING WE SHOULD BE THE SECRET AGENTS?
GOOD IDEA!
SLURP
I'M DOUBLE AGENT NINJA-NAT, MARTIAL ARTS MASTER.
I BREAK BRICKS IN HALF WITH MY COSMIC KICKS...
...I'M STEALTHY AS A GAZELLE...
...AND I'VE SEEN KILL BILL LIKE EIGHT TIMES.
I'M DOCTOR WHATEVER AND I'VE GOT A JET PACK.
THAT'S IT?
YEAH, WHY?
NO, ALL GOOD.
I'VE ALWAYS WANTED TO FLY...
FWOOSH!...
IN OUR MOVIE, THE MASTERMIND MILLIONAIRE MAFIOSO TERRORISTS ARE HOLDING A GIANT BANQUET SLASH FANCY ART AUCTION. OUR MISSION IS TO INFILTRATE THE...
HELLO, MY DOUBLE AGENT COMRADES.
WELL, WELL !
I SEE CANADIAN INTELLIGENCE IS ON THE CASE...
HEY! WE'RE THE SECRET AGENTS!! WHAT'S THIS OLD FART DOING IN OUR MOVIE??
NOT SURE...
...MAYBE HE CAN HELP US WITH OUR MISSION?
YES! LET'S JOIN FORCES!

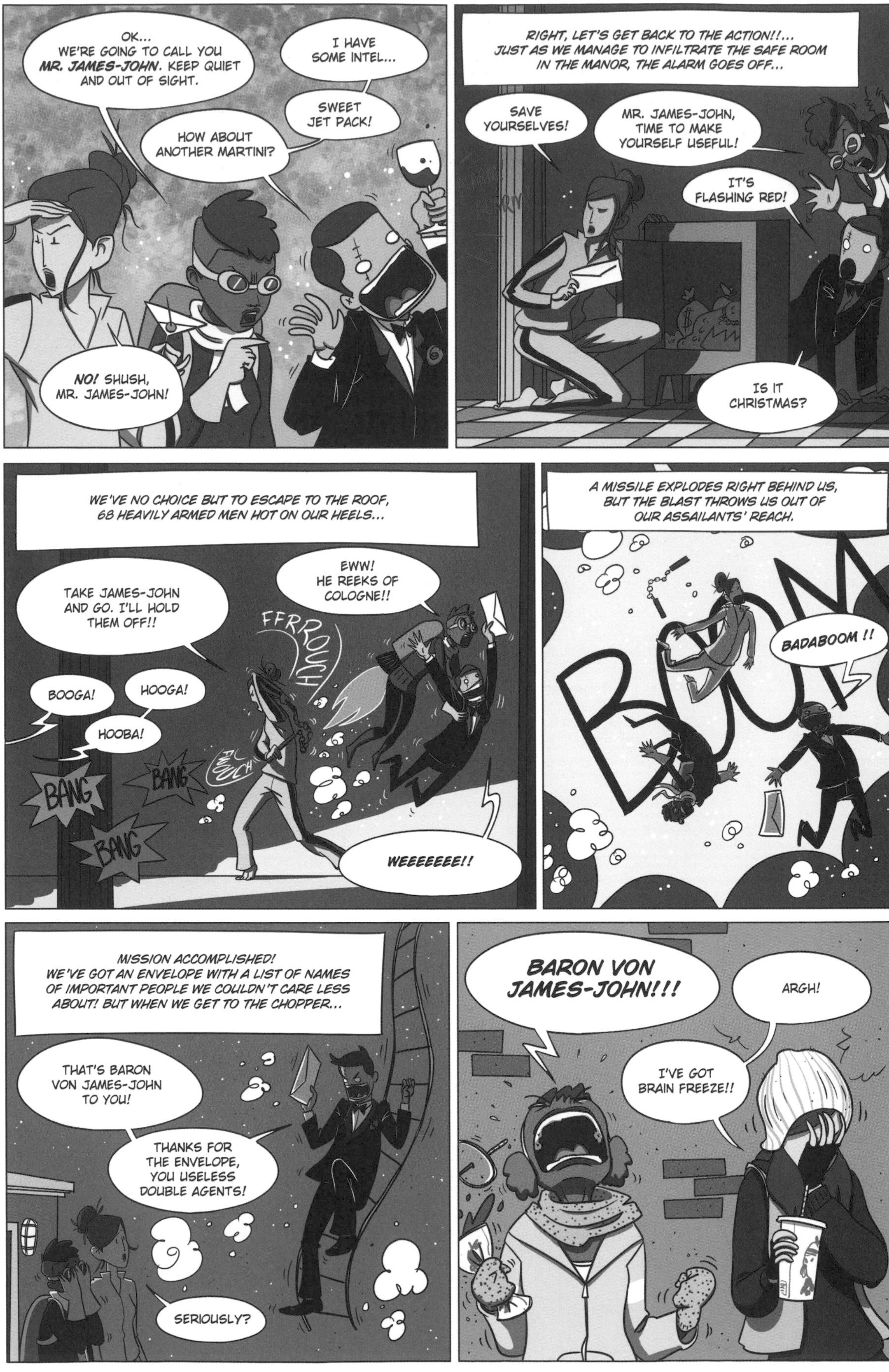
OK...
WE'RE GOING TO CALL YOU **MR. JAMES-JOHN**. KEEP QUIET AND OUT OF SIGHT.
I HAVE SOME INTEL...
SWEET JET PACK!
HOW ABOUT ANOTHER MARTINI?
NO! SHUSH, MR. JAMES-JOHN!
RIGHT, LET'S GET BACK TO THE ACTION!!... JUST AS WE MANAGE TO INFILTRATE THE SAFE ROOM IN THE MANOR, THE ALARM GOES OFF...
SAVE YOURSELVES!
MR. JAMES-JOHN, TIME TO MAKE YOURSELF USEFUL!
IT'S FLASHING RED!
IS IT CHRISTMAS?
WE'VE NO CHOICE BUT TO ESCAPE TO THE ROOF, 68 HEAVILY ARMED MEN HOT ON OUR HEELS...
TAKE JAMES-JOHN AND GO. I'LL HOLD THEM OFF!!
EWW! HE REEKS OF COLOGNE!!
FFRROUCH
BOOGA!
HOOGA!
HOOBA!
BANG
BANG
BANG
WEEEEEEE!!
A MISSILE EXPLODES RIGHT BEHIND US, BUT THE BLAST THROWS US OUT OF OUR ASSAILANTS' REACH.
BOOM
BADABOOM !!
MISSION ACCOMPLISHED!
WE'VE GOT AN ENVELOPE WITH A LIST OF NAMES OF IMPORTANT PEOPLE WE COULDN'T CARE LESS ABOUT! BUT WHEN WE GET TO THE CHOPPER...
THAT'S BARON VON JAMES-JOHN TO YOU!
THANKS FOR THE ENVELOPE, YOU USELESS DOUBLE AGENTS!
SERIOUSLY?
BARON VON JAMES-JOHN!!!
ARGH!
I'VE GOT BRAIN FREEZE!!

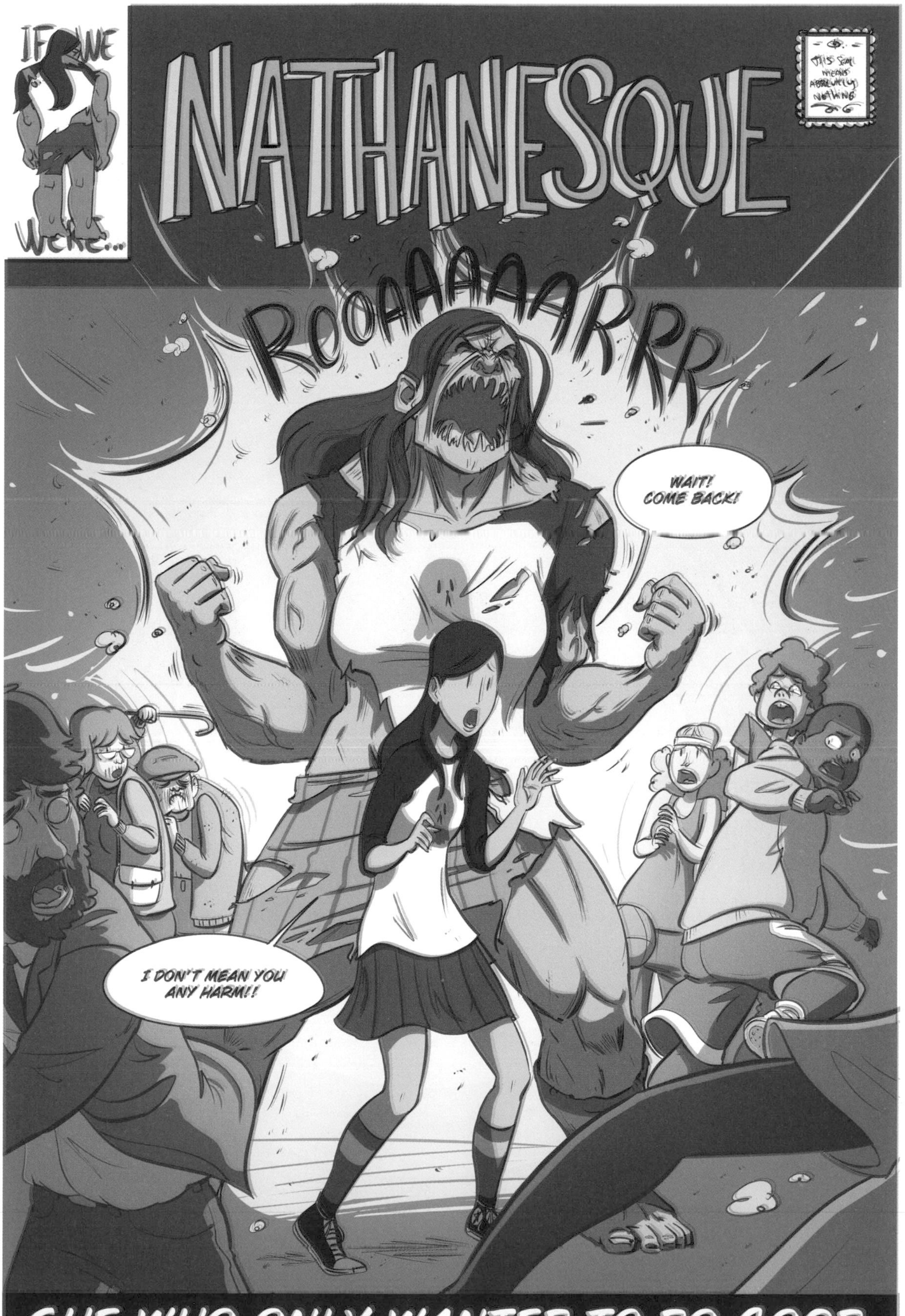
IF SHE WERE...
NATHANESQUE
THIS SEAL MEANS ABSOLUTELY NOTHING
ROOAAAAAARRRR
WAIT! COME BACK!
I DON'T MEAN YOU ANY HARM!!
SHE WHO ONLY WANTED TO DO GOOD.

WHAT IF WE WERE... SUPERHEROINES

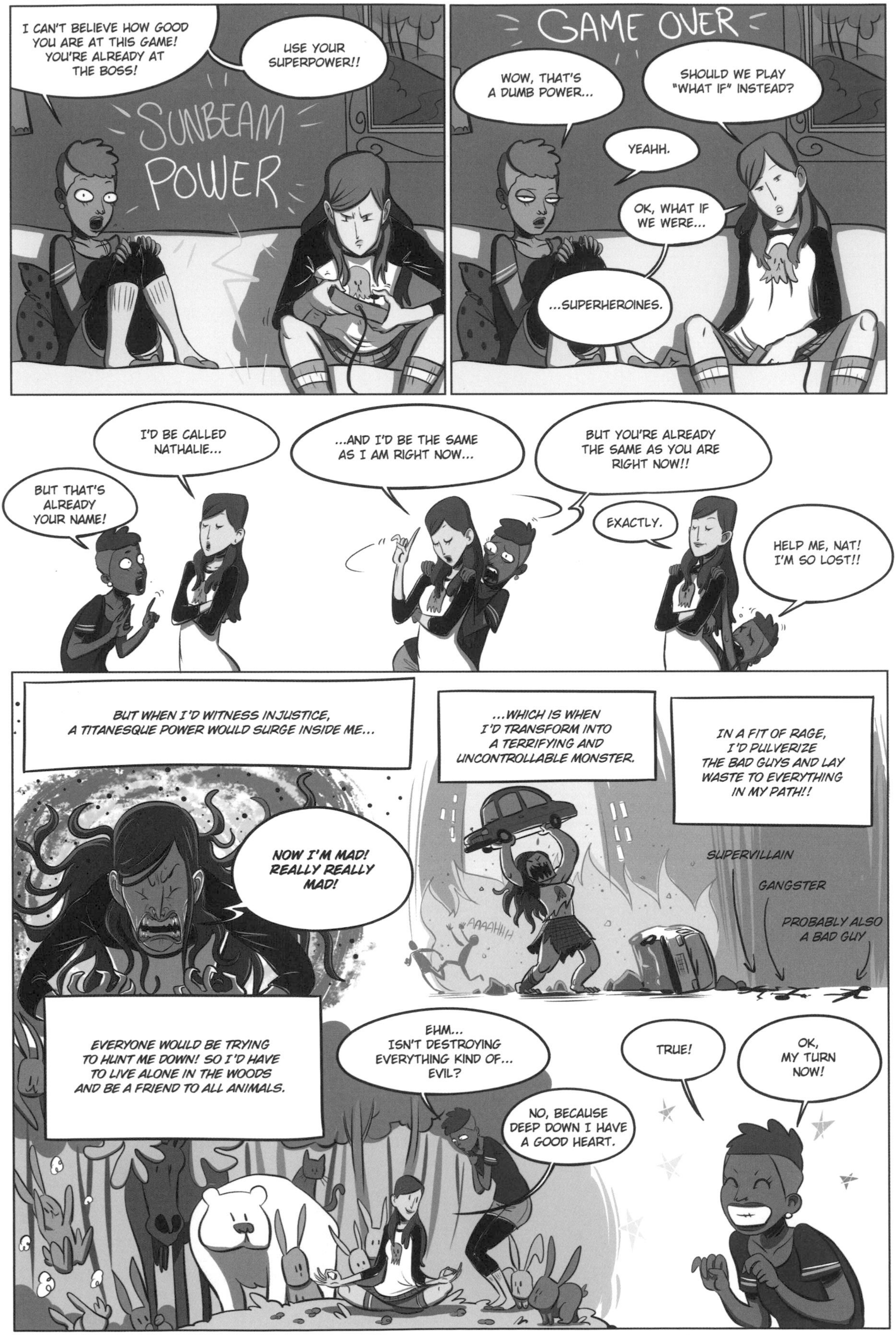

I CAN'T BELIEVE HOW GOOD YOU ARE AT THIS GAME! YOU'RE ALREADY AT THE BOSS!
USE YOUR SUPERPOWER!!
SUNBEAM POWER
GAME OVER
WOW, THAT'S A DUMB POWER...
SHOULD WE PLAY "WHAT IF" INSTEAD?
YEAHH.
OK, WHAT IF WE WERE...
...SUPERHEROINES.
BUT THAT'S ALREADY YOUR NAME!
I'D BE CALLED NATHALIE...
...AND I'D BE THE SAME AS I AM RIGHT NOW...
BUT YOU'RE ALREADY THE SAME AS YOU ARE RIGHT NOW!!
EXACTLY.
HELP ME, NAT! I'M SO LOST!!
BUT WHEN I'D WITNESS INJUSTICE, A TITANESQUE POWER WOULD SURGE INSIDE ME...
NOW I'M MAD! REALLY REALLY MAD!
...WHICH IS WHEN I'D TRANSFORM INTO A TERRIFYING AND UNCONTROLLABLE MONSTER.
IN A FIT OF RAGE, I'D PULVERIZE THE BAD GUYS AND LAY WASTE TO EVERYTHING IN MY PATH!!
AAAAHHH
SUPERVILLAIN
GANGSTER
PROBABLY ALSO A BAD GUY
EVERYONE WOULD BE TRYING TO HUNT ME DOWN! SO I'D HAVE TO LIVE ALONE IN THE WOODS AND BE A FRIEND TO ALL ANIMALS.
EHM... ISN'T DESTROYING EVERYTHING KIND OF... EVIL?
NO, BECAUSE DEEP DOWN I HAVE A GOOD HEART.
TRUE!
OK, MY TURN NOW!

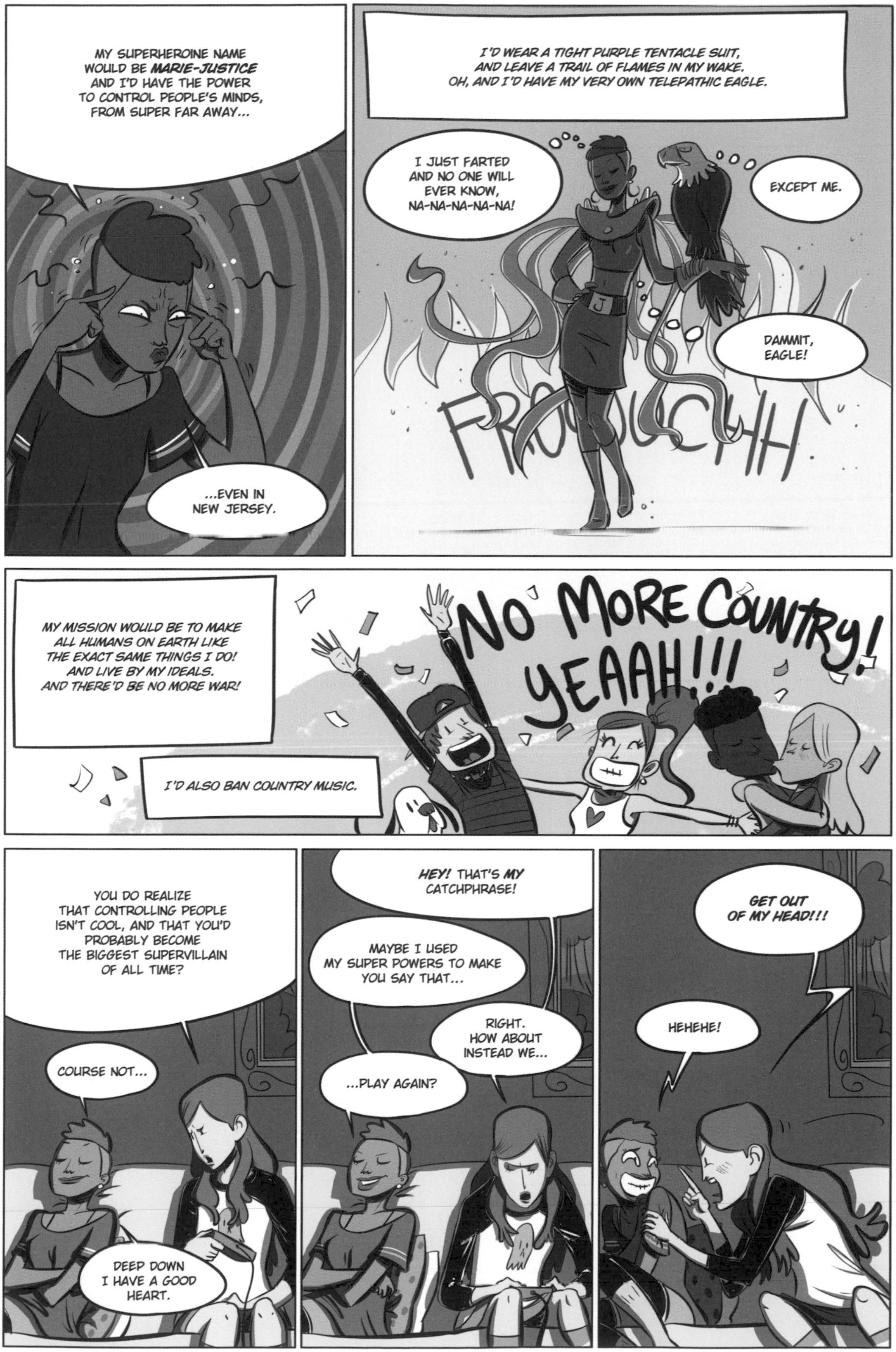
MY SUPERHEROINE NAME WOULD BE MARIE-JUSTICE AND I'D HAVE THE POWER TO CONTROL PEOPLE'S MINDS, FROM SUPER FAR AWAY...
...EVEN IN NEW JERSEY.
I'D WEAR A TIGHT PURPLE TENTACLE SUIT, AND LEAVE A TRAIL OF FLAMES IN MY WAKE. OH, AND I'D HAVE MY VERY OWN TELEPATHIC EAGLE.
I JUST FARTED AND NO ONE WILL EVER KNOW, NA-NA-NA-NA-NA!
EXCEPT ME.
DAMMIT, EAGLE!
FROOUCHH
MY MISSION WOULD BE TO MAKE ALL HUMANS ON EARTH LIKE THE EXACT SAME THINGS I DO! AND LIVE BY MY IDEALS. AND THERE'D BE NO MORE WAR!
I'D ALSO BAN COUNTRY MUSIC.
NO MORE COUNTRY! YEAAH!!!
YOU DO REALIZE THAT CONTROLLING PEOPLE ISN'T COOL, AND THAT YOU'D PROBABLY BECOME THE BIGGEST SUPERVILLAIN OF ALL TIME?
COURSE NOT...
DEEP DOWN I HAVE A GOOD HEART.
HEY! THAT'S MY CATCHPHRASE!
MAYBE I USED MY SUPER POWERS TO MAKE YOU SAY THAT...
RIGHT. HOW ABOUT INSTEAD WE...
...PLAY AGAIN?
GET OUT OF MY HEAD!!!
HEHEHE!

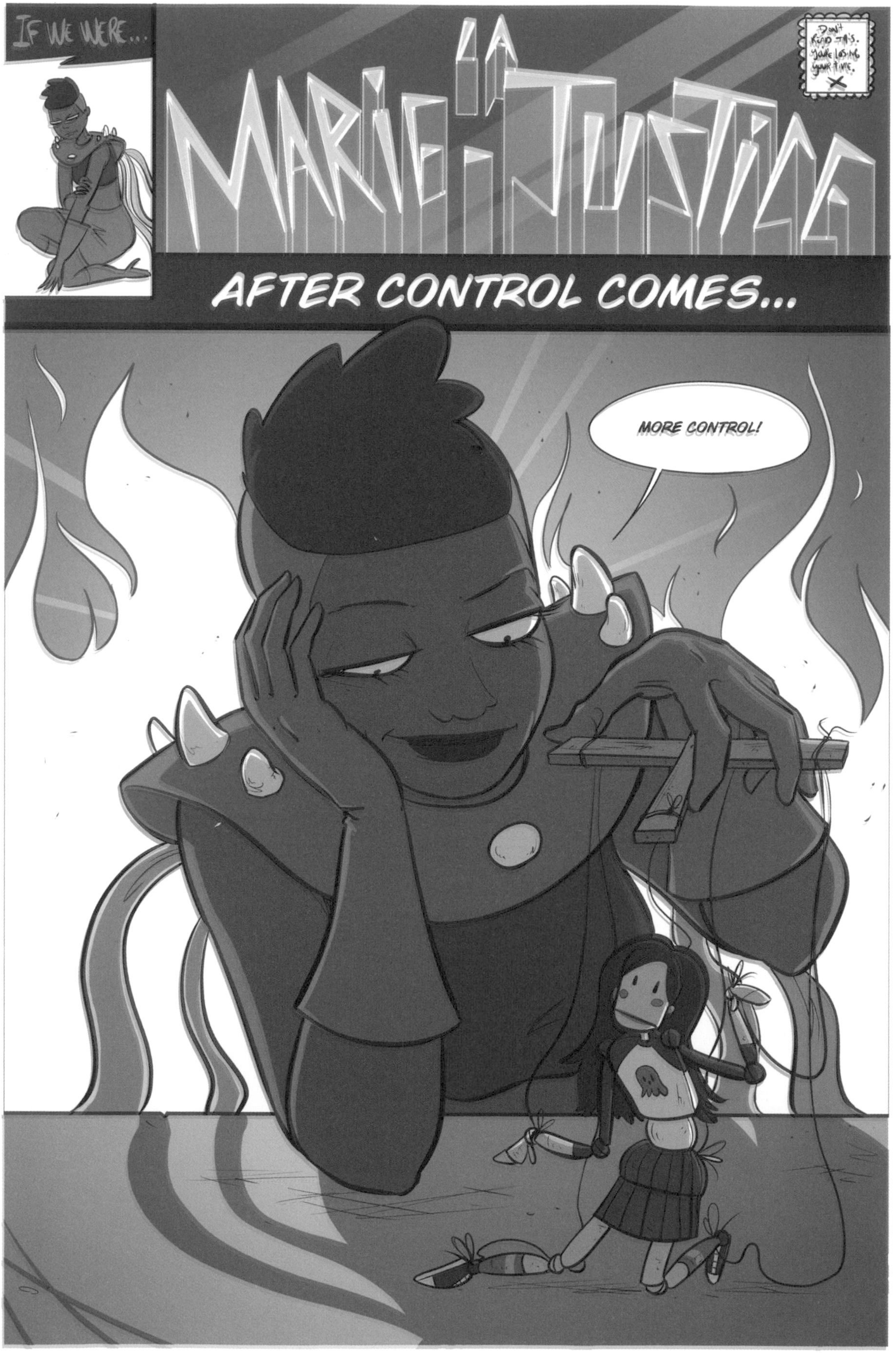
IF WE WERE...
LA MARIE-JUSTICE
Don't read this. You're losing your time.
AFTER CONTROL COMES...
MORE CONTROL!

LET'S GET TO KNOW THE GIRLS BETTER

MARIE: SPONTANEOUS / NATHALIE: LEVEL-HEADED

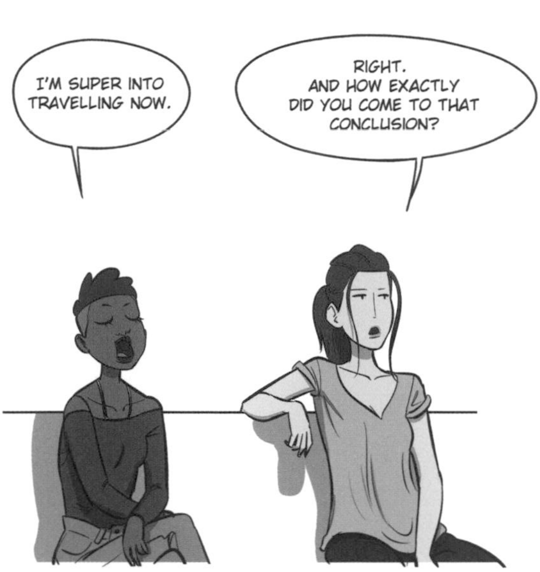
I'M SUPER INTO TRAVELLING NOW.
RIGHT. AND HOW EXACTLY DID YOU COME TO THAT CONCLUSION?

MARIE: IMPULSIVE / NATHALIE: COMPOSED

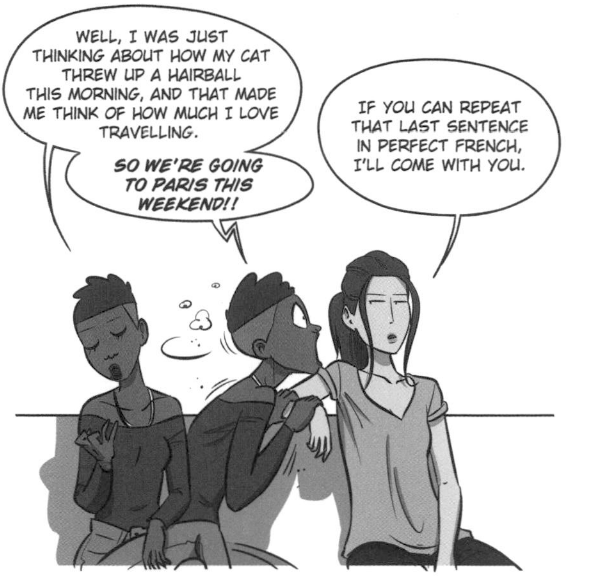
WELL, I WAS JUST THINKING ABOUT HOW MY CAT THREW UP A HAIRBALL THIS MORNING, AND THAT MADE ME THINK OF HOW MUCH I LOVE TRAVELLING.
SO WE'RE GOING TO PARIS THIS WEEKEND!!
IF YOU CAN REPEAT THAT LAST SENTENCE IN PERFECT FRENCH, I'LL COME WITH YOU.

MARIE: BRAVE, DOWN-TO-EARTH / NATHALIE: SARCASTIC

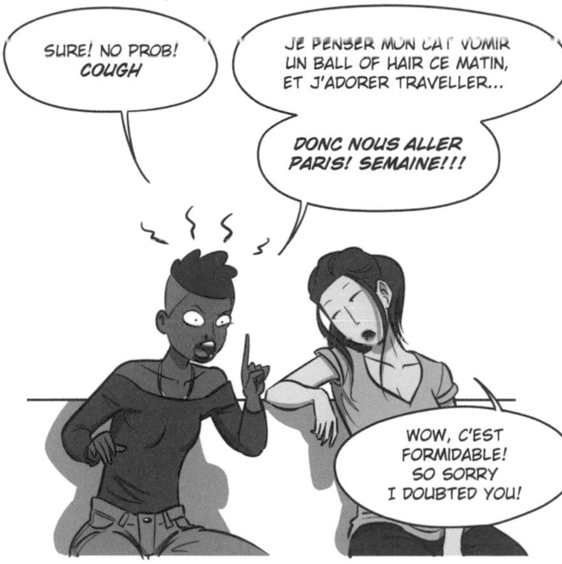
SURE! NO PROB! COUGH
JE PENSER MON CAT VOMIR UN BALL OF HAIR CE MATIN, ET J'ADORER TRAVELLER...
DONC NOUS ALLER PARIS! SEMAINE!!!
WOW, C'EST FORMIDABLE! SO SORRY I DOUBTED YOU!

MARIE: LOST / NATHALIE: CRYPTIC

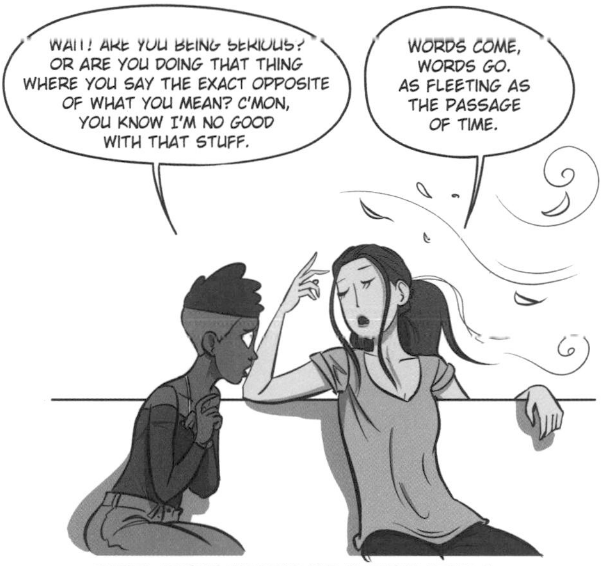
WAIT! ARE YOU BEING SERIOUS? OR ARE YOU DOING THAT THING WHERE YOU SAY THE EXACT OPPOSITE OF WHAT YOU MEAN? C'MON, YOU KNOW I'M NO GOOD WITH THAT STUFF.
WORDS COME, WORDS GO. AS FLEETING AS THE PASSAGE OF TIME.

MARIE: OUTGOING / NATHALIE: LONER

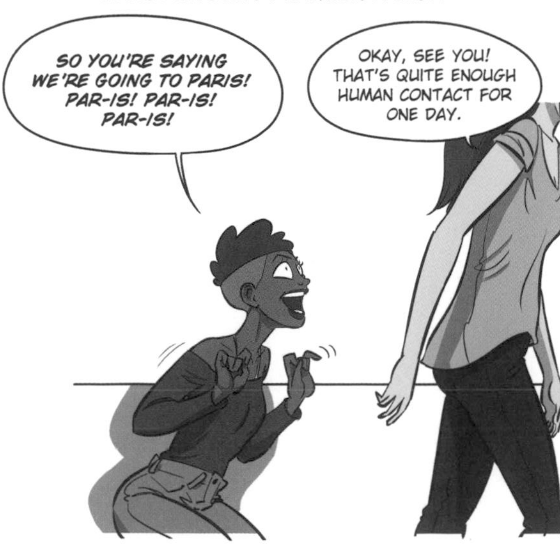
SO YOU'RE SAYING WE'RE GOING TO PARIS! PAR-IS! PAR-IS! PAR-IS!
OKAY, SEE YOU! THAT'S QUITE ENOUGH HUMAN CONTACT FOR ONE DAY.

MARIE: ANGRY BORDERLINE-MANIPULATIVE / NATHALIE: SHY BORDERLINE-ANXIOUS

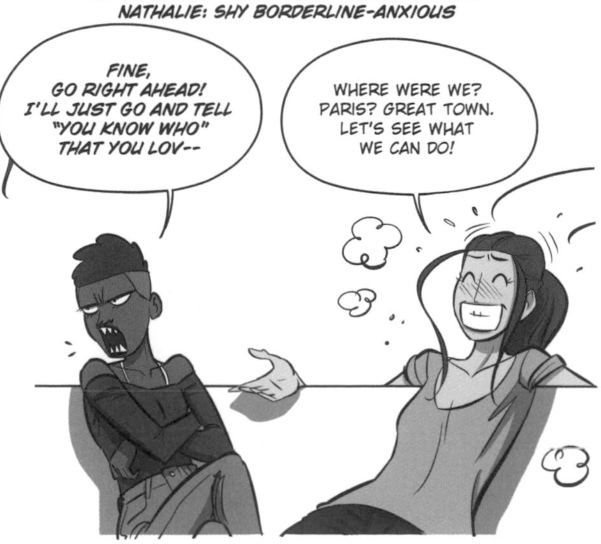
FINE, GO RIGHT AHEAD! I'LL JUST GO AND TELL "YOU KNOW WHO" THAT YOU LOV--
WHERE WERE WE? PARIS? GREAT TOWN. LET'S SEE WHAT WE CAN DO!

WHAT IF, RAPID-FIRE VERSION

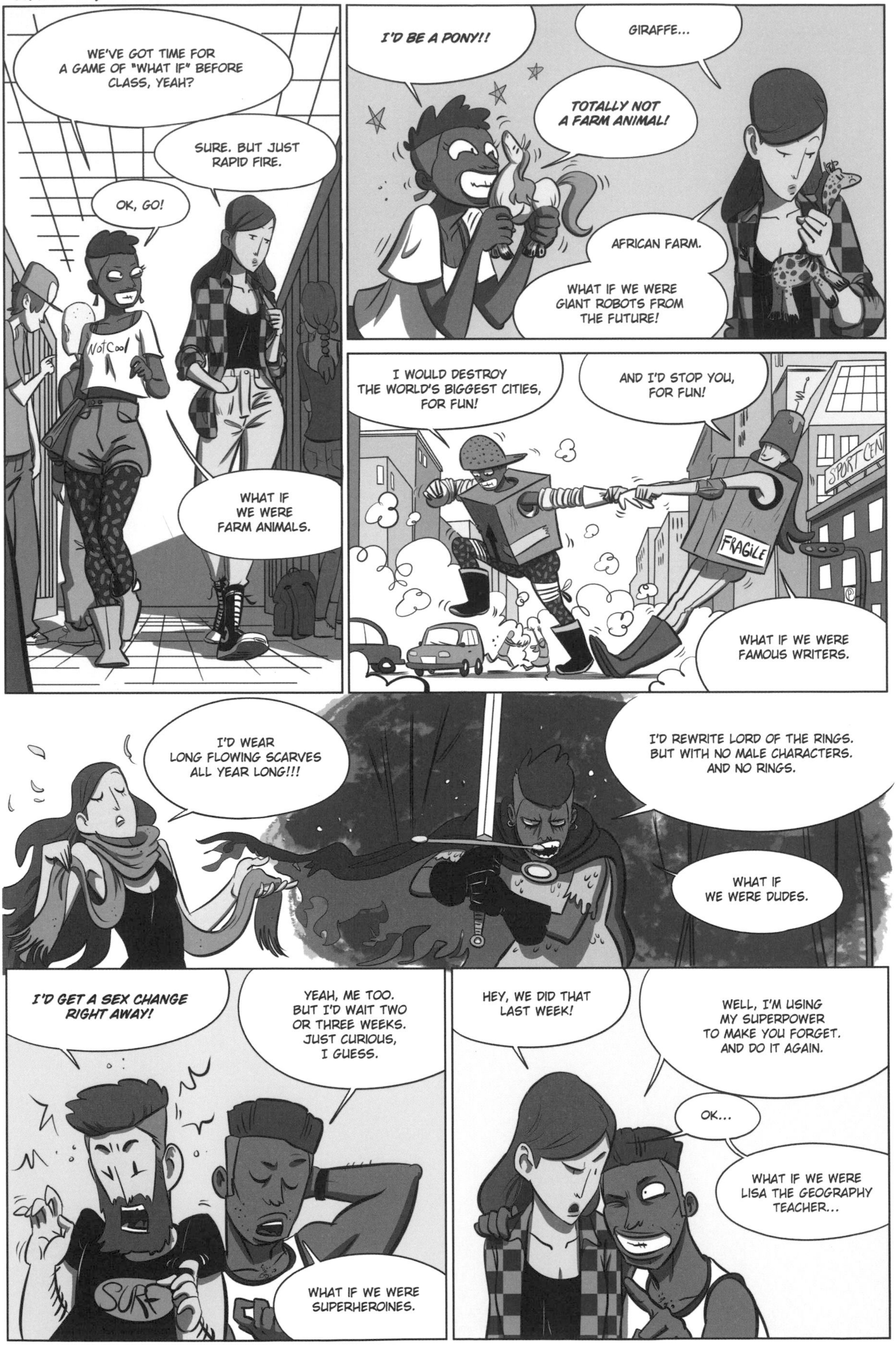
WE'VE GOT TIME FOR A GAME OF "WHAT IF" BEFORE CLASS, YEAH?
SURE. BUT JUST RAPID FIRE.
OK, GO!
Not Cool
WHAT IF WE WERE FARM ANIMALS.
I'D BE A PONY!!
GIRAFFE...
TOTALLY NOT A FARM ANIMAL!
AFRICAN FARM.
WHAT IF WE WERE GIANT ROBOTS FROM THE FUTURE!
I WOULD DESTROY THE WORLD'S BIGGEST CITIES, FOR FUN!
AND I'D STOP YOU, FOR FUN!
FRAGILE
WHAT IF WE WERE FAMOUS WRITERS.
I'D WEAR LONG FLOWING SCARVES ALL YEAR LONG!!!
I'D REWRITE LORD OF THE RINGS. BUT WITH NO MALE CHARACTERS. AND NO RINGS.
WHAT IF WE WERE DUDES.
I'D GET A SEX CHANGE RIGHT AWAY!
YEAH, ME TOO. BUT I'D WAIT TWO OR THREE WEEKS. JUST CURIOUS, I GUESS.
SURF
WHAT IF WE WERE SUPERHEROINES.
HEY, WE DID THAT LAST WEEK!
WELL, I'M USING MY SUPERPOWER TO MAKE YOU FORGET. AND DO IT AGAIN.
OK...
WHAT IF WE WERE LISA THE GEOGRAPHY TEACHER...

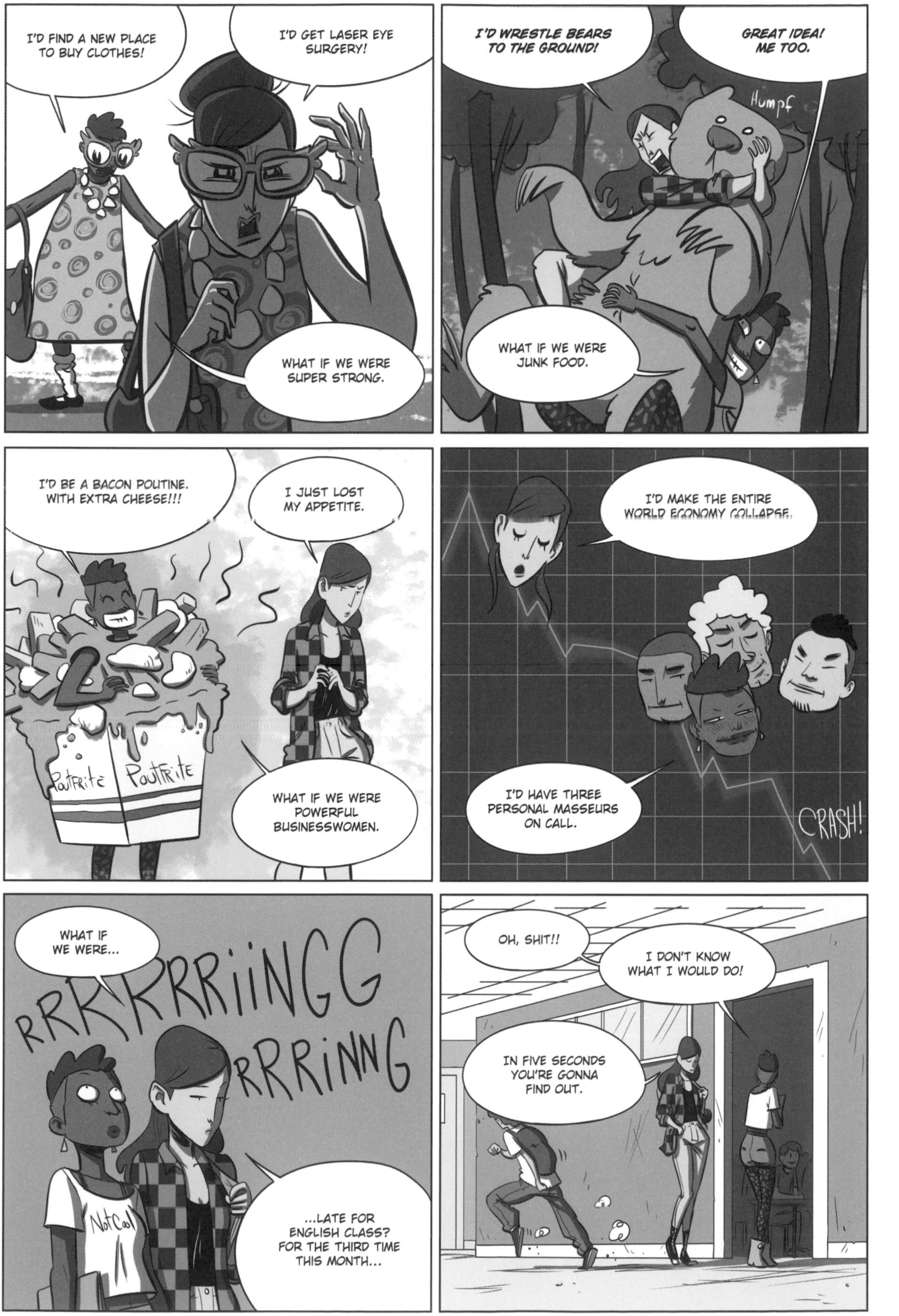
I'D FIND A NEW PLACE TO BUY CLOTHES!
I'D GET LASER EYE SURGERY!
WHAT IF WE WERE SUPER STRONG.
I'D WRESTLE BEARS TO THE GROUND!
GREAT IDEA! ME TOO.
Humpf
WHAT IF WE WERE JUNK FOOD.
I'D BE A BACON POUTINE. WITH EXTRA CHEESE!!!
I JUST LOST MY APPETITE.
Poutrite
Poutrite
WHAT IF WE WERE POWERFUL BUSINESSWOMEN.
I'D MAKE THE ENTIRE WORLD ECONOMY COLLAPSE.
I'D HAVE THREE PERSONAL MASSEURS ON CALL.
CRASH!
WHAT IF WE WERE...
RRRRRRiiNGG
RRRiNNG
NotCool
...LATE FOR ENGLISH CLASS? FOR THE THIRD TIME THIS MONTH...
OH, SHIT!!
I DON'T KNOW WHAT I WOULD DO!
IN FIVE SECONDS YOU'RE GONNA FIND OUT.

WHAT IF WE WERE... IN A COMIC STRIP

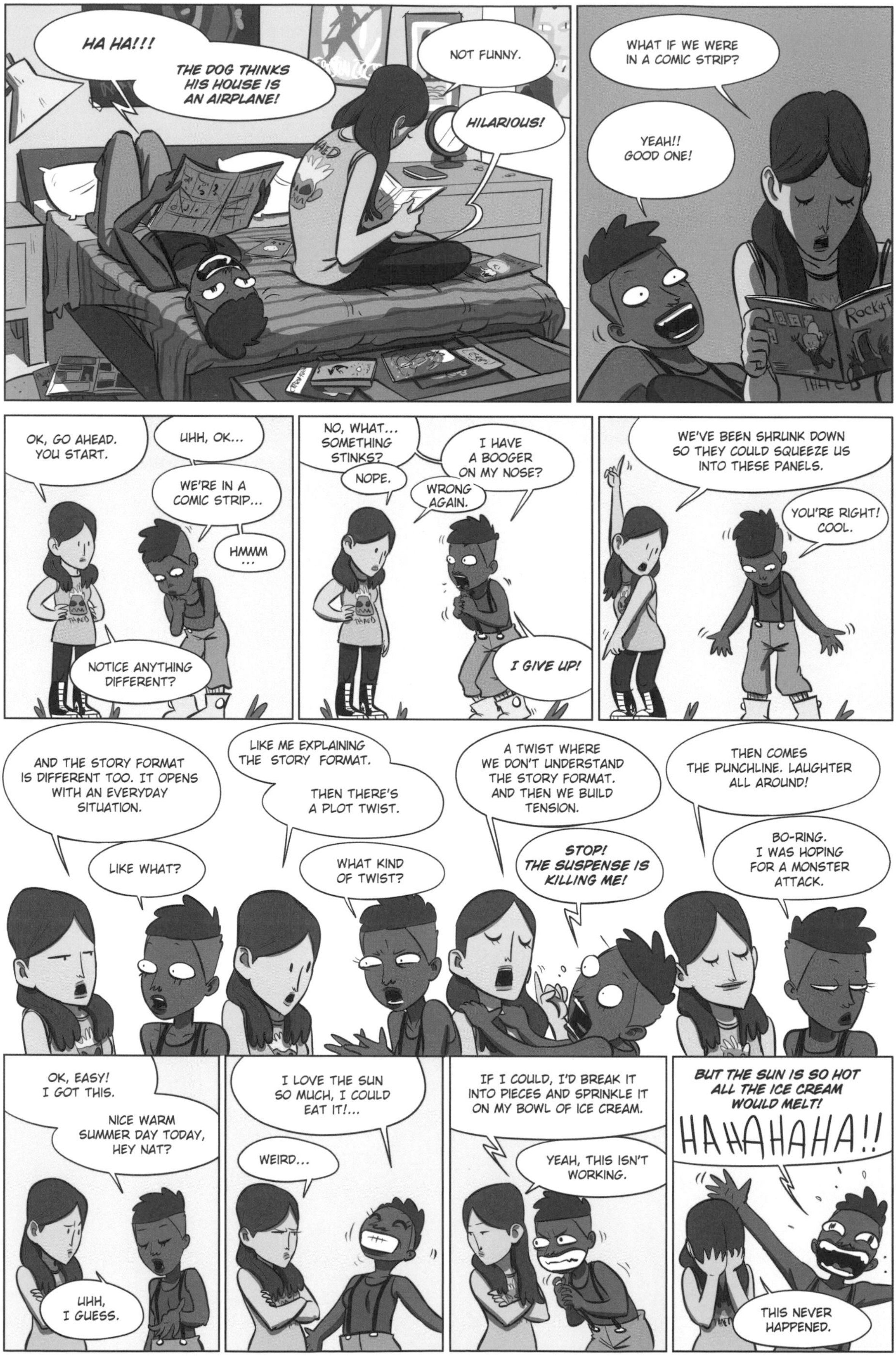
HA HA!!!
THE DOG THINKS HIS HOUSE IS AN AIRPLANE!
NOT FUNNY.
HILARIOUS!
WHAT IF WE WERE IN A COMIC STRIP?
YEAH!! GOOD ONE!
OK, GO AHEAD. YOU START.
UHH, OK...
WE'RE IN A COMIC STRIP...
HMMM ...
NOTICE ANYTHING DIFFERENT?
NO, WHAT... SOMETHING STINKS?
NOPE.
I HAVE A BOOGER ON MY NOSE?
WRONG AGAIN.
I GIVE UP!
WE'VE BEEN SHRUNK DOWN SO THEY COULD SQUEEZE US INTO THESE PANELS.
YOU'RE RIGHT! COOL.
AND THE STORY FORMAT IS DIFFERENT TOO. IT OPENS WITH AN EVERYDAY SITUATION.
LIKE WHAT?
LIKE ME EXPLAINING THE STORY FORMAT.
THEN THERE'S A PLOT TWIST.
WHAT KIND OF TWIST?
A TWIST WHERE WE DON'T UNDERSTAND THE STORY FORMAT. AND THEN WE BUILD TENSION.
STOP! THE SUSPENSE IS KILLING ME!
THEN COMES THE PUNCHLINE. LAUGHTER ALL AROUND!
BO-RING. I WAS HOPING FOR A MONSTER ATTACK.
OK, EASY! I GOT THIS.
NICE WARM SUMMER DAY TODAY, HEY NAT?
UHH, I GUESS.
I LOVE THE SUN SO MUCH, I COULD EAT IT!...
WEIRD...
IF I COULD, I'D BREAK IT INTO PIECES AND SPRINKLE IT ON MY BOWL OF ICE CREAM.
YEAH, THIS ISN'T WORKING.
BUT THE SUN IS SO HOT ALL THE ICE CREAM WOULD MELT!
HAHAHAHA!!
THIS NEVER HAPPENED.

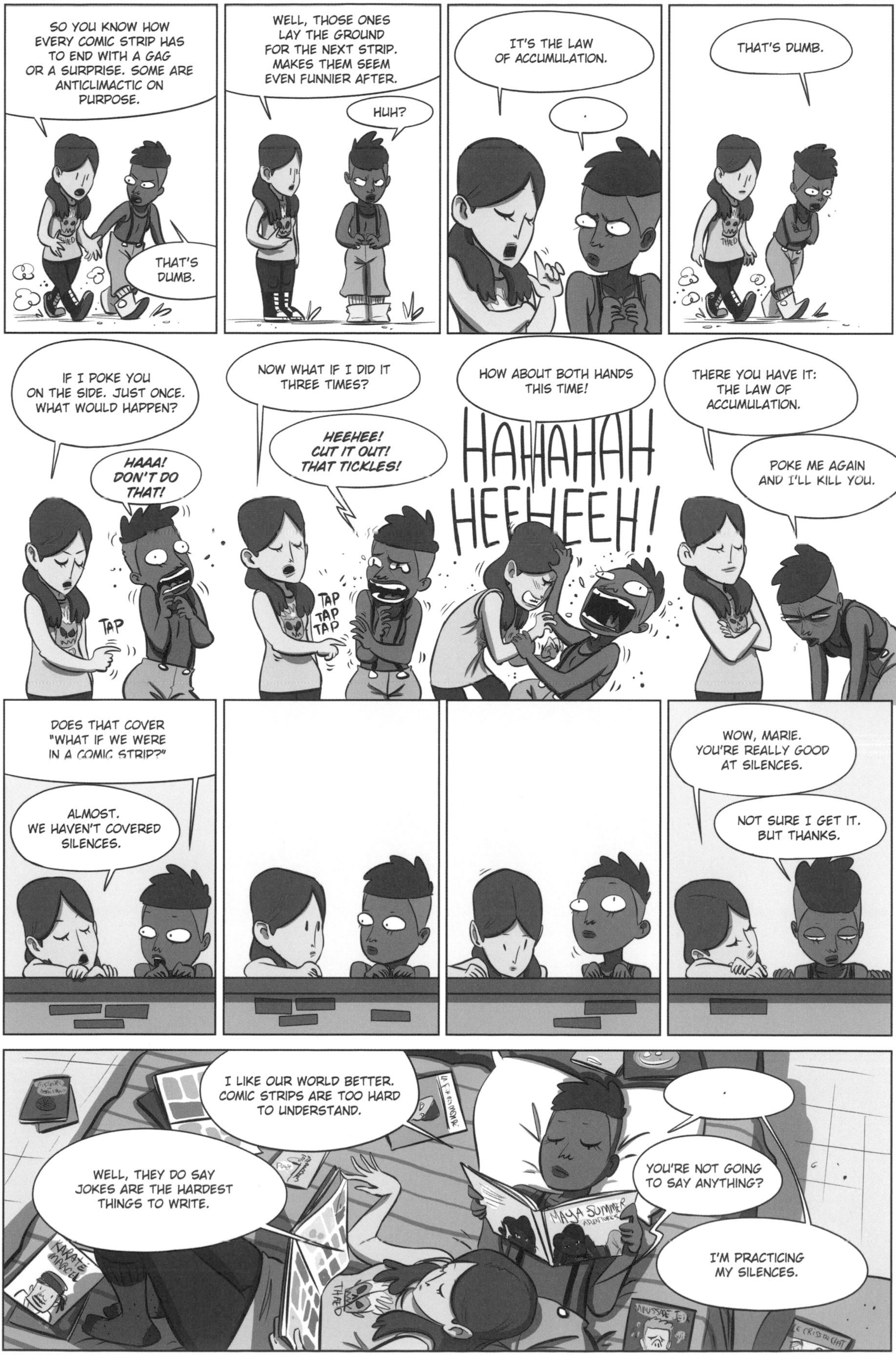
SO YOU KNOW HOW EVERY COMIC STRIP HAS TO END WITH A GAG OR A SURPRISE. SOME ARE ANTICLIMACTIC ON PURPOSE.
THAT'S DUMB.
WELL, THOSE ONES LAY THE GROUND FOR THE NEXT STRIP. MAKES THEM SEEM EVEN FUNNIER AFTER.
HUH?
IT'S THE LAW OF ACCUMULATION.
THAT'S DUMB.
IF I POKE YOU ON THE SIDE. JUST ONCE. WHAT WOULD HAPPEN?
HAAA! DON'T DO THAT!
TAP
NOW WHAT IF I DID IT THREE TIMES?
HEEHEE! CUT IT OUT! THAT TICKLES!
TAP TAP TAP
HOW ABOUT BOTH HANDS THIS TIME!
HAHAHAH HEEHEEH!
THERE YOU HAVE IT: THE LAW OF ACCUMULATION.
POKE ME AGAIN AND I'LL KILL YOU.
DOES THAT COVER "WHAT IF WE WERE IN A COMIC STRIP?"
ALMOST. WE HAVEN'T COVERED SILENCES.
WOW, MARIE. YOU'RE REALLY GOOD AT SILENCES.
NOT SURE I GET IT. BUT THANKS.
I LIKE OUR WORLD BETTER. COMIC STRIPS ARE TOO HARD TO UNDERSTAND.
WELL, THEY DO SAY JOKES ARE THE HARDEST THINGS TO WRITE.
KARATE MARCEL
MAYA SUMMER
YOU'RE NOT GOING TO SAY ANYTHING?
I'M PRACTICING MY SILENCES.

MARIE'S DIARY

DEAR DIARY.
YOU WON'T BELIEVE WHAT I LEARNED TODAY: HOW JOKES ACTUALLY WORK.
I USED TO THINK ALL I HAD TO DO WAS KEEP GOOFING AROUND UNTIL SOMEONE STARTED LAUGHING (PROBABLY BECAUSE THEY CAN'T TAKE IT ANYMORE).

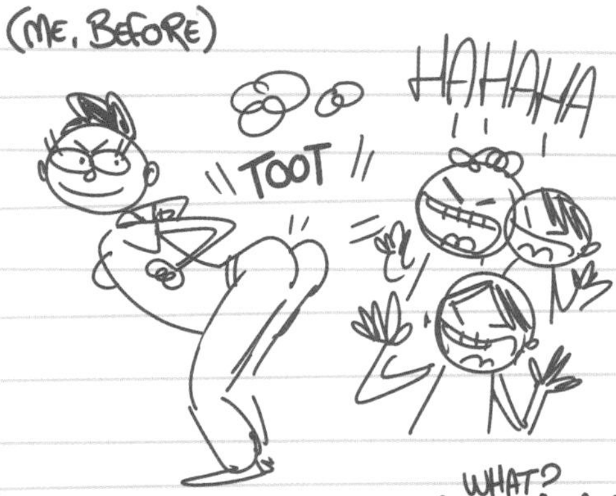
(ME, BEFORE)
TOOT
HAHAHA

BUT APPARENTLY THERE'S SOME KIND OF SCIENCE BEHIND IT. YOU JUST NEED FOUR ELEMENTS – EVERYDAY SITUATION, PLOT TWIST, TENSION, AND A PUNCHLINE. AND THESE FOUR SIMPLE INGREDIENTS CAN BE COMBINED FOR AN INFINITE NUMBER OF JOKES. CHECK OUT THIS KILLER JOKE I JUST MADE UP:

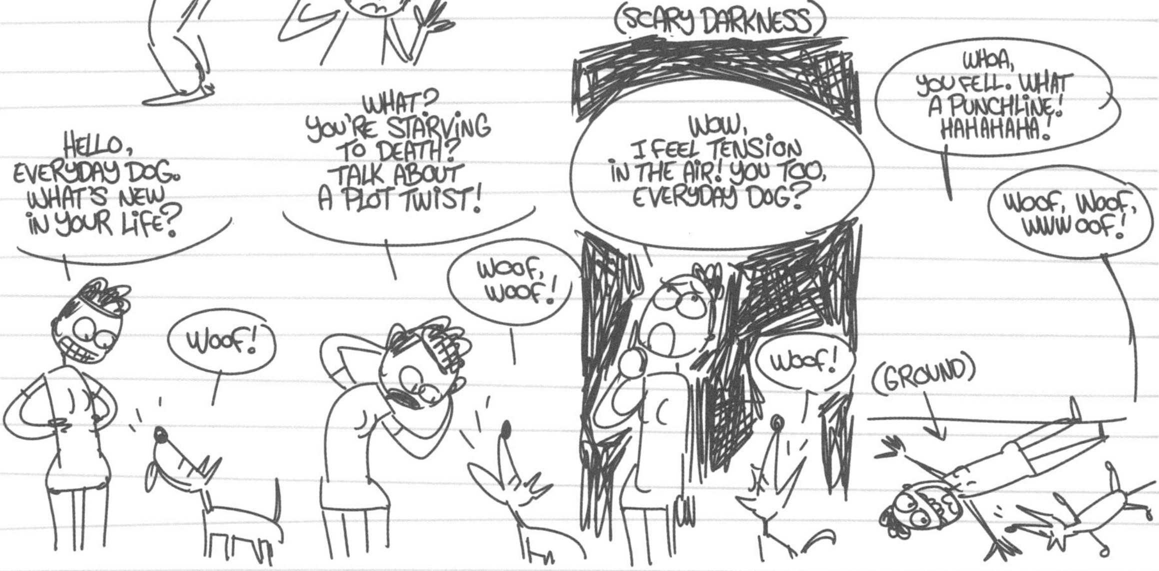
HELLO, EVERYDAY DOG. WHAT'S NEW IN YOUR LIFE?
WOOF!
WHAT? YOU'RE STARVING TO DEATH? TALK ABOUT A PLOT TWIST!
WOOF, WOOF!
(SCARY DARKNESS)
WOW, I FEEL TENSION IN THE AIR! YOU TOO, EVERYDAY DOG?
WOOF!
WHOA, YOU FELL. WHAT A PUNCHLINE! HAHAHAHA!
WOOF, WOOF, WWWOOF!
(GROUND)

HMMM, I STILL HAVE TO WORK OUT A FEW KINKS. MAYBE IT'D BE FUNNIER WITH A CAT INSTEAD OF A DOG? I'LL ASK NAT TOMORROW, SHE'LL KNOW. SHE'S SO SMART!
BUT I DON'T WANT TO TELL HER THAT, BECAUSE THAT WOULD BE LIKE ADMITTING THAT I'M KIND OF DUMB, AND I'D BE WORRIED SHE WOULDN'T WANT TO BE MY FRIEND ANY MORE.
I LIKE HER SO MUCH, I CAN'T IMAGINE WHAT LIFE WOULD BE LIKE WITHOUT HER. SURE, SHE'LL FIGURE IT OUT ONE DAY, BUT I'D RATHER PUSH THAT DAY OFF AS LONG AS I CAN. SHE'S SO BRILLIANT I SOMETIMES WONDER IF SHE CAN READ MY MIND...

NATHALIE... IF YOU CAN READ MINDS, I'M REALLY SUPER SMART!
THAT WAS SOME OTHER MARIE SAYING SHE'S KIND OF DUMB, AND I JUST HAPPENED TO MENTION HER. STOP READING MY THOUGHTS!

SEE YA, DIARY!

BYE, NAT, IF YOU'RE READING MY MIND. AND GET OUT OF MY HEAD! XXX

NATHALIE'S DIARY

Hey you,

How are ya?... Actually, no one cares how you're doing, you're just a diary. I spent the evening reading comics with Marie. She's so funny! She was trying to figure out how to make a joke even though she's already a comic genius. At school, some people think she isn't super smart but she's actually totally brillant. It's just that she doesn't know it yet...
Seriously I don't know what my life would be without her. I know it sounds cheesy, but she really does brighten my days. Sometimes I wish I had her confidence. She doesn't care at all what other people think of her...
I just give the illusion of being in control, but I'm afraid... I'm pretty much afraid all the time.

I can't even bring myself to talk to "You know who" even though I'm sure we'd get along super well. I freeze and I feel myself losing control... And vulnerable. If I was like Marie, I would already have built up the courage... And we'd probably even be going out by now. Maybe I'll work up the courage this year?

Where exactly do you find courage? Is it just something you stumble onto one day?

I'll try to talk to Marie soon. She'll know what to do. xx

Bye diary, even though you're just a diary.

DESPAIR.....
Life is hard...

(message brought to you by sad skeleton)

WHAT IF WE HAD... WEIRD STYLE

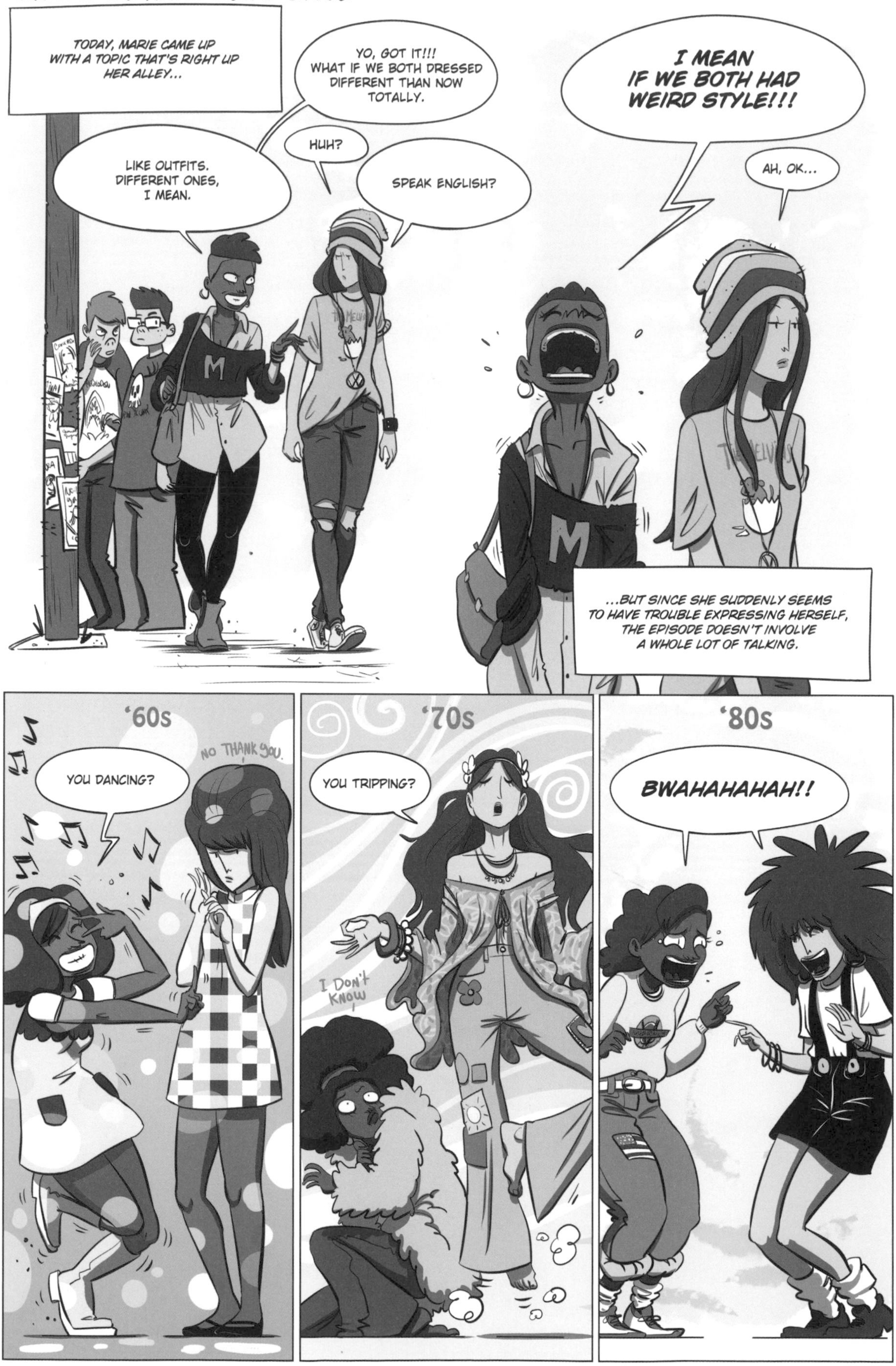
TODAY, MARIE CAME UP WITH A TOPIC THAT'S RIGHT UP HER ALLEY...
LIKE OUTFITS. DIFFERENT ONES, I MEAN.
YO, GOT IT!!! WHAT IF WE BOTH DRESSED DIFFERENT THAN NOW TOTALLY.
HUH?
SPEAK ENGLISH?
I MEAN IF WE BOTH HAD WEIRD STYLE!!!
AH, OK...
...BUT SINCE SHE SUDDENLY SEEMS TO HAVE TROUBLE EXPRESSING HERSELF, THE EPISODE DOESN'T INVOLVE A WHOLE LOT OF TALKING.
'60s
YOU DANCING?
NO THANK YOU.
'70s
YOU TRIPPING?
I DON'T KNOW
'80s
BWAHAHAHAH!!

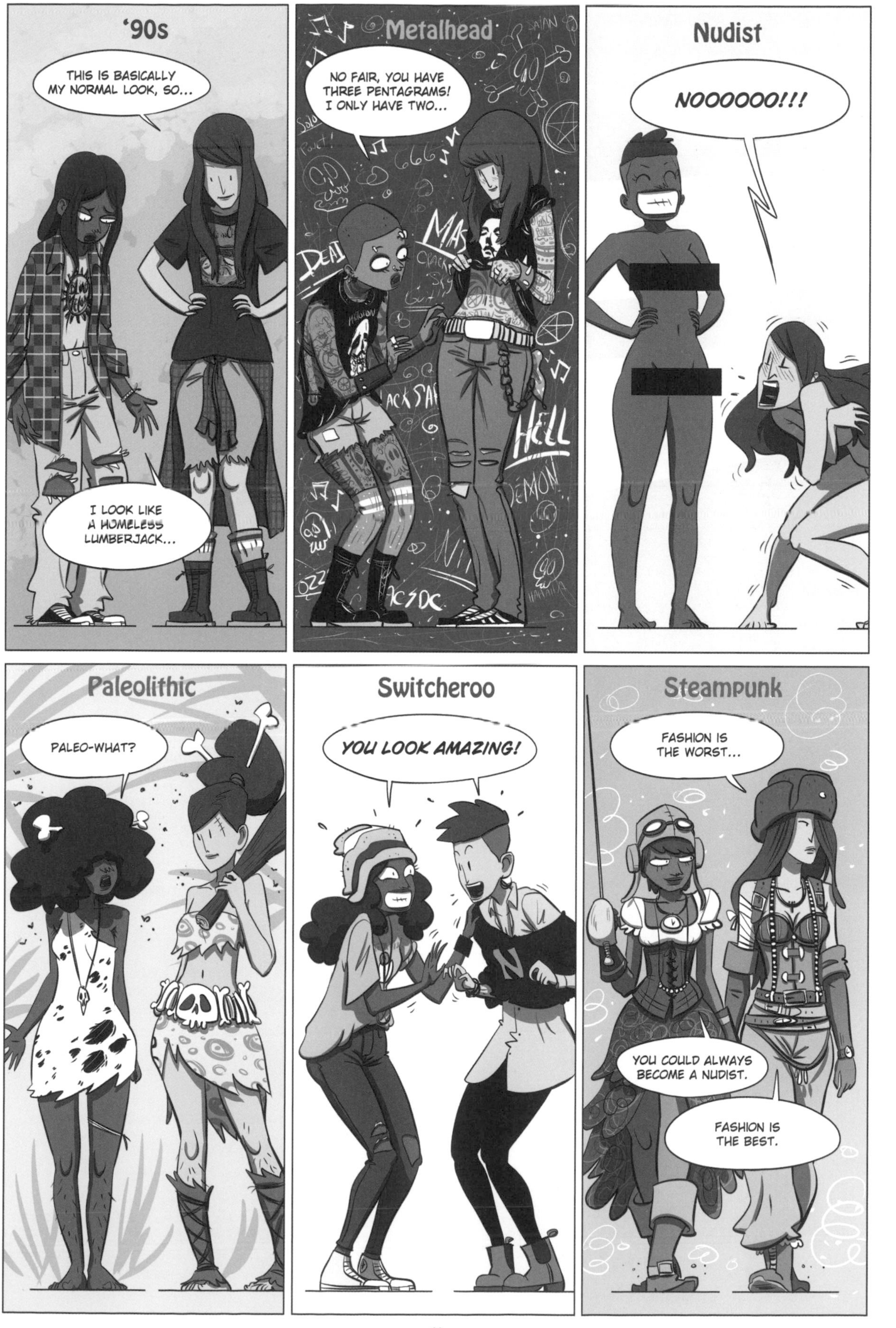
'90s
THIS IS BASICALLY MY NORMAL LOOK, SO...
I LOOK LIKE A HOMELESS LUMBERJACK...
Metalhead
NO FAIR, YOU HAVE THREE PENTAGRAMS! I ONLY HAVE TWO...
Nudist
NOOOOOO!!!
Paleolithic
PALEO-WHAT?
Switcheroo
YOU LOOK AMAZING!
Steampunk
FASHION IS THE WORST...
YOU COULD ALWAYS BECOME A NUDIST.
FASHION IS THE BEST.

NAT'S FAVORITE THINGS

OLD-SCHOOL VIDEO GAMES

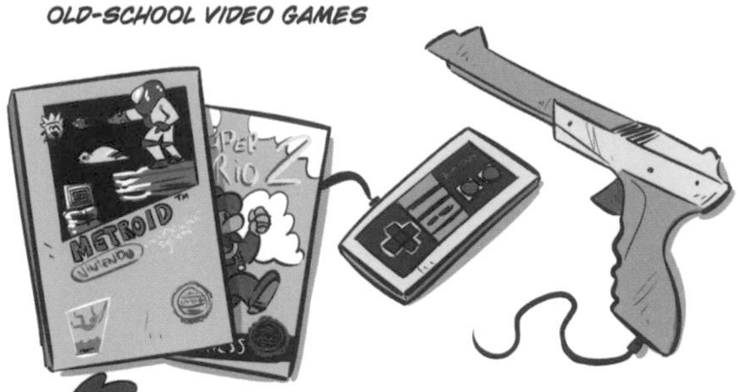
METROID

: YEAH, I DON'T GET IT. NEW GAMES ARE JUST SO MUCH BETTER!

: I DON'T KNOW WHY, BUT THEY GIVE ME A WARM FUZZY FEELING. IT WAS SUCH A NEW WORLD BACK THEN, GAMES WERE SO CREATIVE.

DOOM METAL

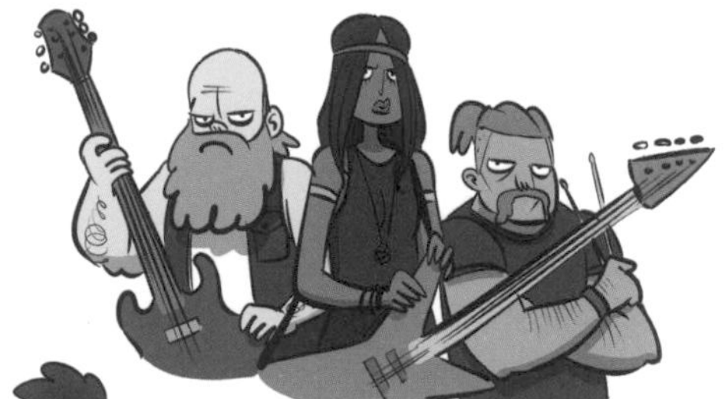

: YEAH, YOU WOULD...

: IT'S NOT LIKE I'M TRYING TO BE COOL. I JUST REALLY LOVE DOOM...

: DIDN'T SAY A THING.

NOVELS, COMICS, AND MOVIES SET IN PARALLEL UNIVERSES

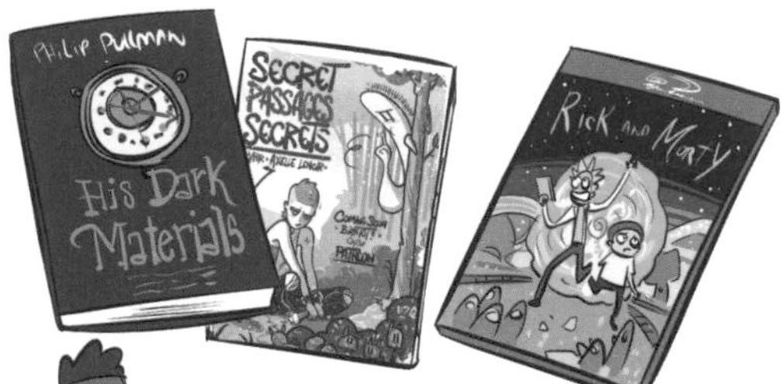
Philip Pullman
His Dark Materials
Secret Passages Secrets
Rick and Morty

: SIGN ME UP!

: WE WATCHING ANNIHILATION AGAIN TONIGHT?

: YEP!

CHELSEA WOLFE, ULTIMATE MUSICAL GODDESS

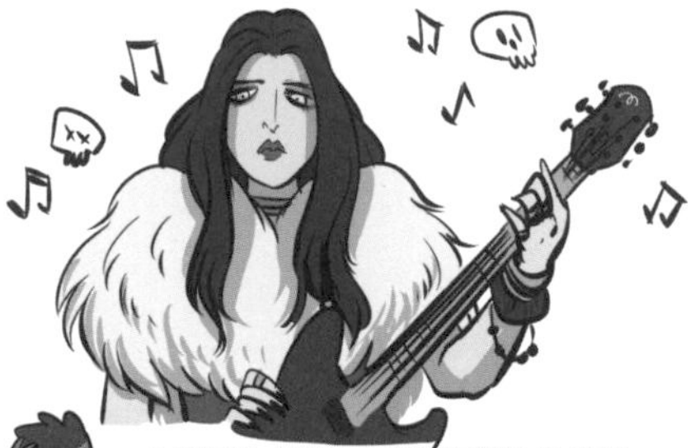

: GREAT, MORE DEPRESSING GLOOM AND DOOM...

: SHUT UP! SHE'S THE ONE I MADE YOU LISTEN TO THE OTHER NIGHT. YOU LOVED IT!

: OH THAT. SHE WAS AWESOME! AND DEPRESSING AS HELL.

PEACE AND QUIET

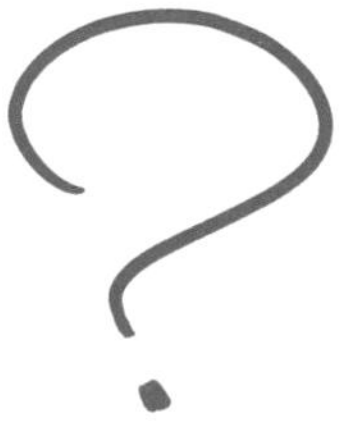

: HOW DO YOU EVEN DRAW PEACE AND QUIET?

: DUNNO. SEEMED TOO CHEESY TO DO A CREEK AND A BUNCH OF CHIRPING BIRDS. SO I LEFT IT BLANK.

: WORKS FOR ME.

YOU KNOW WHO!

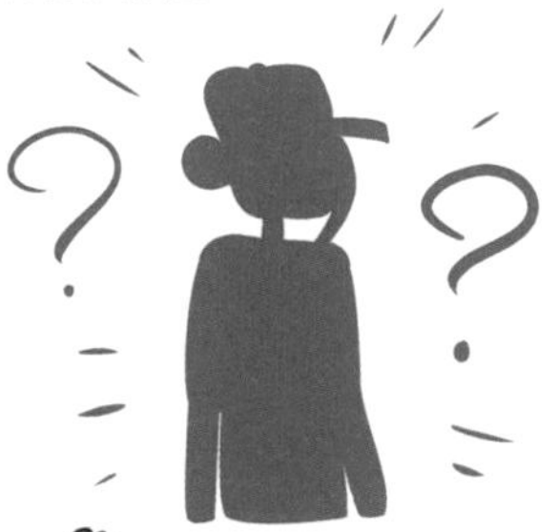

: OH. YOU MEAN THE LOVE OF YOUR LIFE: J...

: DON'T YOU DARE SAY IT!

: WHAT? WHY NOT. IT'S NOT VOLDEMORT OR ANYTHING.

: I DON'T KNOW... IT'S LIKE I HAVE A VISCERAL REACTION EVERY TIME I HEAR IT.

: WOW, NAT. YOU REALLY CAN'T HANDLE BEING IN LOVE. YOU SHOULD GET HELP.

: I KNOW!

MARIE'S FAVORITE THINGS

...

: UHH, WE'RE WAITING.

: I'M DRAWING A BLANK!

: C'MON, YOU LOVE TONS OF STUFF!

: I GUESS, BUT NOTHING THAT DESERVES TO BE ON A LIST!! AHH!! HELP ME OUT!

: ARRRG. OK. BUT YOU OWE ME ONE.

BABY ANIMALS

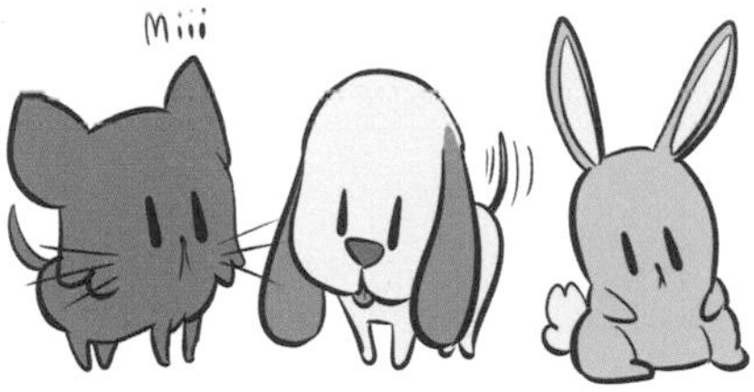
Miii

: YESSSS!! YOU ALWAYS KNOW EXACTLY WHAT I LIKE! YOU'RE THE BEST.

: YEAH, I KNOW...

: DON'T STOP!

GUYS, IN GENERAL?

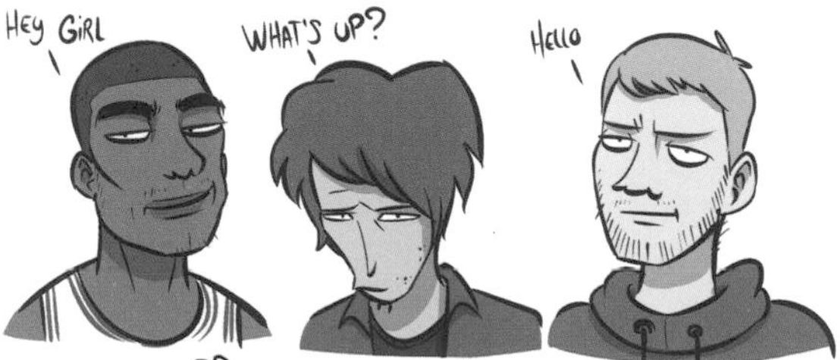
HEY GIRL
WHAT'S UP?
HELLO

: OH HELL YEAH! I DIDN'T KNOW WE COULD HAVE ANSWERS LIKE THAT!

: ...

: WHAT?

: WHY WOULDN'T WE BE ALLOWED TO?

: YOU TELL ME: YOU'RE THE ONE PICKING TOPICS. OKAY, LAST ONE.

MY BROTHER...

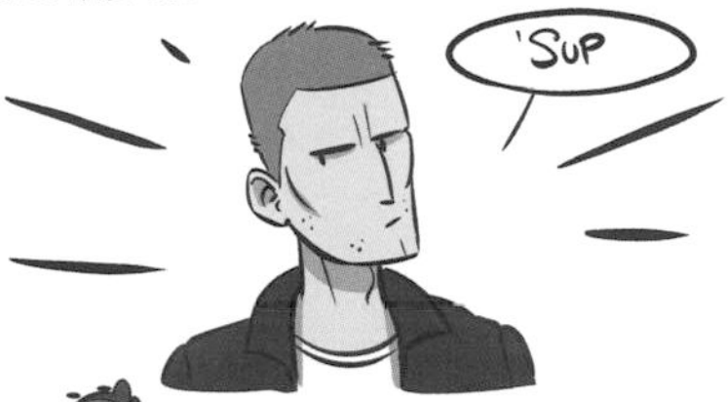
'SUP

: OH HELL YEAH! I AM SO MARRYING YOUR BROTHER IN A FEW YEARS. THANKS FOR THAT ONE!

: NO YOU'RE NOT. HE'S ALREADY MARRIED. WITH KIDS!

: BACK OFF! STOP RUINING MY LIST!

: NOT LIKE YOU NEED MY HELP FOR THAT.

: OK, NEXT! WHAT ELSE?

KARATE?

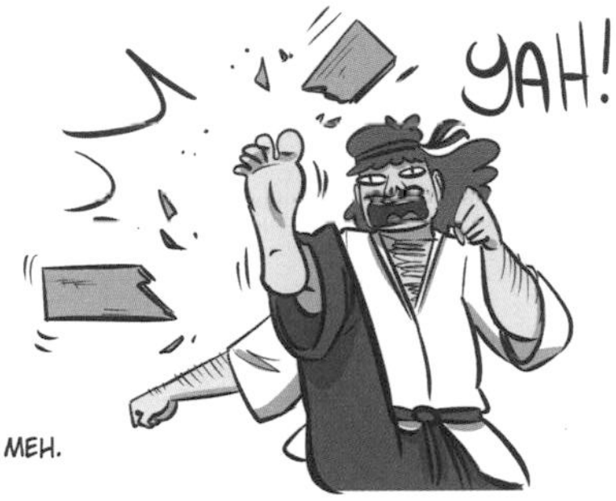
YAH!

: MEH.

: YOU'VE GOT AN ENTIRE ROOM AT HOME FOR YOUR KARATE TROPHIES!

: MY PARENTS MADE ME DO IT, FOR LIKE 10 YEARS. IT'S EASY FOR ME, AND YEAH I KICK ASS. BUT I'M HONESTLY NOT THAT INTO IT.

: NOTHING'S TOO GOOD FOR OUR PRINCESS.

: C'MON, TWO MORE TO GO!

...

: C'MON!

: NO!

: C'MON NAT. QUIT POUTING.

: NOPE! MAYBE TRY BEING A LITTLE NICER!

: YOU CAN'T LEAVE ME HANGING LIKE THAT! I NEED TO KNOW WHAT I LIKE.

: NOPE, SORRY.

: THAT'S TOTALLY IRRESPONSIBLE! YOU'RE A ***BAD FRIEND!***

: OH YEAH? YOU REALLY WANT TO TALK RESPONSIBILITY?

: BRING IT ON! I'M LISTENING!

WHAT IF WE WERE... RESPONSIBLE

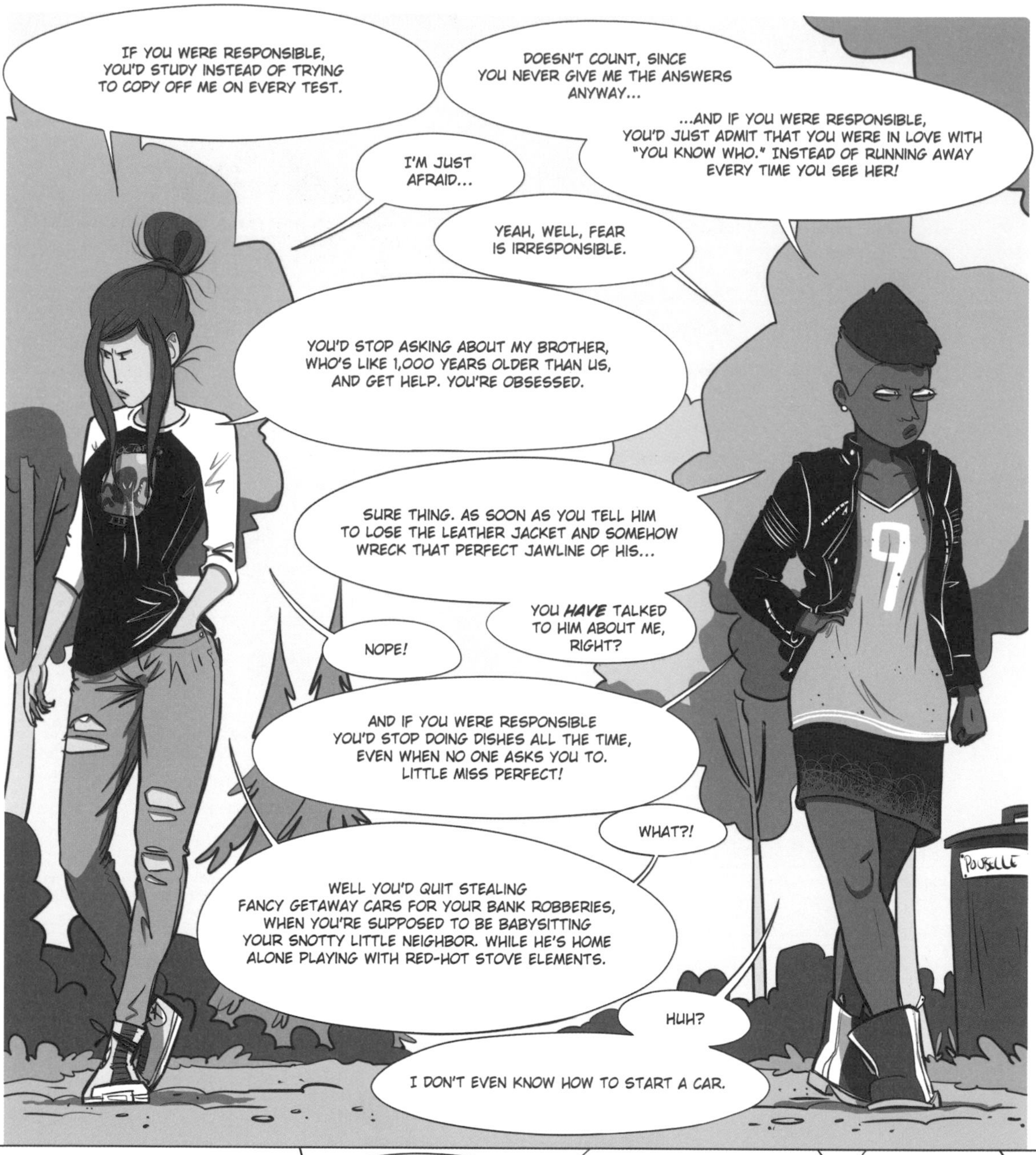
IF YOU WERE RESPONSIBLE, YOU'D STUDY INSTEAD OF TRYING TO COPY OFF ME ON EVERY TEST.
DOESN'T COUNT, SINCE YOU NEVER GIVE ME THE ANSWERS ANYWAY...
...AND IF YOU WERE RESPONSIBLE, YOU'D JUST ADMIT THAT YOU WERE IN LOVE WITH "YOU KNOW WHO." INSTEAD OF RUNNING AWAY EVERY TIME YOU SEE HER!
I'M JUST AFRAID...
YEAH, WELL, FEAR IS IRRESPONSIBLE.
YOU'D STOP ASKING ABOUT MY BROTHER, WHO'S LIKE 1,000 YEARS OLDER THAN US, AND GET HELP. YOU'RE OBSESSED.
SURE THING. AS SOON AS YOU TELL HIM TO LOSE THE LEATHER JACKET AND SOMEHOW WRECK THAT PERFECT JAWLINE OF HIS...
YOU *HAVE* TALKED TO HIM ABOUT ME, RIGHT?
NOPE!
AND IF YOU WERE RESPONSIBLE YOU'D STOP DOING DISHES ALL THE TIME, EVEN WHEN NO ONE ASKS YOU TO. LITTLE MISS PERFECT!
WHAT?!
WELL YOU'D QUIT STEALING FANCY GETAWAY CARS FOR YOUR BANK ROBBERIES, WHEN YOU'RE SUPPOSED TO BE BABYSITTING YOUR SNOTTY LITTLE NEIGHBOR. WHILE HE'S HOME ALONE PLAYING WITH RED-HOT STOVE ELEMENTS.
HUH?
I DON'T EVEN KNOW HOW TO START A CAR.

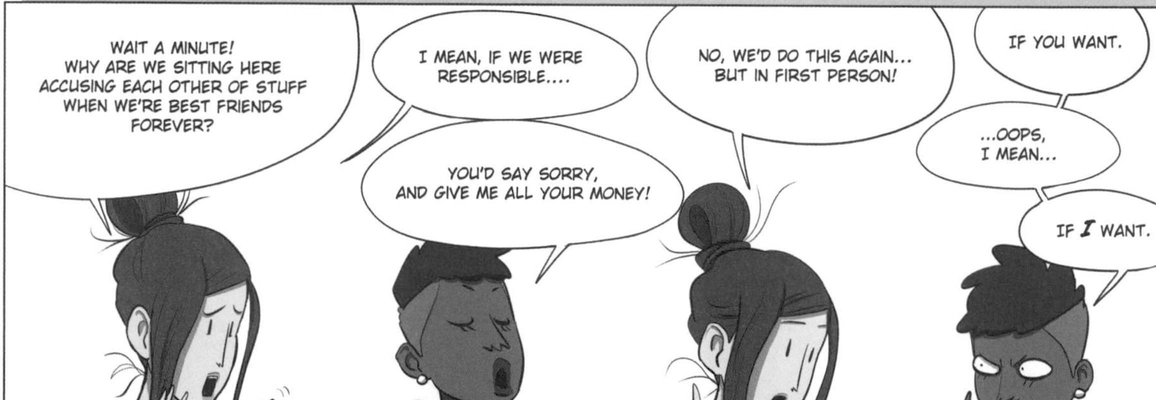
WAIT A MINUTE! WHY ARE WE SITTING HERE ACCUSING EACH OTHER OF STUFF WHEN WE'RE BEST FRIENDS FOREVER?
I MEAN, IF WE WERE RESPONSIBLE....
YOU'D SAY SORRY, AND GIVE ME ALL YOUR MONEY!
NO, WE'D DO THIS AGAIN... BUT IN FIRST PERSON!
IF YOU WANT.
...OOPS, I MEAN...
IF *I* WANT.

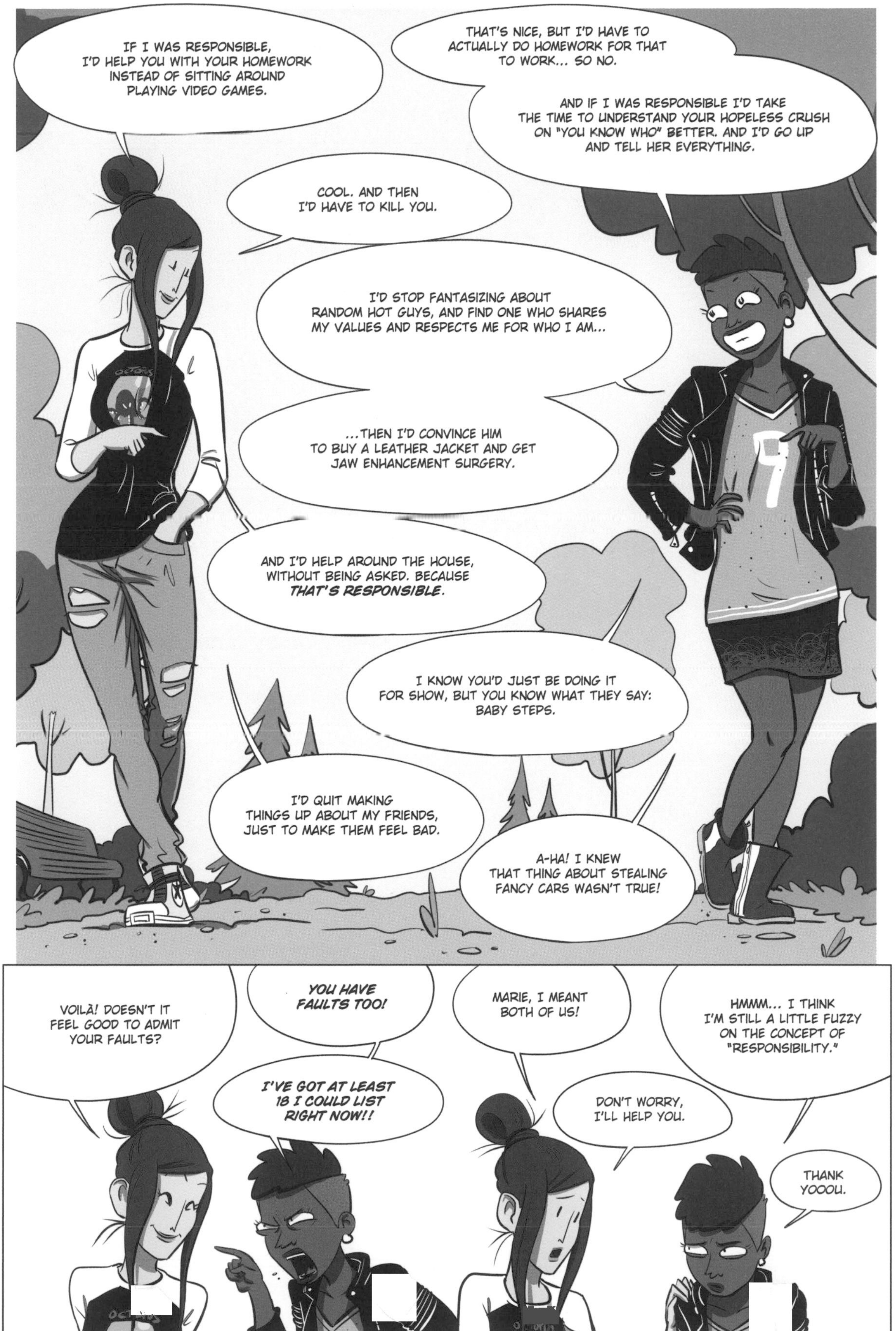
IF I WAS RESPONSIBLE, I'D HELP YOU WITH YOUR HOMEWORK INSTEAD OF SITTING AROUND PLAYING VIDEO GAMES.
THAT'S NICE, BUT I'D HAVE TO ACTUALLY DO HOMEWORK FOR THAT TO WORK... SO NO.
AND IF I WAS RESPONSIBLE I'D TAKE THE TIME TO UNDERSTAND YOUR HOPELESS CRUSH ON "YOU KNOW WHO" BETTER. AND I'D GO UP AND TELL HER EVERYTHING.
COOL. AND THEN I'D HAVE TO KILL YOU.
I'D STOP FANTASIZING ABOUT RANDOM HOT GUYS, AND FIND ONE WHO SHARES MY VALUES AND RESPECTS ME FOR WHO I AM...
...THEN I'D CONVINCE HIM TO BUY A LEATHER JACKET AND GET JAW ENHANCEMENT SURGERY.
AND I'D HELP AROUND THE HOUSE, WITHOUT BEING ASKED. BECAUSE ***THAT'S RESPONSIBLE***.
I KNOW YOU'D JUST BE DOING IT FOR SHOW, BUT YOU KNOW WHAT THEY SAY: BABY STEPS.
I'D QUIT MAKING THINGS UP ABOUT MY FRIENDS, JUST TO MAKE THEM FEEL BAD.
A-HA! I KNEW THAT THING ABOUT STEALING FANCY CARS WASN'T TRUE!
VOILÀ! DOESN'T IT FEEL GOOD TO ADMIT YOUR FAULTS?
YOU HAVE FAULTS TOO!
I'VE GOT AT LEAST 18 I COULD LIST RIGHT NOW!!
MARIE, I MEANT BOTH OF US!
HMMM... I THINK I'M STILL A LITTLE FUZZY ON THE CONCEPT OF "RESPONSIBILITY."
DON'T WORRY, I'LL HELP YOU.
THANK YOOOU.

WHAT NATHALIE HATES MOST: A NON-EXHAUSTIVE LIST

BEING SURROUNDED BY PEOPLE

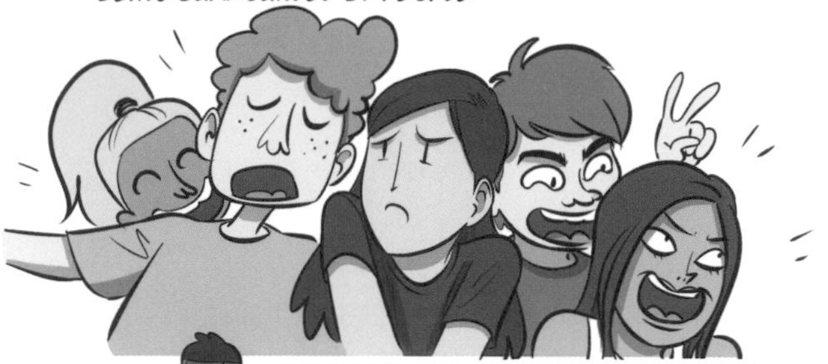

: YOU KNOW THAT'S A MENTAL ILLNESS, RIGHT?

: IT'S NOT AN "ILLNESS." I'M JUST AN INTROVERT.

: ANOTHER SERIOUS ILLNESS!

: WHATEVER.

MACHOS

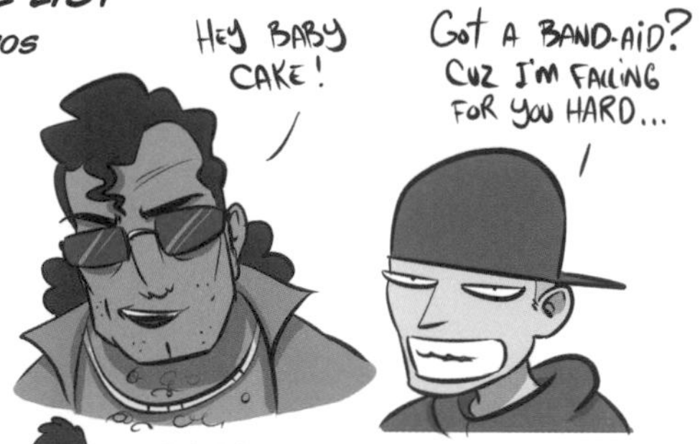
HEY BABY CAKE!
GOT A BAND-AID? CUZ I'M FALLING FOR YOU HARD...

: BUT THEY'RE SO GOOD WITH SALSA.

: MARIE, THOSE ARE "NACHOS." NOT "MACHOS."

: HEH-HEH-HEH

: WOW, I WALKED RIGHT INTO THAT ONE!

: HOW ABOUT MACHO MEN COVERED IN SALSA. YUM!

: DON'T MAKE ME PUKE.

HATERS

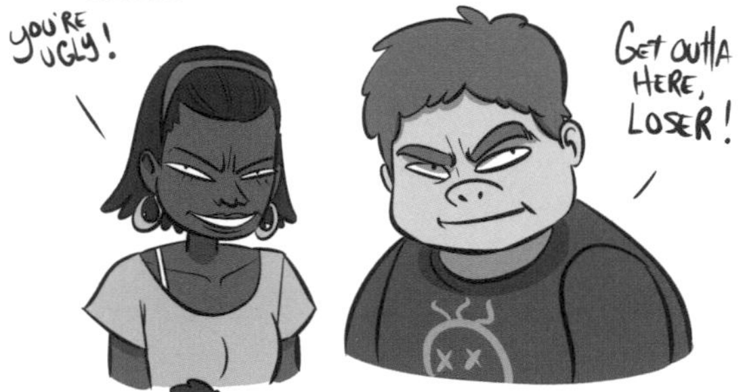
YOU'RE UGLY!
GET OUTTA HERE, LOSER!

: WAIT – I'M A TOTAL HATER!

: YEAH, BUT IT'S THE GOOD KIND OF HATE!

: COOL. MAKES ABSOLUTELY NO SENSE, BUT THANKS!

BIGOTRY

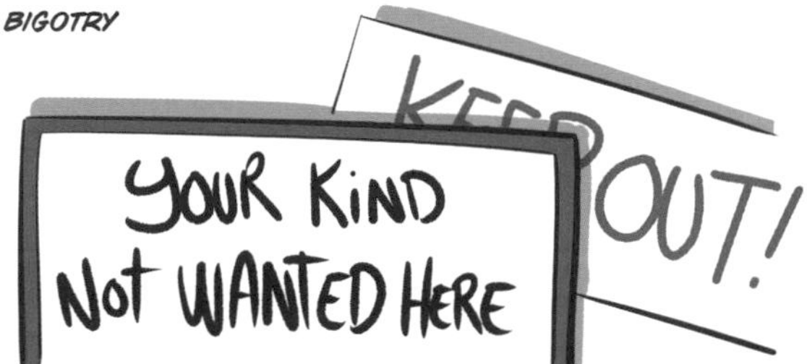
YOUR KIND NOT WANTED HERE
OUT!

: WE DON'T TOLERATE BIGOTRY HERE.

: NOPE.

: MAYBE WE SHOULD ROUND UP ALL THE BIGOTS AND KILL THEM!

: WHOA. EASY THERE, MARIE!!

SUNDAYS

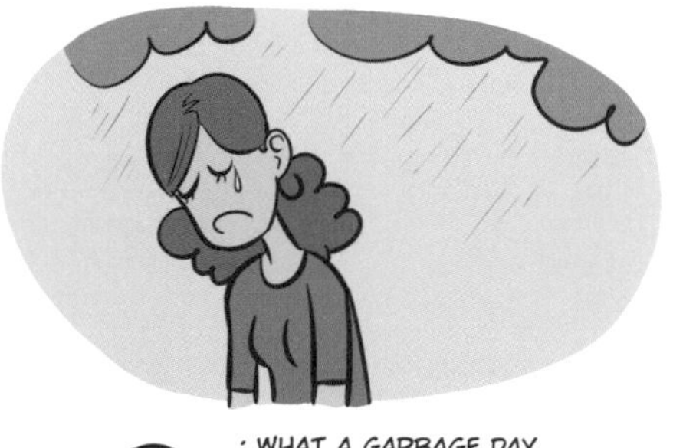

: WHAT A GARBAGE DAY.
THE WEATHER'S ALWAYS GREY, AND NO MATTER HOW MUCH FUN STUFF YOU'VE GOT PLANNED, THERE'S NO GETTING AROUND IT: TOMORROW'S MONDAY.

: OH THANKS! NOW I'LL NEVER BE ABLE TO ENJOY SUNDAYS EVER AGAIN!

REALITY SHOWS

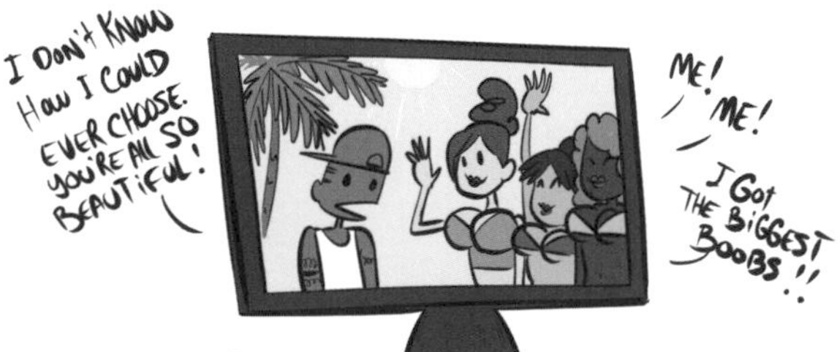
I DON'T KNOW HOW I COULD EVER CHOOSE. YOU'RE ALL SO BEAUTIFUL!
ME! ME!
I GOT THE BIGGEST BOOBS!!

: REALLY?

: YUP. THEY EPITOMIZE THE DECADENCE OF OUR POSTMODERN ERA. AND I CAN'T STOP WATCHING THEM.

THE THINGS MARIE HATES ABOVE ALL

PROCESSED CHEESE SLICES

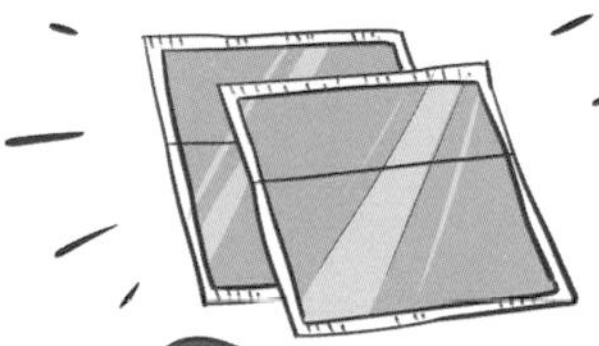

: REALLY? I HAD NO IDEA. IS IT THE CHEMICAL TASTE?

: NAH, MORE LIKE A VISCERAL HATRED. SOMETHING ABOUT THEIR SHAPE. AND THE TEXTURE. AND THE WAY THEY STARE BACK AT YOU WHEN YOU UNWRAP THEM! I WISH I COULD ERASE EVERY TRACE OF PROCESSED CHEESE FROM THE HISTORY BOOKS!

: IF IT MAKES YOU FEEL ANY BETTER, I DOUBT PROCESSED CHEESE GETS MANY MENTIONS IN THE HISTORY BOOKS.

: GOOD!

CLOWNS

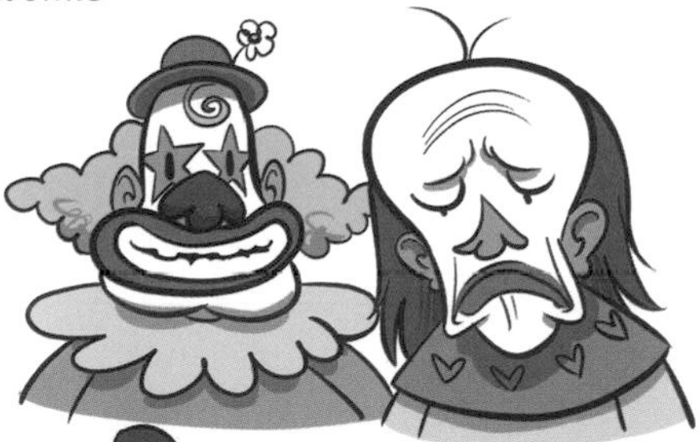

: IF THERE'S ONE THING WE CAN'T STAND, IT'S CLOWNS!

: WHEN I STARE AT SOMEONE LONG ENOUGH, I CAN PICTURE THEIR FACE AS A CLOWN. AND I GET THE SUDDEN URGE TO INFLICT PAIN ON THEM.

: REALLY?! EVEN WITH ME?

: SOMETIMES.

MANIPULATORS

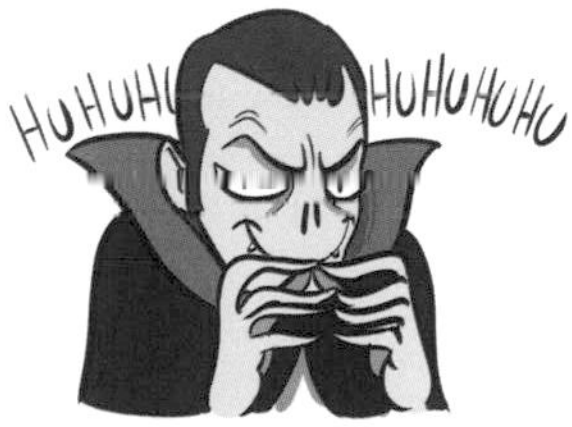
HUHUH
HUHUHUHU

: MARIE, YOU DO REALIZE YOU'RE A BIT OF A MANIPULATOR YOURSELF, RIGHT?

: YEAH, BUT WHEN I MANIPULATE PEOPLE IT'S OUT IN THE OPEN. THAT MAKES IT OKAY.

: NO, THAT IN NO WAY MAKES IT OKAY.

: IT DOES SO! IT TAKES SO MUCH MORE TALENT. AND SINCE BOTH OF US KNOW I'M DOING IT, IT MEANS MY BEST FRIEND MUST BE A STONE COLD GENIUS TO SEE THROUGH MY ELABORATE SCHEMES.

: AW SHUCKS.

NEVER BEING COMPLETELY SURE I'M NOT WALKING OVER BURIED TREASURE

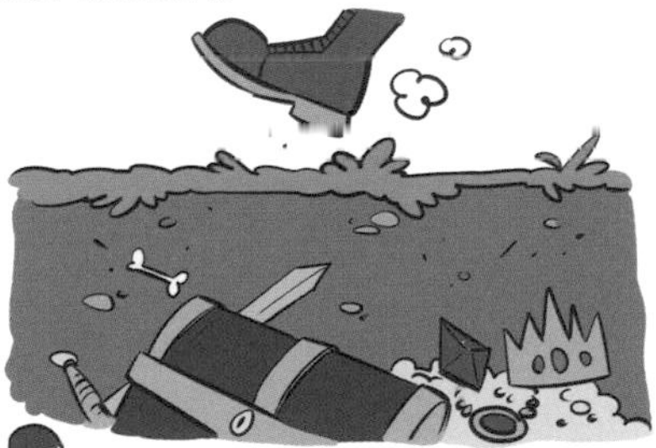

: UHH... WEIRD?

: YEAH, I KNOW.

: ...

: ADMIT IT, THOUGH. IT'S UNBEARABLE!

: I'LL NEVER LOOK AT THINGS THE SAME WAY AGAIN!

WHEN I NEED TO TALK TO YOU BUT YOU'RE NOT THERE, AND YOU WON'T PICK UP THE PHONE, SO I GO OVER AND WAIT UNDER YOUR BEDROOM WINDOW, BUT YOU'RE SLEEPING

: UUUH. DO YOU DO THAT A LOT?

: DUNNO, MAYBE ONCE OR TWICE A MONTH?

: WHAT? AND WHAT DO YOU DO ONCE YOU'RE THERE?

: I DON'T WANT TO WAKE YOU UP, SO I SIT DOWN ON THE GROUND AND TALK TO YOU THROUGH THE WINDOW. THEN, I LOOK AT YOU AND TRY TO IMAGINE YOUR ANSWERS.

: OK, BASICALLY THE CREEPIEST THING I'VE EVER HEARD. AND THE CUTEST.

: THANKS!!!

WHEN YOU'RE SAD

: HUH?

: YEAH...

: C'MON MARIE! I'M A BIG GIRL.

: YEAH, I KNOW... BUT I DON'T LIKE HOW SOMETIMES I CAN TELL YOU'RE SAD, AND THERE'S NOTHING I CAN DO TO HELP. YOU KNOW, LIKE WHEN YOU THINK ABOUT "YOU KNOW WHO"–AND I'M NOT TALKING ABOUT VOLDEMORT. I JUST WISH I COULD TAKE ALL YOUR SADNESS FROM YOU SO YOU'D FEEL BETTER.

: MARIE, I LOVE YOU SO MUCH...
: NO, I LOVE YOU SO MUCH!! WAA HAAA HA!

WHAT IF WE WERE... SCIENTISTS

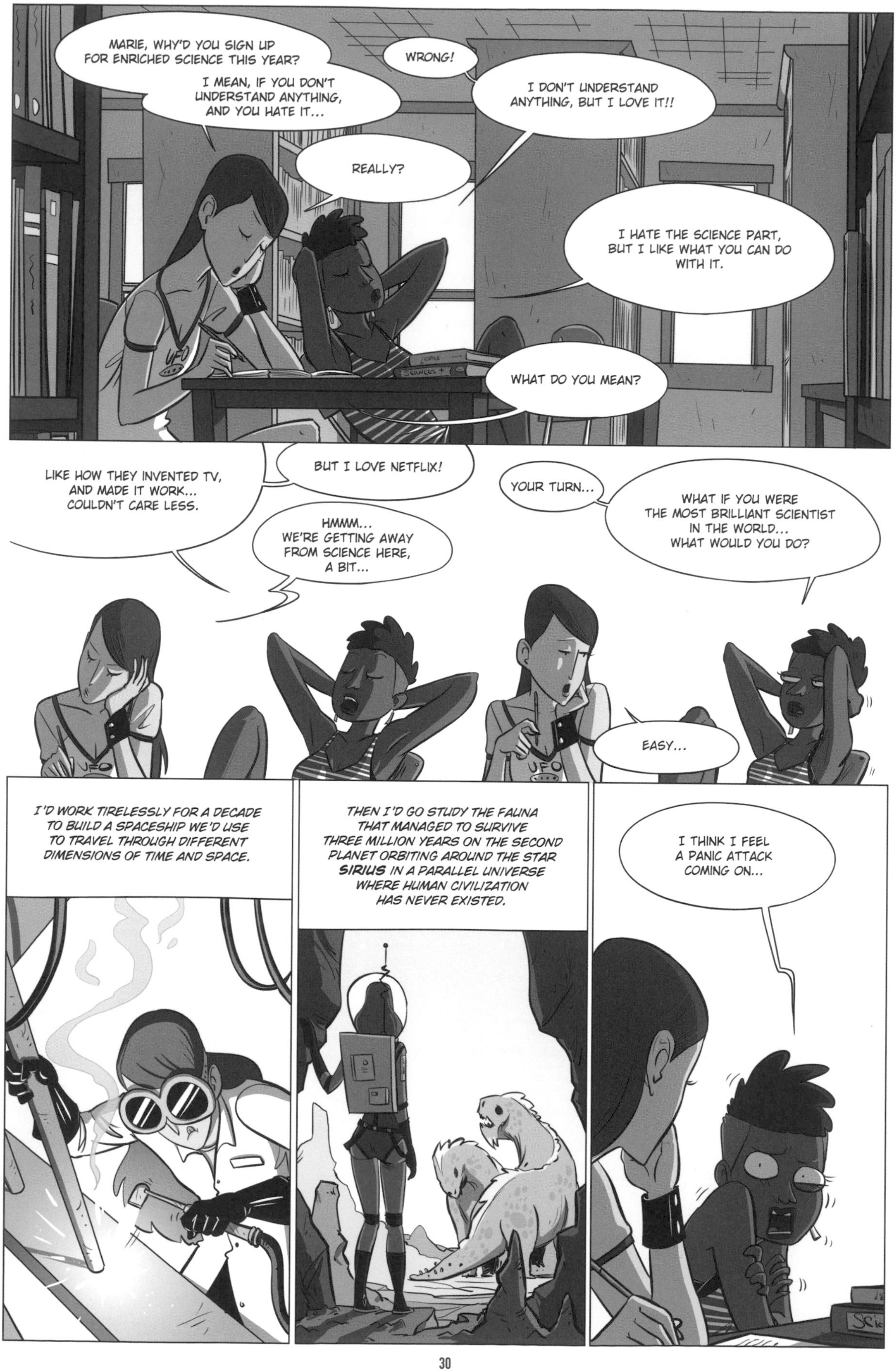
MARIE, WHY'D YOU SIGN UP FOR ENRICHED SCIENCE THIS YEAR?
I MEAN, IF YOU DON'T UNDERSTAND ANYTHING, AND YOU HATE IT...
WRONG!
I DON'T UNDERSTAND ANYTHING, BUT I LOVE IT!!
REALLY?
I HATE THE SCIENCE PART, BUT I LIKE WHAT YOU CAN DO WITH IT.
WHAT DO YOU MEAN?
LIKE HOW THEY INVENTED TV, AND MADE IT WORK... COULDN'T CARE LESS.
BUT I LOVE NETFLIX!
HMMM... WE'RE GETTING AWAY FROM SCIENCE HERE, A BIT...
YOUR TURN...
WHAT IF YOU WERE THE MOST BRILLIANT SCIENTIST IN THE WORLD... WHAT WOULD YOU DO?
EASY...
I'D WORK TIRELESSLY FOR A DECADE TO BUILD A SPACESHIP WE'D USE TO TRAVEL THROUGH DIFFERENT DIMENSIONS OF TIME AND SPACE.
THEN I'D GO STUDY THE FAUNA THAT MANAGED TO SURVIVE THREE MILLION YEARS ON THE SECOND PLANET ORBITING AROUND THE STAR SIRIUS IN A PARALLEL UNIVERSE WHERE HUMAN CIVILIZATION HAS NEVER EXISTED.
I THINK I FEEL A PANIC ATTACK COMING ON...

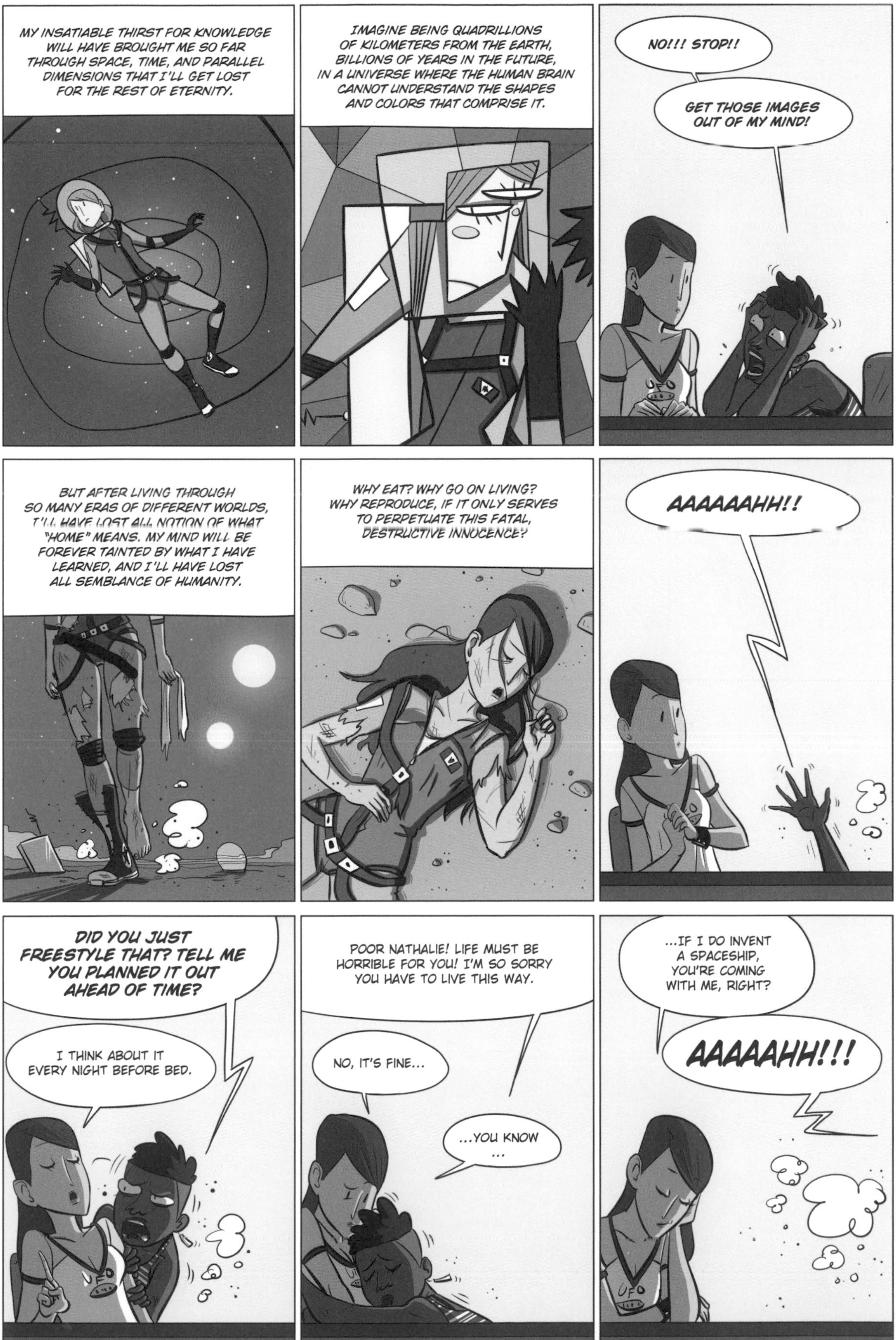
MY INSATIABLE THIRST FOR KNOWLEDGE WILL HAVE BROUGHT ME SO FAR THROUGH SPACE, TIME, AND PARALLEL DIMENSIONS THAT I'LL GET LOST FOR THE REST OF ETERNITY.
IMAGINE BEING QUADRILLIONS OF KILOMETERS FROM THE EARTH, BILLIONS OF YEARS IN THE FUTURE, IN A UNIVERSE WHERE THE HUMAN BRAIN CANNOT UNDERSTAND THE SHAPES AND COLORS THAT COMPRISE IT.
NO!!! STOP!!
GET THOSE IMAGES OUT OF MY MIND!
BUT AFTER LIVING THROUGH SO MANY ERAS OF DIFFERENT WORLDS, I'LL HAVE LOST ALL NOTION OF WHAT "HOME" MEANS. MY MIND WILL BE FOREVER TAINTED BY WHAT I HAVE LEARNED, AND I'LL HAVE LOST ALL SEMBLANCE OF HUMANITY.
WHY EAT? WHY GO ON LIVING? WHY REPRODUCE, IF IT ONLY SERVES TO PERPETUATE THIS FATAL, DESTRUCTIVE INNOCENCE?
AAAAAAHH!!
DID YOU JUST FREESTYLE THAT? TELL ME YOU PLANNED IT OUT AHEAD OF TIME?
I THINK ABOUT IT EVERY NIGHT BEFORE BED.
POOR NATHALIE! LIFE MUST BE HORRIBLE FOR YOU! I'M SO SORRY YOU HAVE TO LIVE THIS WAY.
NO, IT'S FINE...
...YOU KNOW ...
...IF I DO INVENT A SPACESHIP, YOU'RE COMING WITH ME, RIGHT?
AAAAAHH!!!

WHAT IF WE WERE... SCIENTISTS. PART 2

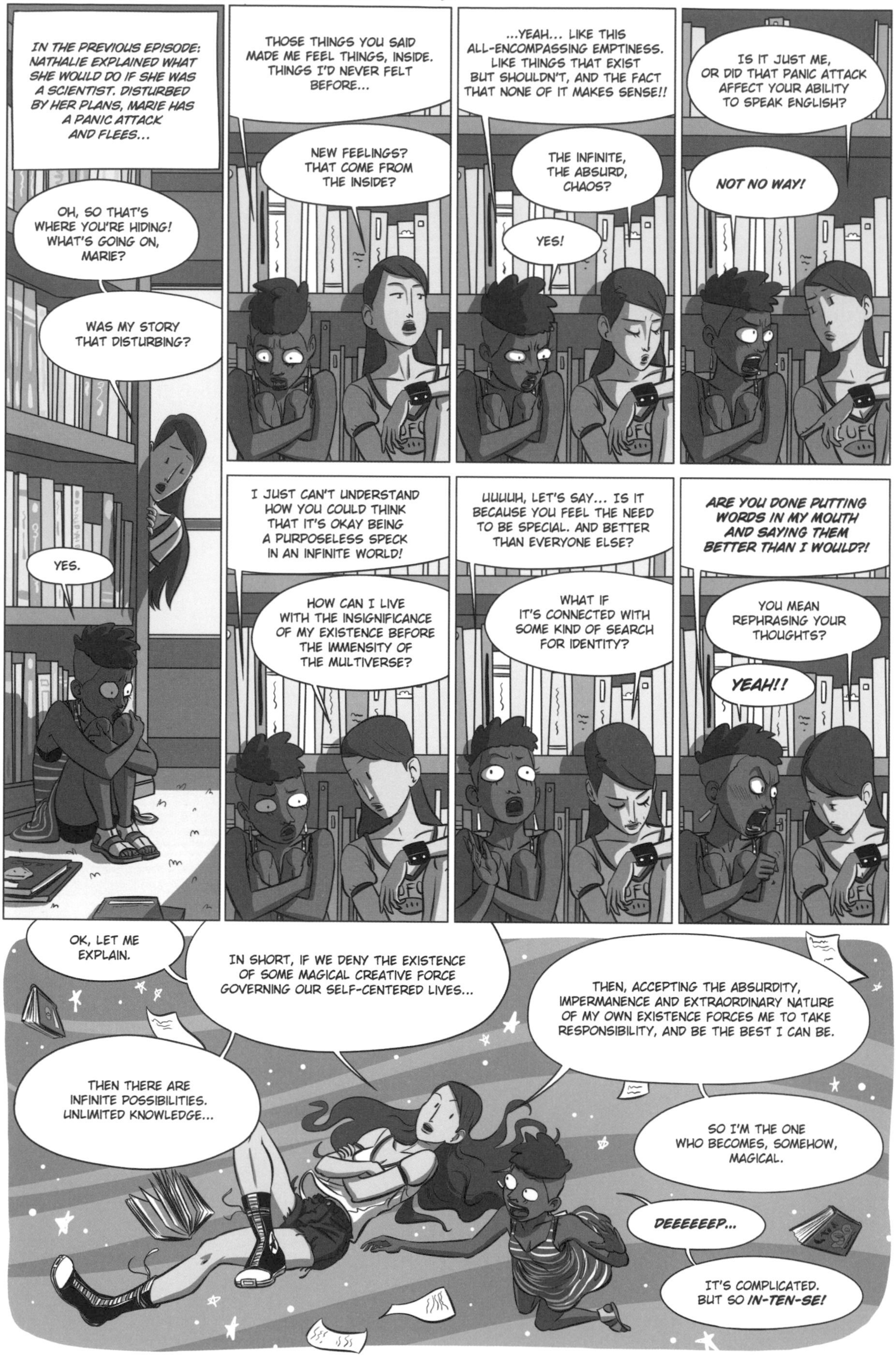
IN THE PREVIOUS EPISODE: NATHALIE EXPLAINED WHAT SHE WOULD DO IF SHE WAS A SCIENTIST. DISTURBED BY HER PLANS, MARIE HAS A PANIC ATTACK AND FLEES...
OH, SO THAT'S WHERE YOU'RE HIDING! WHAT'S GOING ON, MARIE?
WAS MY STORY THAT DISTURBING?
YES.
THOSE THINGS YOU SAID MADE ME FEEL THINGS, INSIDE. THINGS I'D NEVER FELT BEFORE...
NEW FEELINGS? THAT COME FROM THE INSIDE?
...YEAH... LIKE THIS ALL-ENCOMPASSING EMPTINESS. LIKE THINGS THAT EXIST BUT SHOULDN'T, AND THE FACT THAT NONE OF IT MAKES SENSE!!
THE INFINITE, THE ABSURD, CHAOS?
YES!
IS IT JUST ME, OR DID THAT PANIC ATTACK AFFECT YOUR ABILITY TO SPEAK ENGLISH?
NOT NO WAY!
I JUST CAN'T UNDERSTAND HOW YOU COULD THINK THAT IT'S OKAY BEING A PURPOSELESS SPECK IN AN INFINITE WORLD!
HOW CAN I LIVE WITH THE INSIGNIFICANCE OF MY EXISTENCE BEFORE THE IMMENSITY OF THE MULTIVERSE?
UUUUH, LET'S SAY... IS IT BECAUSE YOU FEEL THE NEED TO BE SPECIAL. AND BETTER THAN EVERYONE ELSE?
WHAT IF IT'S CONNECTED WITH SOME KIND OF SEARCH FOR IDENTITY?
ARE YOU DONE PUTTING WORDS IN MY MOUTH AND SAYING THEM BETTER THAN I WOULD?!
YOU MEAN REPHRASING YOUR THOUGHTS?
YEAH!!
OK, LET ME EXPLAIN.
IN SHORT, IF WE DENY THE EXISTENCE OF SOME MAGICAL CREATIVE FORCE GOVERNING OUR SELF-CENTERED LIVES...
THEN THERE ARE INFINITE POSSIBILITIES. UNLIMITED KNOWLEDGE...
THEN, ACCEPTING THE ABSURDITY, IMPERMANENCE AND EXTRAORDINARY NATURE OF MY OWN EXISTENCE FORCES ME TO TAKE RESPONSIBILITY, AND BE THE BEST I CAN BE.
SO I'M THE ONE WHO BECOMES, SOMEHOW, MAGICAL.
DEEEEEEP...
IT'S COMPLICATED. BUT SO IN-TEN-SE!

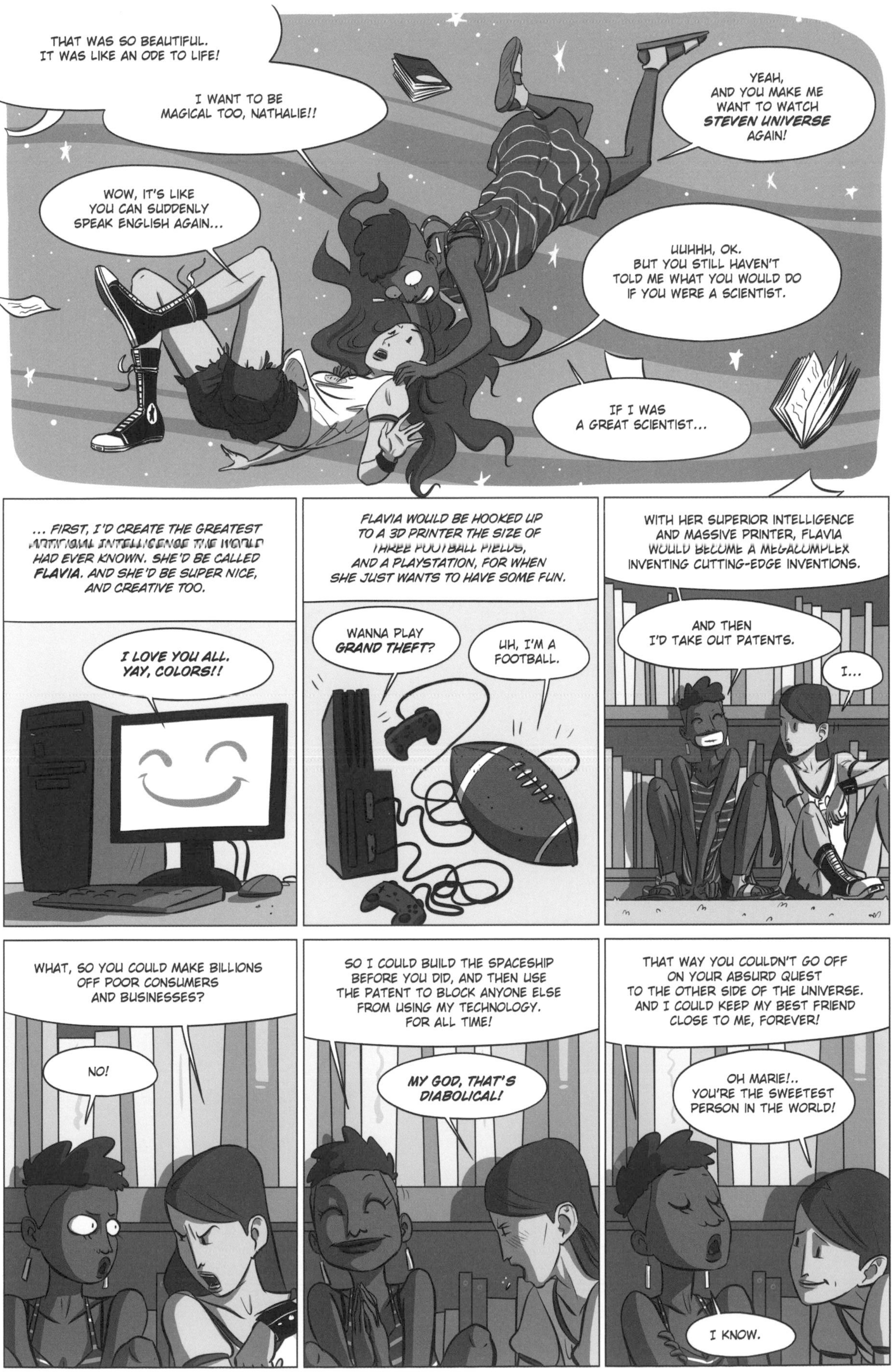
THAT WAS SO BEAUTIFUL. IT WAS LIKE AN ODE TO LIFE!
I WANT TO BE MAGICAL TOO, NATHALIE!!
YEAH, AND YOU MAKE ME WANT TO WATCH **STEVEN UNIVERSE** AGAIN!
WOW, IT'S LIKE YOU CAN SUDDENLY SPEAK ENGLISH AGAIN...
UHHHH, OK. BUT YOU STILL HAVEN'T TOLD ME WHAT YOU WOULD DO IF YOU WERE A SCIENTIST.
IF I WAS A GREAT SCIENTIST...
*... FIRST, I'D CREATE THE GREATEST ARTIFICIAL INTELLIGENCE THE WORLD HAD EVER KNOWN. SHE'D BE CALLED **FLAVIA**. AND SHE'D BE SUPER NICE, AND CREATIVE TOO.*
I LOVE YOU ALL. YAY, COLORS!!
FLAVIA WOULD BE HOOKED UP TO A 3D PRINTER THE SIZE OF THREE FOOTBALL FIELDS, AND A PLAYSTATION, FOR WHEN SHE JUST WANTS TO HAVE SOME FUN.
WANNA PLAY **GRAND THEFT**?
UH, I'M A FOOTBALL.
WITH HER SUPERIOR INTELLIGENCE AND MASSIVE PRINTER, FLAVIA WOULD BECOME A MEGACOMPLEX INVENTING CUTTING-EDGE INVENTIONS.
AND THEN I'D TAKE OUT PATENTS.
I...
WHAT, SO YOU COULD MAKE BILLIONS OFF POOR CONSUMERS AND BUSINESSES?
NO!
SO I COULD BUILD THE SPACESHIP BEFORE YOU DID, AND THEN USE THE PATENT TO BLOCK ANYONE ELSE FROM USING MY TECHNOLOGY. FOR ALL TIME!
MY GOD, THAT'S DIABOLICAL!
THAT WAY YOU COULDN'T GO OFF ON YOUR ABSURD QUEST TO THE OTHER SIDE OF THE UNIVERSE. AND I COULD KEEP MY BEST FRIEND CLOSE TO ME, FOREVER!
OH MARIE!.. YOU'RE THE SWEETEST PERSON IN THE WORLD!
I KNOW.

NATHALIE'S 4 FAVORITE MOVIES

STARDUST

STARDUST

: WHAT? WHAT'S THAT?

: YOU KNOW, THE ONE WITH THE PIRATES CHASING LIGHTNING BOLTS AND THE BROTHERS WHO MURDER EACH OTHER FOR THE THRONE?

: AREN'T THEY, LIKE, TRYING TO SAVE A PRINCESS?

: SHE'S NOT A PRINCESS, SHE'S A SHOOTING STAR!

: OH SORRY, THAT MAKES IT WAY LESS CHEESY! HAHAHA!

: YOU KNOW THE MAIN CHARACTER IS THE GUY WHO PLAYS DAREDEVIL?

: ***WHAT?! WE ARE SO WATCHING IT TONIGHT!!***

PRINCESS MONONOKE

PRINCESS
MONONOKÉ

: OH MY GOD! SERIOUSLY, MORE PRINCESSES?

: IT'S THAT JAPANESE ANIME MOVIE, WITH THE GIANT HUMAN DEER WHO GETS HIS HEAD CUT OFF.

: OH MY GOD! NOT THAT ONE! IT'S SO CREEPY AND DISTURBING!

ARRIVAL

ARRIVAL

: SO GOOD!! SO SAD! WITH ALIENS AND EVERYTHING! JUST WOW.

: BEST MOVIE EVER!!

: I DIDN'T GET IT AT ALL. BUT AGREED!

MAD MAX : FURY ROAD

MAD
MAX
FURY ROAD

: NO FAIR! THAT ONE'S MINE!

: IMPOSSIBLE! AND I HAVE PROOF...

: OH YEAH, WHAT?

: FURIOSA IS AN IMPERATOR, WHICH IS BASICALLY A PRINCESS.

: FINE... BUT I GET TO BE HER FOR HALLOWEEN!

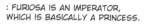

: DEAL.

MARIE'S 4 FAVORITE MOVIES (ACTUALLY, THERE ARE 3)

SHE-RA AND THE PRINCESSES OF POWER SERIES

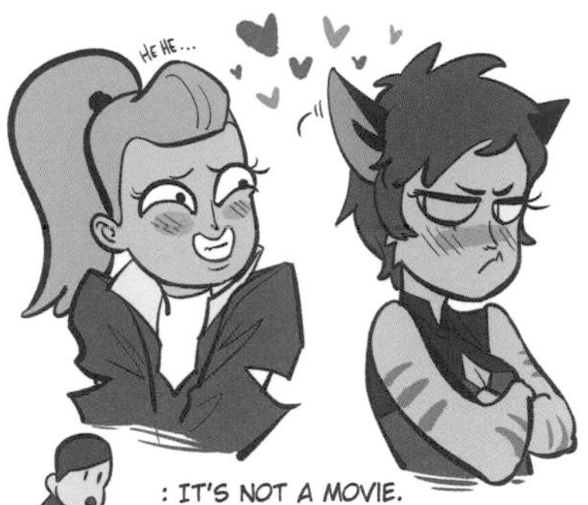
HE HE...

: IT'S NOT A MOVIE.

: I DON'T CARE!
THEY'RE ALL THE BEST!!

: YEAH, TRUE.

: STOP AGREEING WITH ME!

: WHICH SEASON IS YOUR FAVORITE THOUGH?

: ALL OF THEM!!

: OKAY, OKAY, ALL OF THEM...
BUT IF YOU HAD TO PUT THEM IN ORD...

: 5, 3, 1, 2, 4!

: IMPRESSIVE.

FROZEN

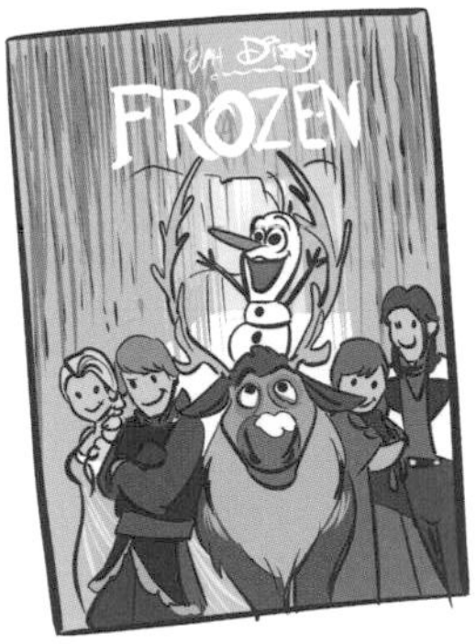
FROZEN

: AND YOU'RE TEASING ***ME*** ABOUT PRINCESSES?

: DIFFERENCE IS, I'M NOT EMBARRASSED
OF LIKING PRINCESSES.

: I DON'T LIKE PRINCESSES!
IT'S CHEESY AS...

: SEE? YOU'RE EMBARRASSED!

: HMPH!

HUNGER GAMES

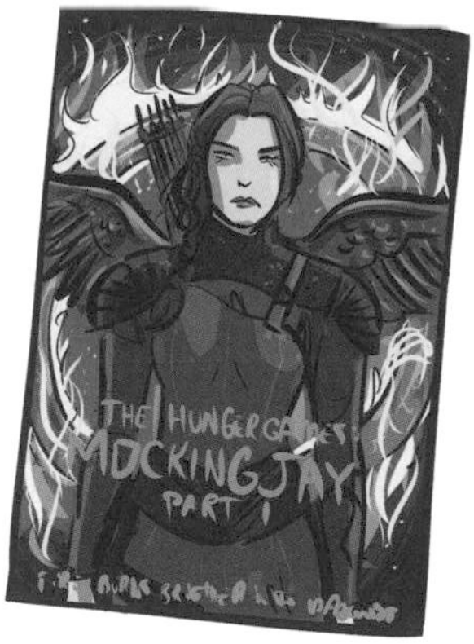
THE HUNGER GAMES
MOCKINGJAY
PART 1

: MMMM... JENNIFER LAWRENCE...

: MMMM... THE GUY WHO PLAYS
JENNIFER LAWRENCE'S BOYFRIEND...

: I'M GLAD YOU'RE MY BEST FRIEND,
WE NEVER HAVE TO FIGHT OVER
CELEB CRUSHES.

: HEH HEH!

TWILIGHT

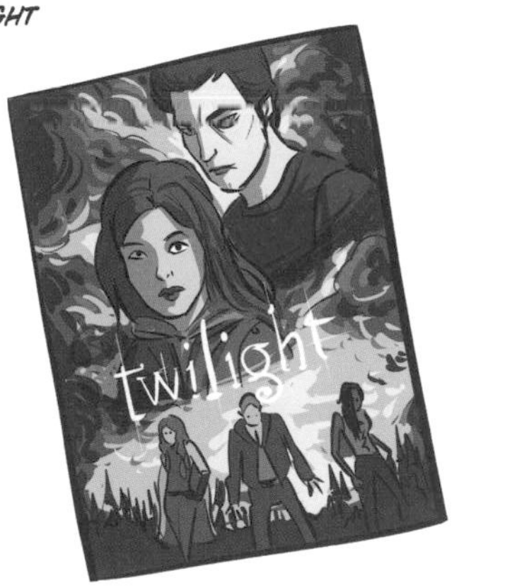
twilight

: NEVER SEEN IT.

: ME NEITHER, BUT I GET THE FEELING
IT'S LIKE, AMAZING.

: YOU KNOW I THINK WE MIGHT BE
THE ONLY TWO GIRLS IN SCHOOL
WHO HAVEN'T SEEN IT?

: YOU THINK?

: IT'S PLAYING IN THAT THEATRE
THAT SHOWS OLD MOVIES. WANNA GO?

: I'M WORRIED IT WON'T LIVE UP
TO MY EXPECTATIONS.

: IT WILL TOTALLY EXCEED THEM!

: OKAY, LET'S DO IT!!

WHAT IF WE WERE... MAGICAL CREATURES

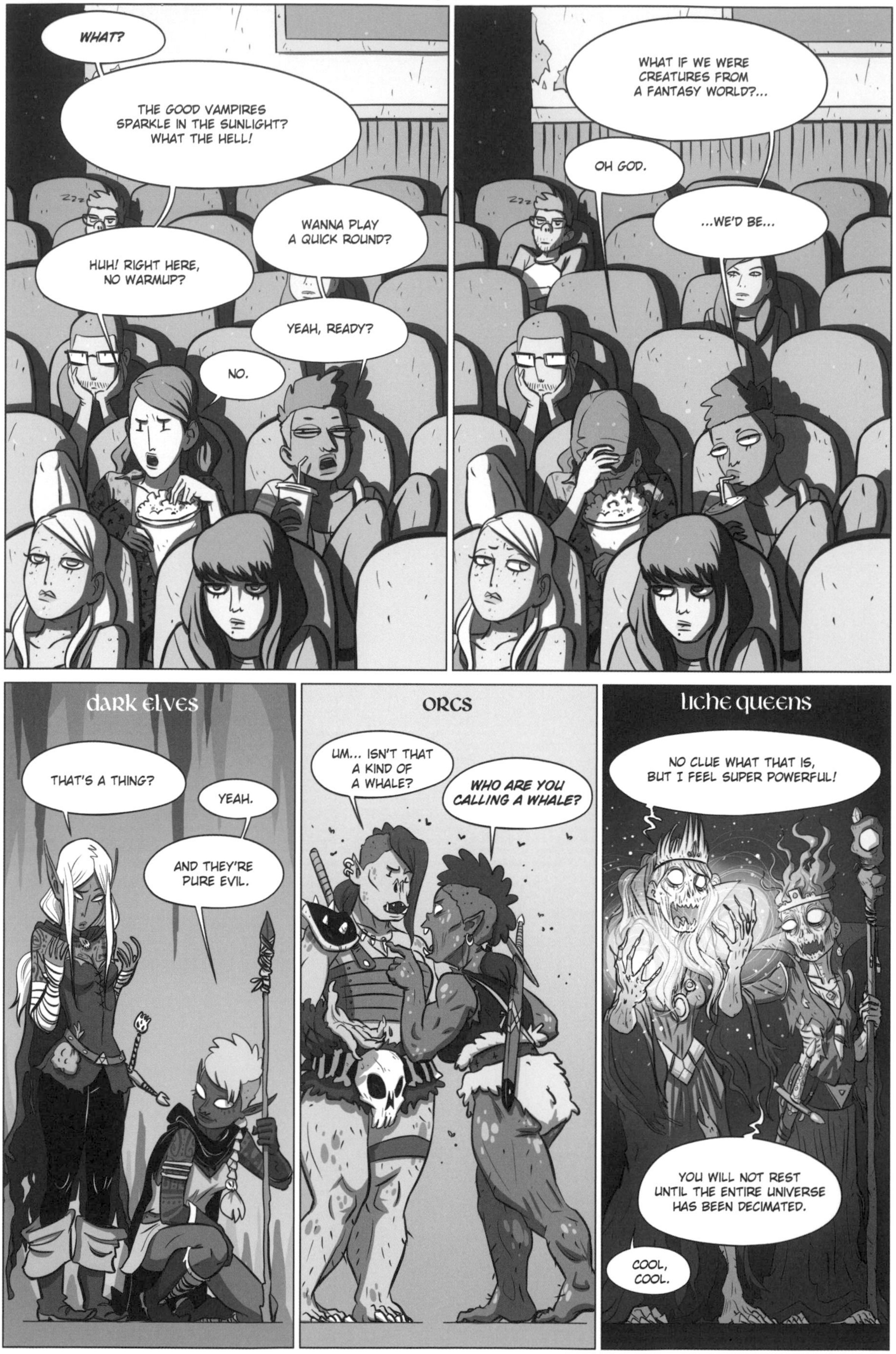
WHAT?
THE GOOD VAMPIRES SPARKLE IN THE SUNLIGHT? WHAT THE HELL!
WANNA PLAY A QUICK ROUND?
HUH! RIGHT HERE, NO WARMUP?
YEAH, READY?
NO.
WHAT IF WE WERE CREATURES FROM A FANTASY WORLD?...
OH GOD.
...WE'D BE...
dark elves
THAT'S A THING?
YEAH.
AND THEY'RE PURE EVIL.
ORCS
UM... ISN'T THAT A KIND OF A WHALE?
WHO ARE YOU CALLING A WHALE?
liche queens
NO CLUE WHAT THAT IS, BUT I FEEL SUPER POWERFUL!
YOU WILL NOT REST UNTIL THE ENTIRE UNIVERSE HAS BEEN DECIMATED.
COOL, COOL.

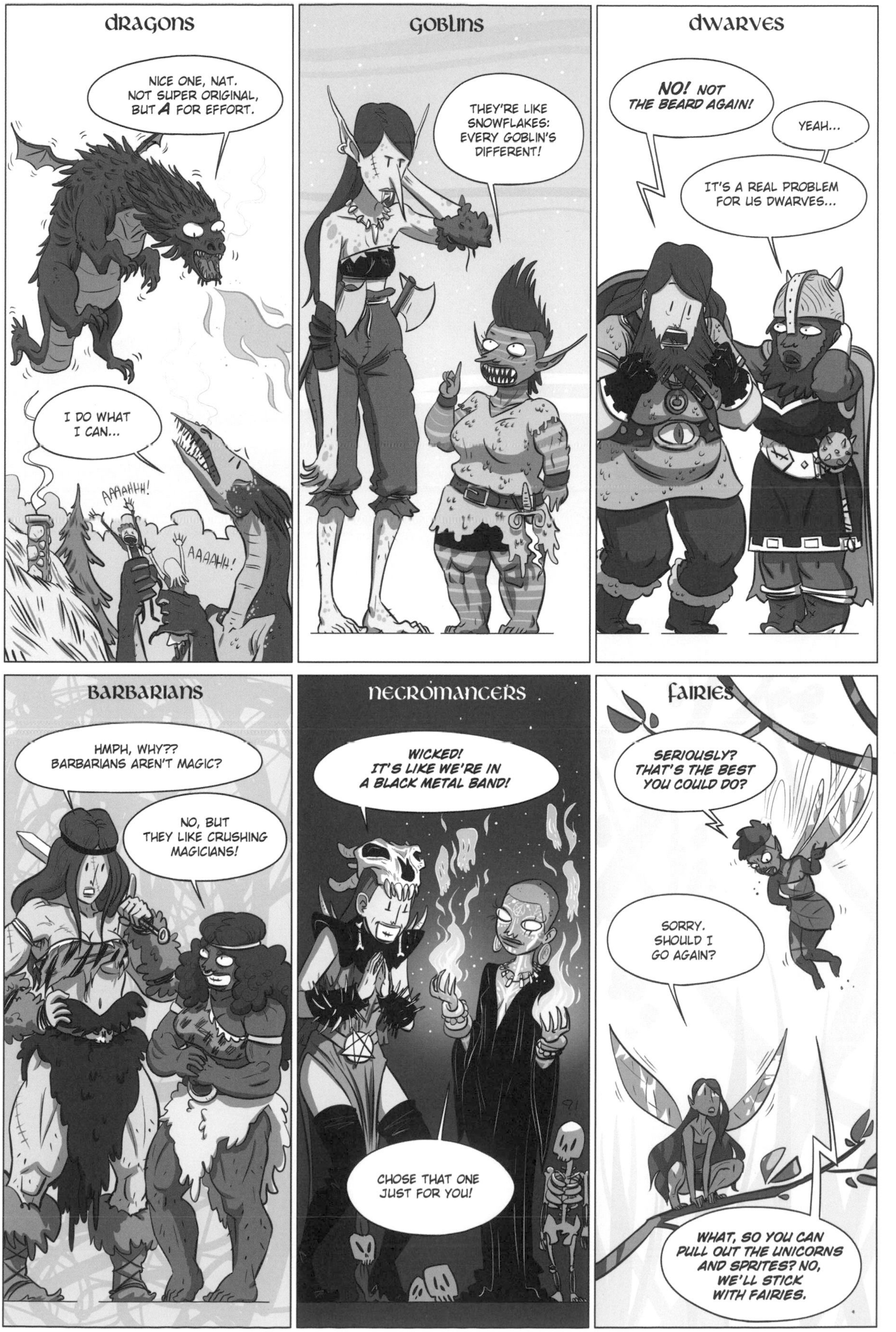
DRAGONS
NICE ONE, NAT. NOT SUPER ORIGINAL, BUT A FOR EFFORT.
I DO WHAT I CAN...
AAAAHHH!
AAAAHH!
GOBLINS
THEY'RE LIKE SNOWFLAKES: EVERY GOBLIN'S DIFFERENT!
DWARVES
NO! NOT THE BEARD AGAIN!
YEAH...
IT'S A REAL PROBLEM FOR US DWARVES...
BARBARIANS
HMPH, WHY?? BARBARIANS AREN'T MAGIC?
NO, BUT THEY LIKE CRUSHING MAGICIANS!
NECROMANCERS
WICKED! IT'S LIKE WE'RE IN A BLACK METAL BAND!
CHOSE THAT ONE JUST FOR YOU!
FAIRIES
SERIOUSLY? THAT'S THE BEST YOU COULD DO?
SORRY. SHOULD I GO AGAIN?
WHAT, SO YOU CAN PULL OUT THE UNICORNS AND SPRITES? NO, WE'LL STICK WITH FAIRIES.

MARIE'S ALL-TIME GREATEST HALLOWEEN COSTUMES

AGE 5: CLOWN-BALLOONS

SHE DIDN'T REALLY GET THE WHOLE HALLOWEEN THING. BUT SHE SURE LIKED KNOCKING ON DOORS FOR CANDY. FOR THREE MONTHS AFTER HALLOWEEN, MARIE KEPT KNOCKING ON DOORS – MINUS THE COSTUME.

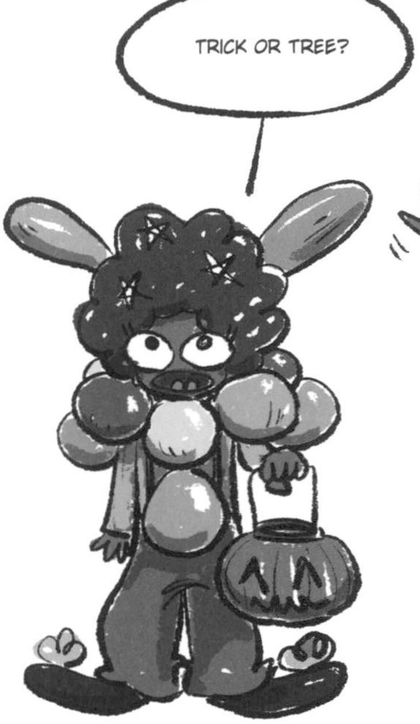
TRICK OR TREE?

AGE 7: STAR WITCH

MARIE INSISTED ON BEING A WITCH, EVEN THOUGH HER MOM HAD ALREADY BOUGHT HER A COSTUME.

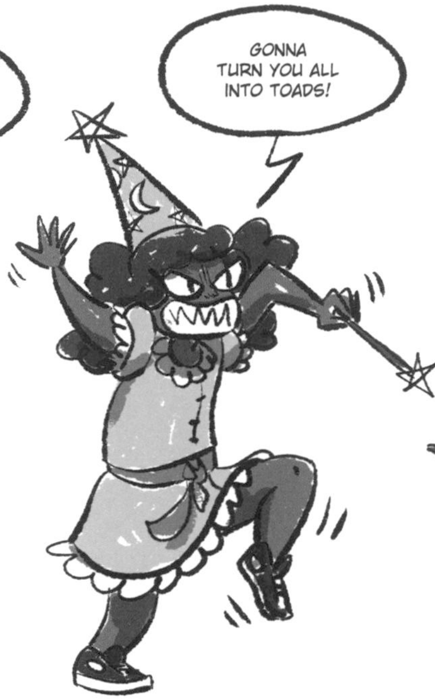
GONNA TURN YOU ALL INTO TOADS!

AGE 9: COWBOY-WITCH

MARIE'S MOTHER NEVER UNDERSTOOD THAT ALL HER DAUGHTER WANTED WAS TO DRESS UP AS A WITCH.

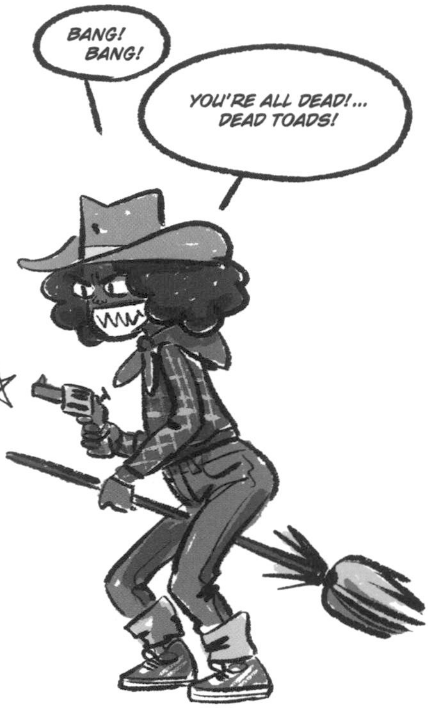
BANG! BANG!
YOU'RE ALL DEAD!... DEAD TOADS!

AGE 10: KICK-ASS WITCH

THIS TIME MARIE MADE HER COSTUME SIX MONTHS IN ADVANCE. UNFORTUNATELY, IT WAS FREEZING AND SNOWING THAT HALLOWEEN.

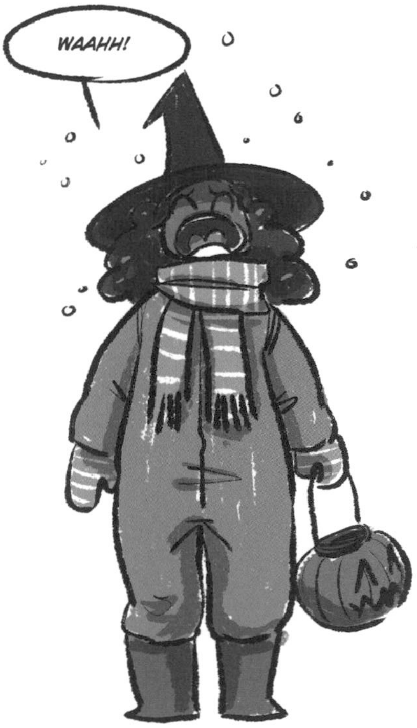
WAAHH!

AGE 14: HIPPIE

GOT KICKED OUT OF THREE CLASSES BECAUSE SHE WAS TOO INTO HER CHARACTER AND HER TEACHERS DIDN'T APPRECIATE BEING TOLD TO "*JUST RELAX, MAN,*" "*PEACE OUT,*" LET ALONE "*DOWN WITH THE MAN, LET'S DANCE NAKED!*"

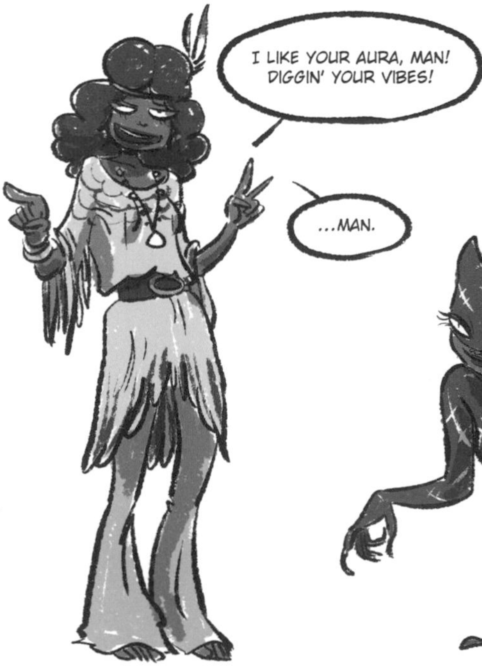
I LIKE YOUR AURA, MAN! DIGGIN' YOUR VIBES!
...MAN.

AGE 16: CATWOMAN

SHE MANAGED TO GET THROUGH ONE AND A HALF CLASSES BEFORE SHE GOT SENT HOME TO CHANGE. HER COSTUME WAS TOO DISTRACTING FOR EVERYONE.

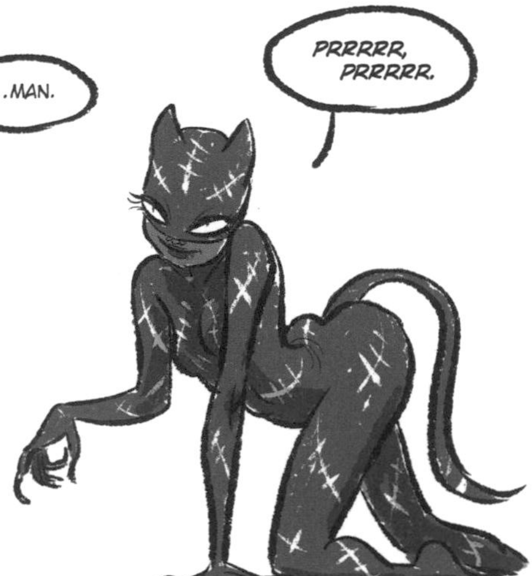
PRRRRR, PRRRRR.

NAT'S BEST HALLOWEEN COSTUMES

AGE 4: SOMETHING

WHAT HAPPENS WHEN 2 PARENTS MAKE 1 CONFUSING COSTUME.

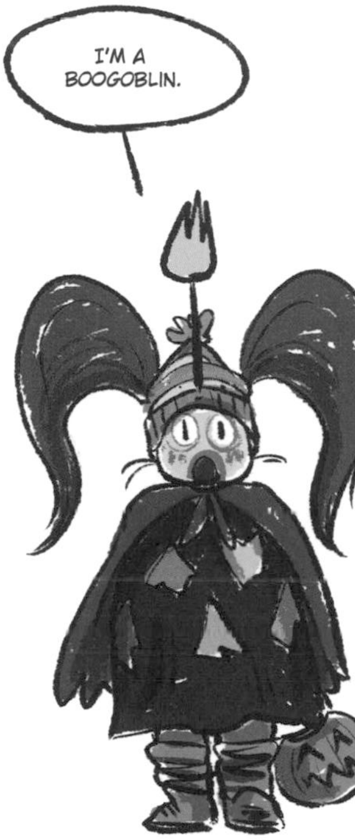
I'M A BOOGOBLIN.

AGE 8: PIPPI LONGSTOCKING

GOT INTO FIGHTS TWO RECESSES IN A ROW BECAUSE THE BOYS WERE PULLING HER PIGTAILS. POOR FOOLS DIDN'T REALIZE PIPPI HAS SUPERHUMAN STRENGTH.

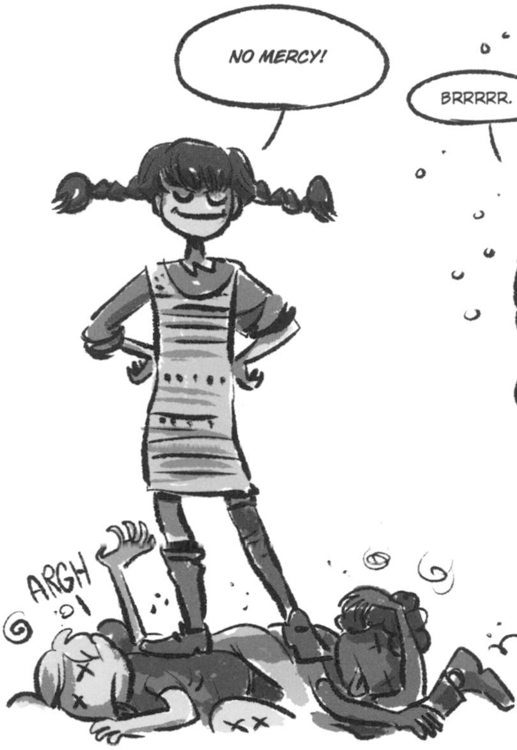
NO MERCY!
ARGH

AGE 10: BAD GUY

DRESSING UP LIKE A BAD GUY FROM A CHEESY '80S MOVIE NO ONE HAS SEEN IS RISKY. LUCKILY IT WAS FREEZING COLD, AND HER SNOWSUIT SAVED HER FROM HUMILIATION.

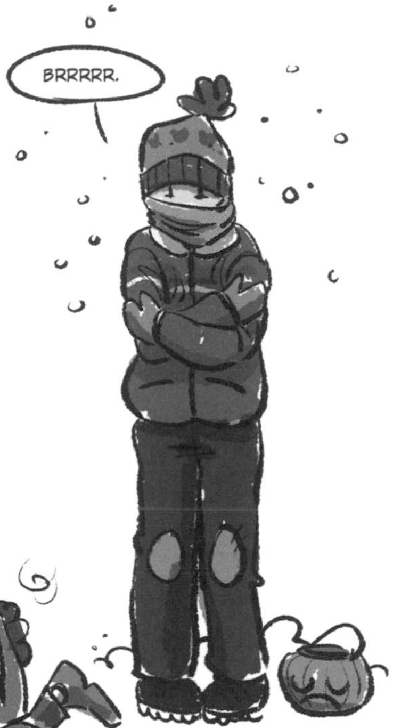
BRRRRR.

AGE 12: SHY PIRATE-ZOMBIE

WON THE PRIZE FOR BEST COSTUME AT SCHOOL, BUT WAS TOO SHY TO GO UP ON STAGE TO GET IT. (A GIANT BAG OF CANDY AND TWO MOVIE TICKETS FOR ***GUARDIANS OF THE GALAXY***). MARIE STILL HASN'T FORGIVEN HER.

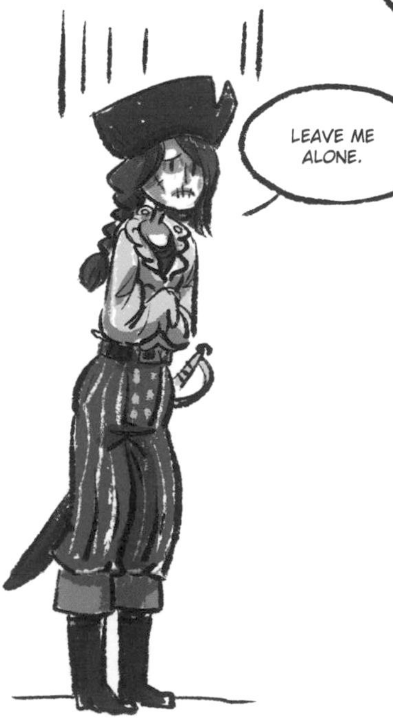
LEAVE ME ALONE.

AGE 14: HIPPIE

IN SOLIDARITY WITH MARIE, SHE GOT KICKED OUT OF THE SAME THREE CLASSES.

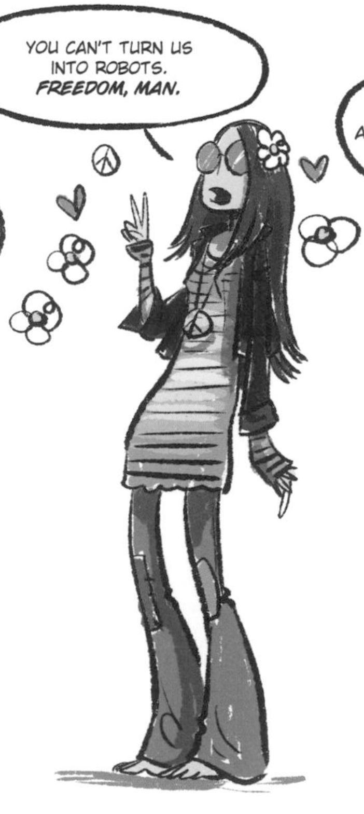
YOU CAN'T TURN US INTO ROBOTS. ***FREEDOM, MAN.***

AGE 16: POISON IVY

AFTER SHE WAS SENT HOME TO CHANGE, MARIE COMPLAINED TO THE PRINCIPAL THAT NATHALIE'S COSTUME WAS JUST AS PROVOCATIVE. NO DICE.

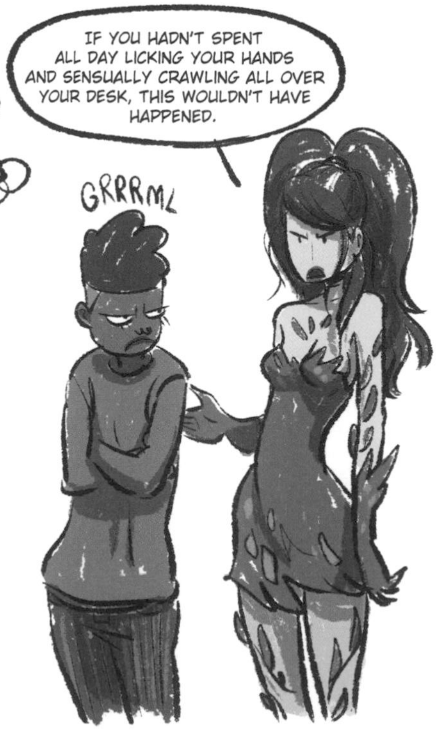
IF YOU HADN'T SPENT ALL DAY LICKING YOUR HANDS AND SENSUALLY CRAWLING ALL OVER YOUR DESK, THIS WOULDN'T HAVE HAPPENED.
GRRRML

WHAT IF... HALLOWEEN EDITION

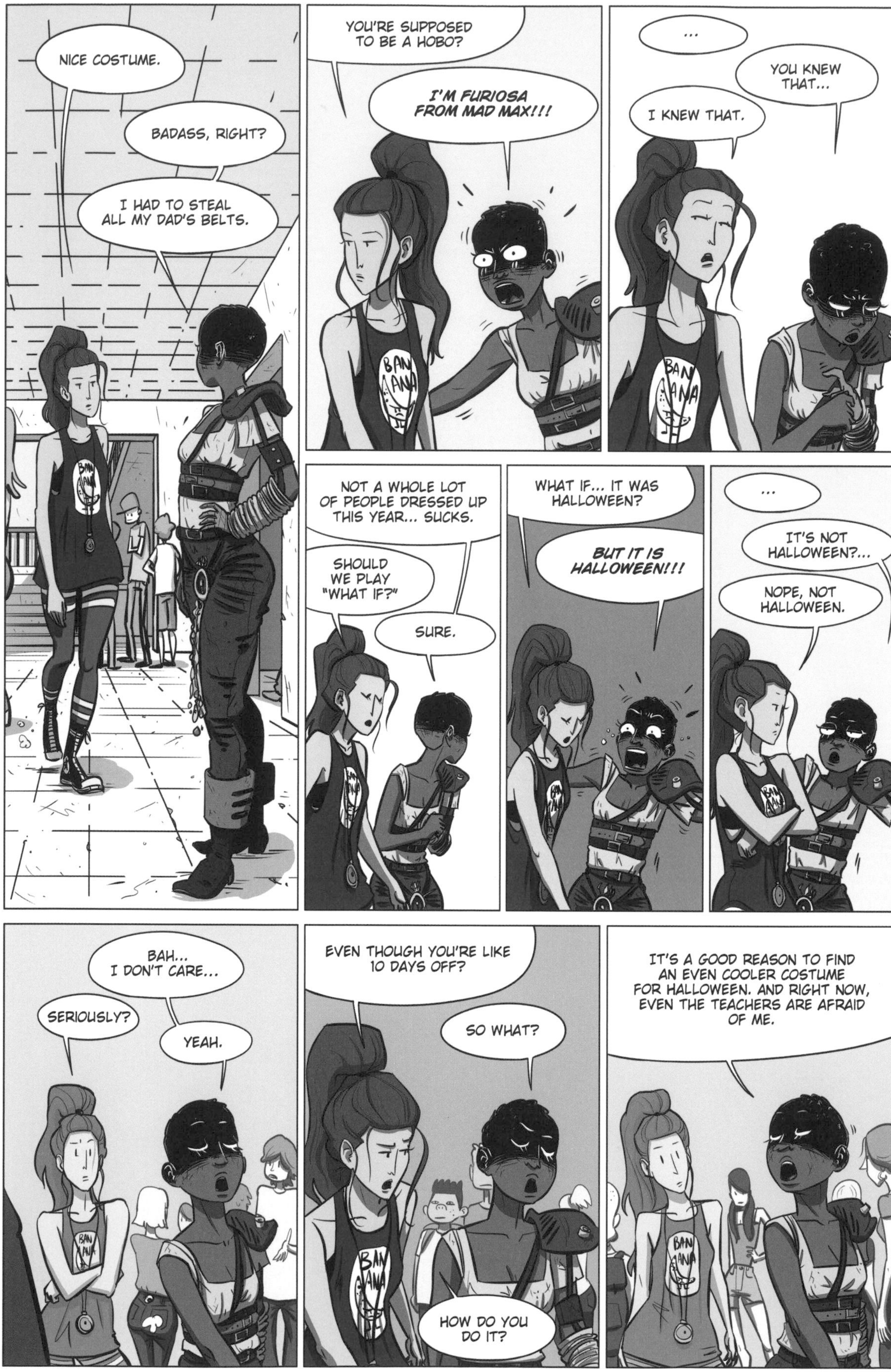
NICE COSTUME.
BADASS, RIGHT?
I HAD TO STEAL ALL MY DAD'S BELTS.
YOU'RE SUPPOSED TO BE A HOBO?
I'M FURIOSA FROM MAD MAX!!!
...
YOU KNEW THAT...
I KNEW THAT.
NOT A WHOLE LOT OF PEOPLE DRESSED UP THIS YEAR... SUCKS.
SHOULD WE PLAY "WHAT IF?"
SURE.
WHAT IF... IT WAS HALLOWEEN?
BUT IT IS HALLOWEEN!!!
...
IT'S NOT HALLOWEEN?...
NOPE, NOT HALLOWEEN.
BAH... I DON'T CARE...
SERIOUSLY?
YEAH.
EVEN THOUGH YOU'RE LIKE 10 DAYS OFF?
SO WHAT?
HOW DO YOU DO IT?
IT'S A GOOD REASON TO FIND AN EVEN COOLER COSTUME FOR HALLOWEEN. AND RIGHT NOW, EVEN THE TEACHERS ARE AFRAID OF ME.

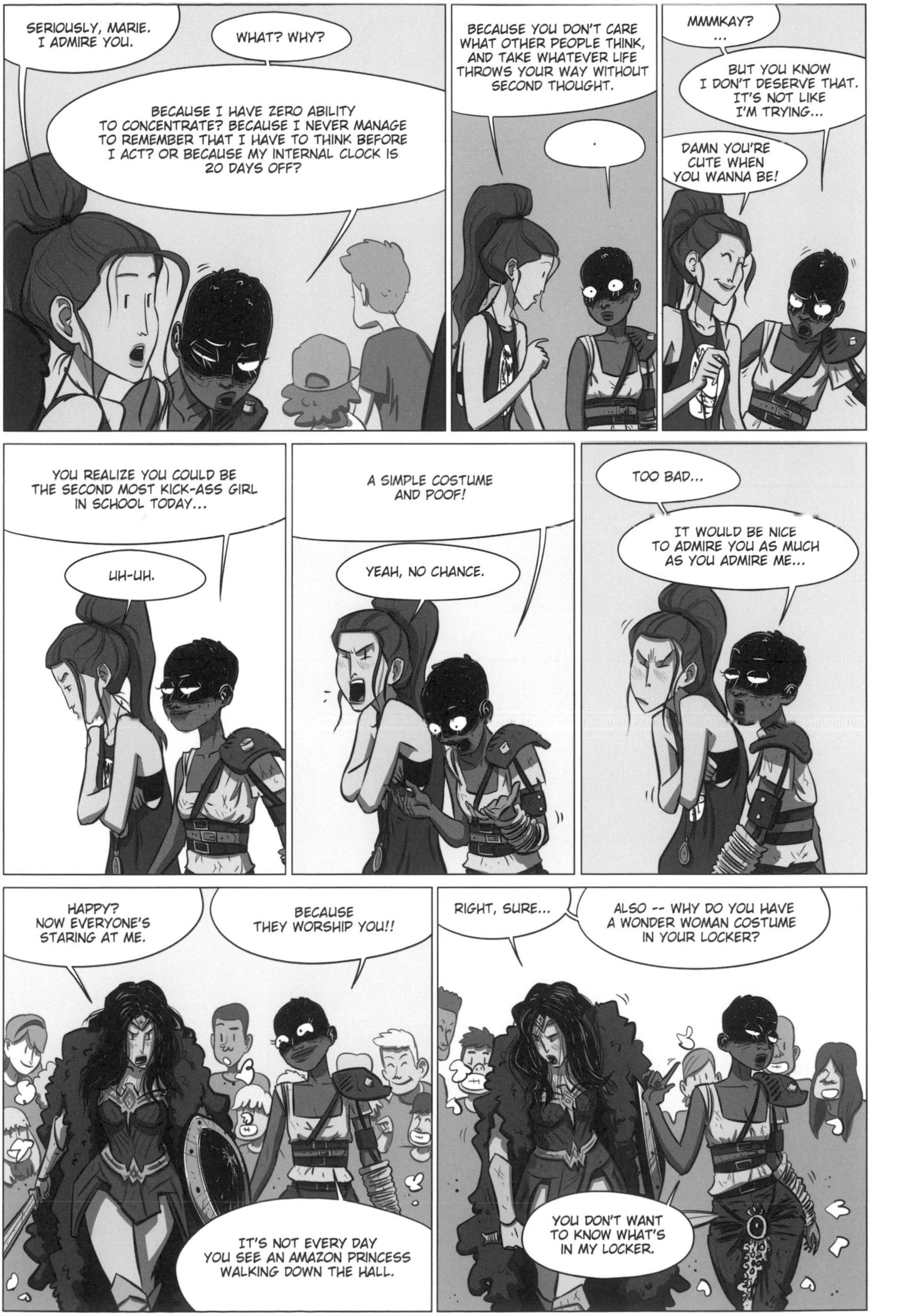
SERIOUSLY, MARIE. I ADMIRE YOU.
WHAT? WHY?
BECAUSE I HAVE ZERO ABILITY TO CONCENTRATE? BECAUSE I NEVER MANAGE TO REMEMBER THAT I HAVE TO THINK BEFORE I ACT? OR BECAUSE MY INTERNAL CLOCK IS 20 DAYS OFF?
BECAUSE YOU DON'T CARE WHAT OTHER PEOPLE THINK, AND TAKE WHATEVER LIFE THROWS YOUR WAY WITHOUT SECOND THOUGHT.
.
MMMKAY? ...
BUT YOU KNOW I DON'T DESERVE THAT. IT'S NOT LIKE I'M TRYING...
DAMN YOU'RE CUTE WHEN YOU WANNA BE!
YOU REALIZE YOU COULD BE THE SECOND MOST KICK-ASS GIRL IN SCHOOL TODAY...
UH-UH.
A SIMPLE COSTUME AND POOF!
YEAH, NO CHANCE.
TOO BAD...
IT WOULD BE NICE TO ADMIRE YOU AS MUCH AS YOU ADMIRE ME...
HAPPY? NOW EVERYONE'S STARING AT ME.
BECAUSE THEY WORSHIP YOU!!
IT'S NOT EVERY DAY YOU SEE AN AMAZON PRINCESS WALKING DOWN THE HALL.
RIGHT, SURE...
ALSO -- WHY DO YOU HAVE A WONDER WOMAN COSTUME IN YOUR LOCKER?
YOU DON'T WANT TO KNOW WHAT'S IN MY LOCKER.

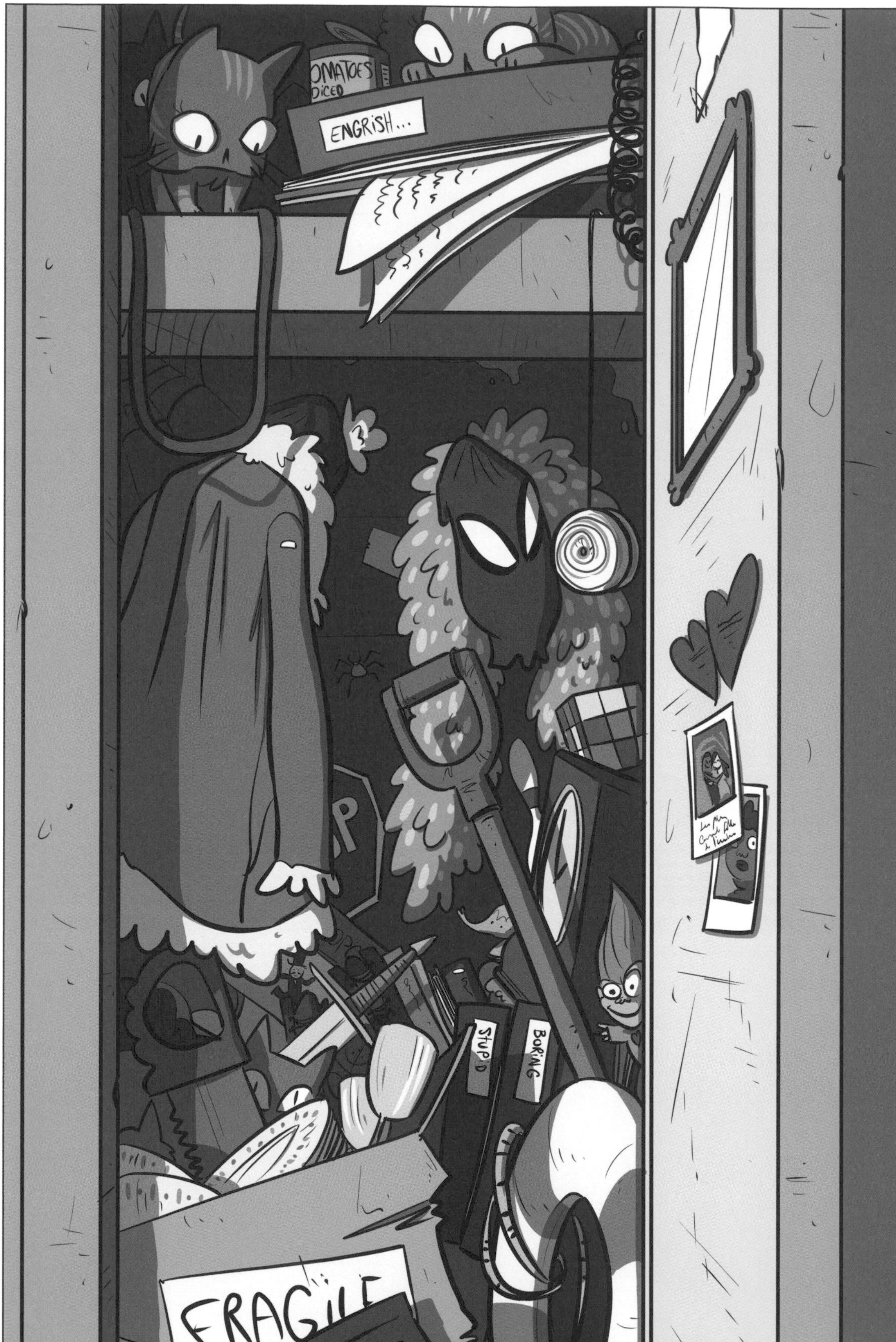
OMATOES
DICED
ENGRISH...
STUPID
BORING
FRAGILE

LET'S WELCOME OUR NEW CHALLENGER!

-NAME: ???

-NICKNAME: JANE DOE

-AGE: ??? (SHE LOOKS AROUND 17, RIGHT?)

-HEIGHT: A LITTLE TALLER THAN MARIE, A BIT SHORTER THAN NATHALIE.

-WEIGHT: ???

-ZODIAC SIGN: NO IDEA. NATHALIE LIKES TO THINK SHE'S A LEO, BUT MARIE SAYS SHE'S A VIRGO.

-FAVORITE ANIMAL: RIGHT, LIKE WE'D REALLY KNOW THAT BEFORE WE EVEN KNOW HER REAL NAME.

-SPECIAL MOVE: ???

-ANYTHING ELSE? SHE LIKES TO WEAR BASEBALL HATS... AND... UH... THAT'S ABOUT ALL WE KNOW.

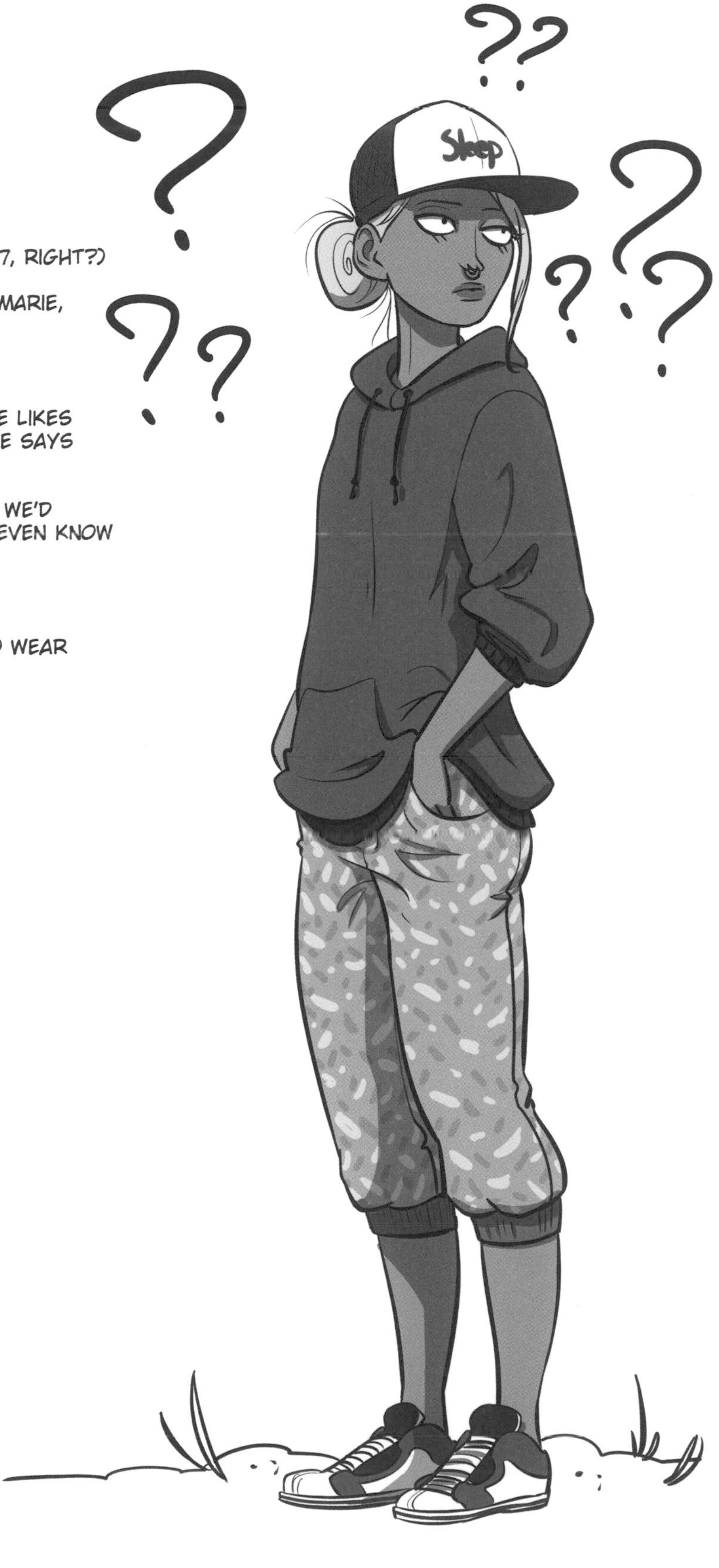
Sleep

WHAT IF WE WERE... CRYPTOLOGISTS

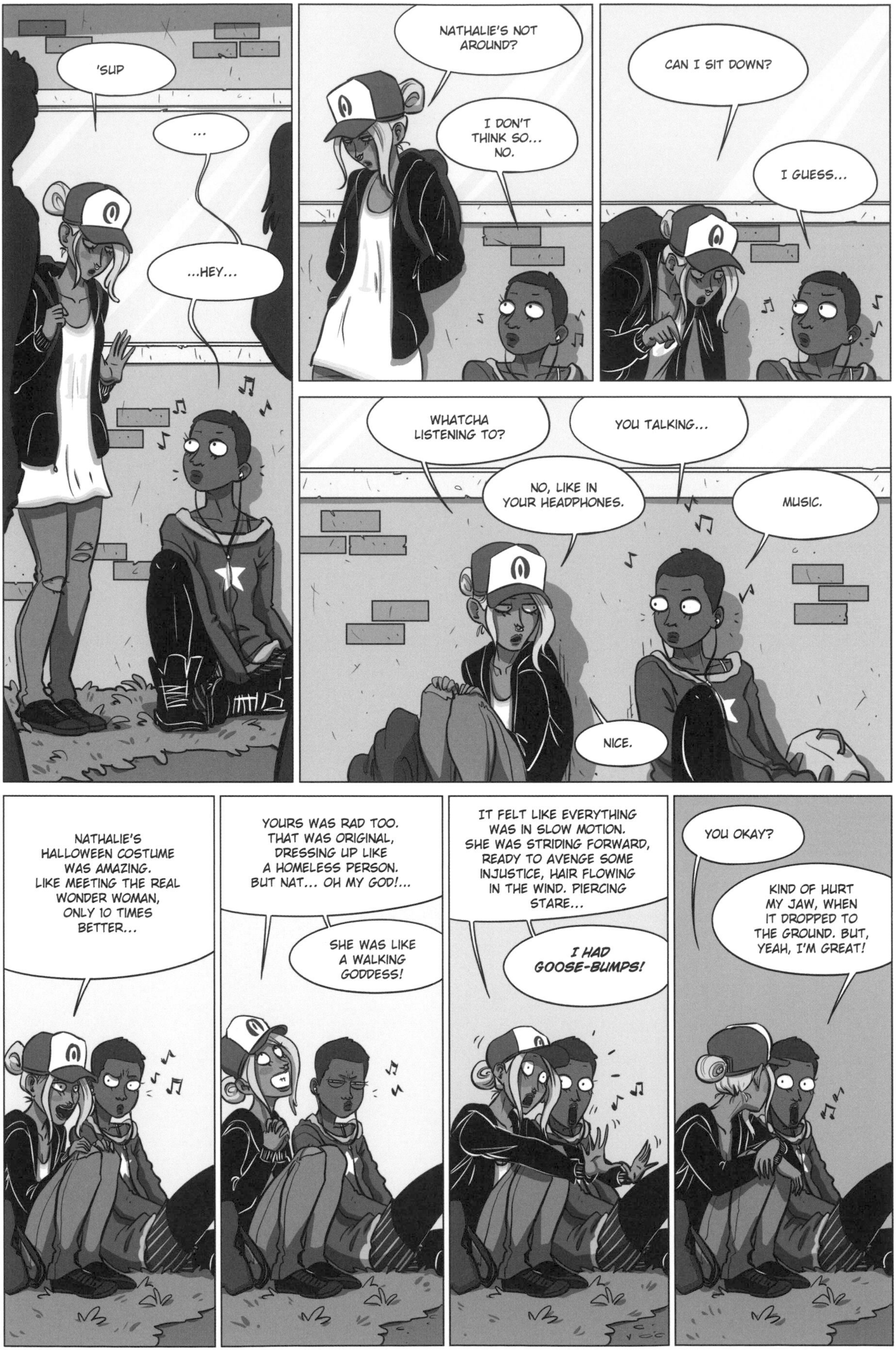
'SUP
...
...HEY...
NATHALIE'S NOT AROUND?
I DON'T THINK SO... NO.
CAN I SIT DOWN?
I GUESS...
WHATCHA LISTENING TO?
YOU TALKING...
NO, LIKE IN YOUR HEADPHONES.
MUSIC.
NICE.
NATHALIE'S HALLOWEEN COSTUME WAS AMAZING. LIKE MEETING THE REAL WONDER WOMAN, ONLY 10 TIMES BETTER...
YOURS WAS RAD TOO. THAT WAS ORIGINAL, DRESSING UP LIKE A HOMELESS PERSON. BUT NAT... OH MY GOD!...
SHE WAS LIKE A WALKING GODDESS!
IT FELT LIKE EVERYTHING WAS IN SLOW MOTION. SHE WAS STRIDING FORWARD, READY TO AVENGE SOME INJUSTICE, HAIR FLOWING IN THE WIND. PIERCING STARE...
I HAD GOOSE-BUMPS!
YOU OKAY?
KIND OF HURT MY JAW, WHEN IT DROPPED TO THE GROUND. BUT, YEAH, I'M GREAT!

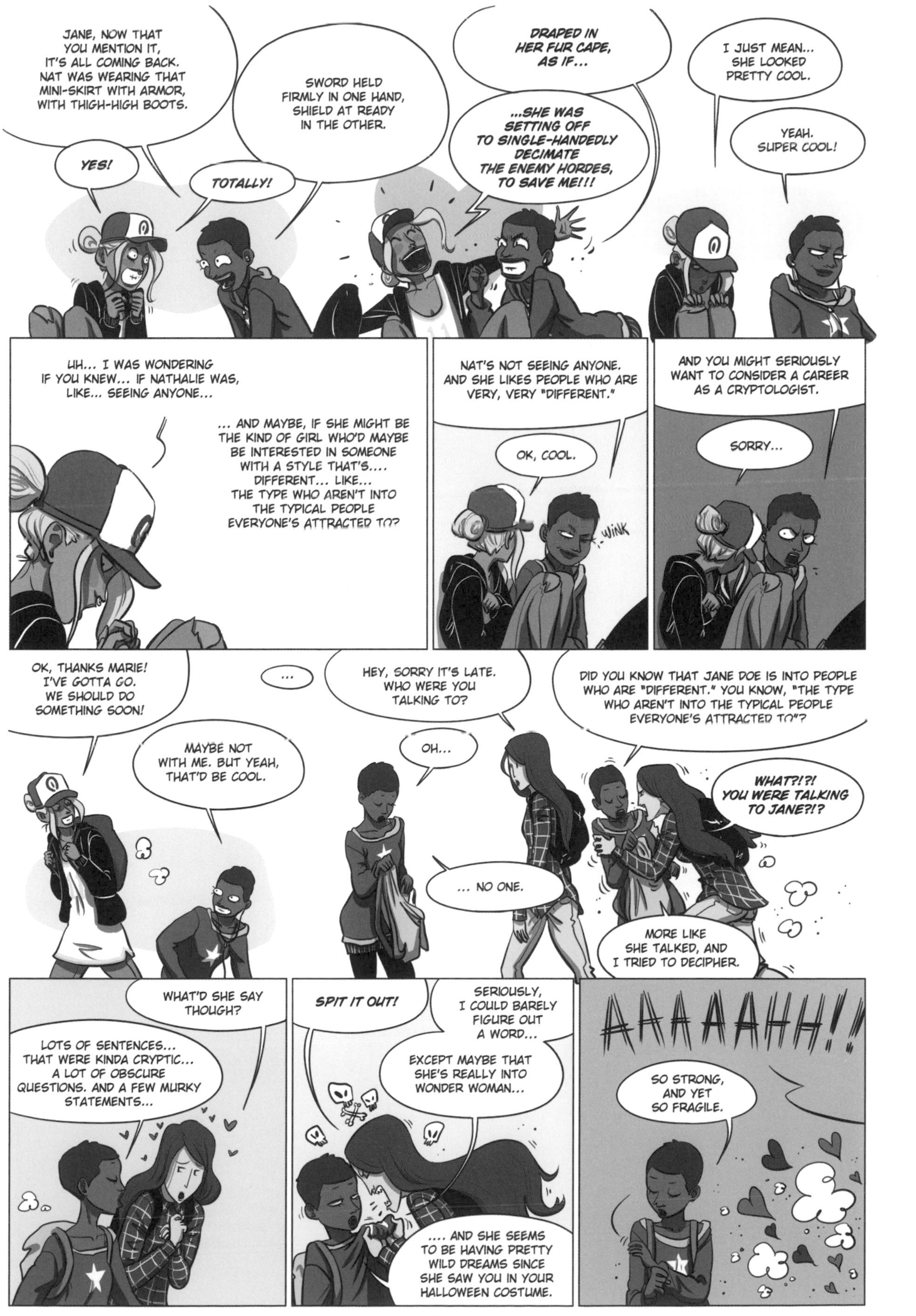
JANE, NOW THAT YOU MENTION IT, IT'S ALL COMING BACK. NAT WAS WEARING THAT MINI-SKIRT WITH ARMOR, WITH THIGH-HIGH BOOTS.
YES!
SWORD HELD FIRMLY IN ONE HAND, SHIELD AT READY IN THE OTHER.
TOTALLY!
DRAPED IN HER FUR CAPE, AS IF...
...SHE WAS SETTING OFF TO SINGLE-HANDEDLY DECIMATE THE ENEMY HORDES, TO SAVE ME!!!
I JUST MEAN... SHE LOOKED PRETTY COOL.
YEAH. SUPER COOL!
UH... I WAS WONDERING IF YOU KNEW... IF NATHALIE WAS, LIKE... SEEING ANYONE...
... AND MAYBE, IF SHE MIGHT BE THE KIND OF GIRL WHO'D MAYBE BE INTERESTED IN SOMEONE WITH A STYLE THAT'S.... DIFFERENT... LIKE... THE TYPE WHO AREN'T INTO THE TYPICAL PEOPLE EVERYONE'S ATTRACTED TO?
NAT'S NOT SEEING ANYONE. AND SHE LIKES PEOPLE WHO ARE VERY, VERY "DIFFERENT."
OK, COOL.
WINK
AND YOU MIGHT SERIOUSLY WANT TO CONSIDER A CAREER AS A CRYPTOLOGIST.
SORRY...
OK, THANKS MARIE! I'VE GOTTA GO. WE SHOULD DO SOMETHING SOON!
MAYBE NOT WITH ME. BUT YEAH, THAT'D BE COOL.
...
HEY, SORRY IT'S LATE. WHO WERE YOU TALKING TO?
OH...
... NO ONE.
DID YOU KNOW THAT JANE DOE IS INTO PEOPLE WHO ARE "DIFFERENT." YOU KNOW, "THE TYPE WHO AREN'T INTO THE TYPICAL PEOPLE EVERYONE'S ATTRACTED TO"?
WHAT?!?! YOU WERE TALKING TO JANE?!?
MORE LIKE SHE TALKED, AND I TRIED TO DECIPHER.
WHAT'D SHE SAY THOUGH?
LOTS OF SENTENCES... THAT WERE KINDA CRYPTIC... A LOT OF OBSCURE QUESTIONS. AND A FEW MURKY STATEMENTS...
SPIT IT OUT!
SERIOUSLY, I COULD BARELY FIGURE OUT A WORD...
EXCEPT MAYBE THAT SHE'S REALLY INTO WONDER WOMAN...
.... AND SHE SEEMS TO BE HAVING PRETTY WILD DREAMS SINCE SHE SAW YOU IN YOUR HALLOWEEN COSTUME.
AAAAAHH!!
SO STRONG, AND YET SO FRAGILE.

NATHALIE'S DIARY

November 2nd

My life is over. My only hope is to turn into a vampire and go into hiding in the northern mountains. It'd be easy: I'd just have to find a pack of wolves to lead and drink the blood of the few travellers foolhardy enough to venture onto my lands, and then everything will be peachy.
...

Don't you get it, diary? I'm sorry. You must be wondering why I'm freaking out like this. OK, I'll tell you, but once I do my life is over. Swear to god! Today, Jane Doe asked Marie all kinds of questions about me. Marie said she was trying to find out if I was a "different" type of person, who was into other "different" people!! What does that even mean?!?!?
Who's "different?" Why me? I'm not "different!!"

Yeah, I know - I know what it means, but I'm freaking out! I've been dreaming about this for years, and now, the day it finally happens I'm paralyzed. To the point where my one wish is to sever all human contact. Is that what love is? SHIT! this is so much less fun than in the movies! I feel like my body is sick, like really sick, you know... Like level 8 mono, with 3 swollen tonsils and a 49-degree fever and a final boss you can never beat!

I could just sabotage the whole thing by playing dumb. Marie would kill me. And she won't let me off the hook until I talk to Jane!!

So there you have it. My only chance is to find a pack of wolves and run with them.
Bye diary. My life is over

PS: Marie, if the information you gave me isn't true, I'll send my wolves

TO EAT YOU!!!!

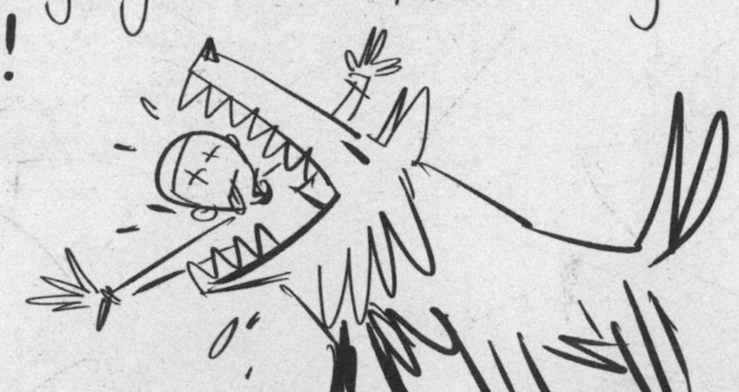

JANE'S DIARY

Hey dude,

You'll never guess what I just found out! Nathalie's into girls! I know: told you so, right? Marie just confirmed it! OK, I guess what she actually said is that Nathalie is into people who are "different", but you know, it's obvious what that means right?

I can't believe it! We are so going to be going out soon. And totally in love.

Nathalie, here's a poem just for you:

Long legs, red hair,
Sweet apparition in the night,
My body trembles, but stays still,
Come to me, beautiful valkyrie,

Luminescent light, your silhouette,
your gaze has hypnotized me,
In your bed you pull your quilt,
Against me, and I move no more.

Nathalie, I love you,
Nathalie, take me now,
Passion will be ours,
Free of doubt, free of fear.

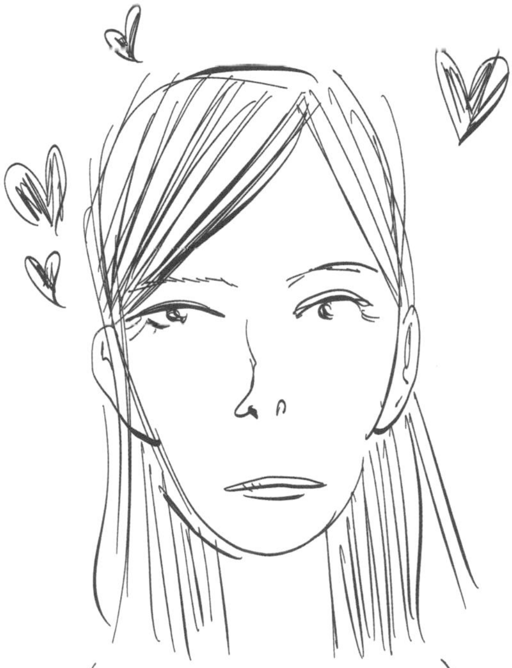

(She's prettier in real life...)

...

All this gets me super hot!

Bye dude!

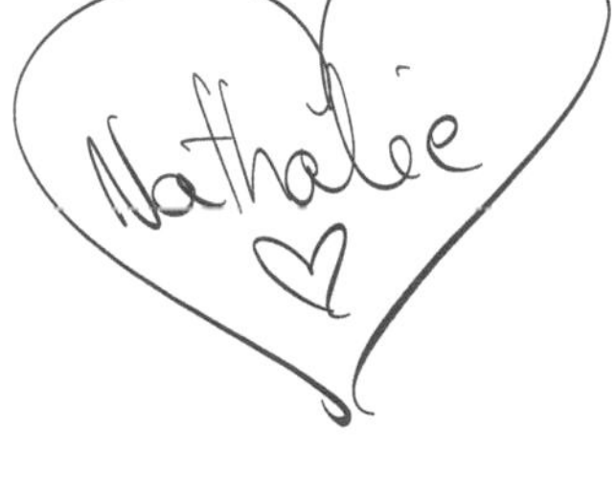
Nathalie

MARIE'S DIARY

DEAR DIARY,

NOTHING MUCH HAPPENED TODAY. SCHOOL WAS BORING AS EVER, BUT AT LEAST THERE WAS PIZZA IN THE CAF. SMALL CONSOLATION. I LOVE PIZZA. HERE'S A POEM THAT EXPRESSES MY DEEP LOVE OF PIZZA:

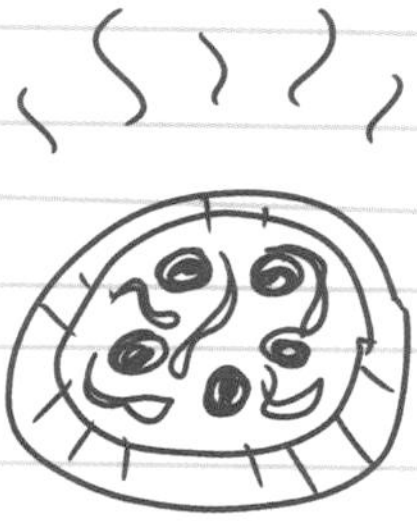

(IT'S SUPPOSED TO BE A PIZZA.)

(IT LOOKS LIKE A BOWL OF WORMS...)

PEPPERONI, MUSHROOMS, MOZZA SLICE,
WHEN I DON'T GET SOME, I'M NOT NICE,
PEPPERS, SAUSAGE, OR VEGETARIAN,
IF I DON'T GET PIZZA I'M DESPAIRIN.'

ARTICHOKES, CANADIAN BACON,
ALL TOPPINGS ARE MINE FOR THE TAKIN...

AARGH! MY STUPID CAT IS STARING AT ME, AND IT'S DISTRACTING!
GET OUT OF HERE, DUMB CAT!
ALRIGHT, THAT'S PRETTY MUCH THAT. I HOPE TOMORROW WILL BE A LITTLE MORE EXCITING.

AND THAT THERE'LL BE PIZZA AT THE CAF AGAIN! YEAH, I LOVE PIZZA!!!

PIZZA, PIZZA, PIZZA, PIZZA, PIZZA!!!...

...PIZZA!!!

GOOD NIGHT XXX

AAAAAAAAAAAAHHH!!! I FORGOT!!!
JANE DOE LOVES NATHALIE!!!!

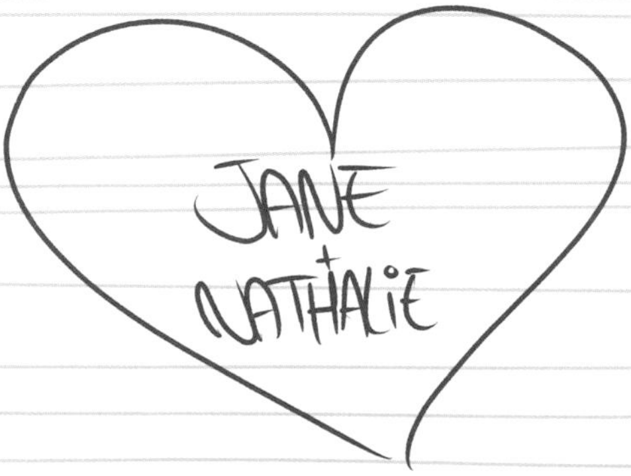
JANE
+
NATHALIE

WHAT IF WE WERE... IN A ROCK GROUP

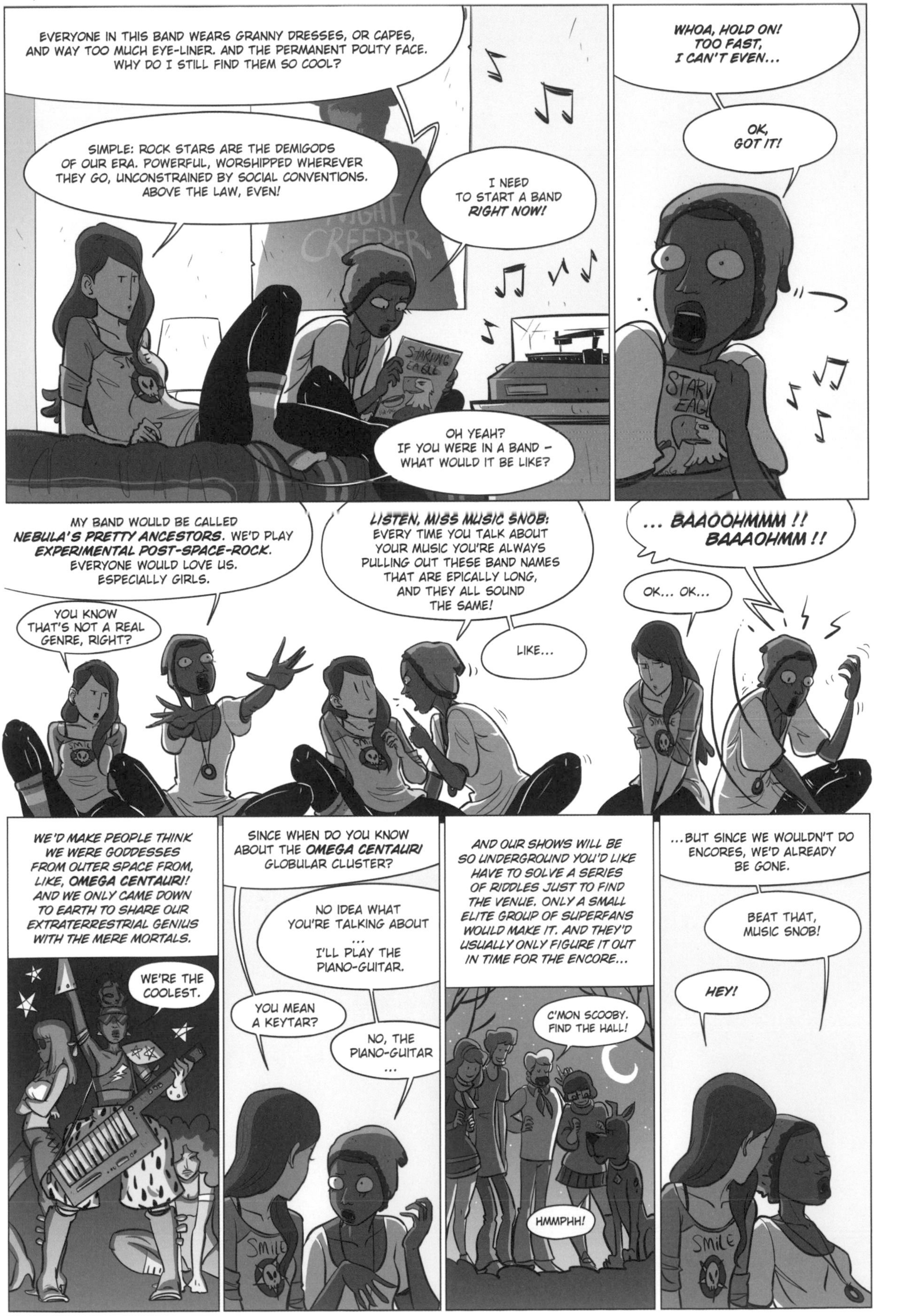
EVERYONE IN THIS BAND WEARS GRANNY DRESSES, OR CAPES, AND WAY TOO MUCH EYE-LINER. AND THE PERMANENT POUTY FACE. WHY DO I STILL FIND THEM SO COOL?
SIMPLE: ROCK STARS ARE THE DEMIGODS OF OUR ERA. POWERFUL, WORSHIPPED WHEREVER THEY GO, UNCONSTRAINED BY SOCIAL CONVENTIONS. ABOVE THE LAW, EVEN!
I NEED TO START A BAND ***RIGHT NOW!***
OH YEAH? IF YOU WERE IN A BAND – WHAT WOULD IT BE LIKE?
WHOA, HOLD ON! TOO FAST, I CAN'T EVEN...
OK, GOT IT!
MY BAND WOULD BE CALLED ***NEBULA'S PRETTY ANCESTORS***. WE'D PLAY ***EXPERIMENTAL POST-SPACE-ROCK***. EVERYONE WOULD LOVE US. ESPECIALLY GIRLS.
YOU KNOW THAT'S NOT A REAL GENRE, RIGHT?
LISTEN, MISS MUSIC SNOB: EVERY TIME YOU TALK ABOUT YOUR MUSIC YOU'RE ALWAYS PULLING OUT THESE BAND NAMES THAT ARE EPICALLY LONG, AND THEY ALL SOUND THE SAME!
LIKE...
... BAAOOHMMM !! BAAAOHMM !!
OK... OK...
*WE'D MAKE PEOPLE THINK WE WERE GODDESSES FROM OUTER SPACE FROM, LIKE, **OMEGA CENTAURI**! AND WE ONLY CAME DOWN TO EARTH TO SHARE OUR EXTRATERRESTRIAL GENIUS WITH THE MERE MORTALS.*
WE'RE THE COOLEST.
SINCE WHEN DO YOU KNOW ABOUT THE ***OMEGA CENTAURI*** GLOBULAR CLUSTER?
NO IDEA WHAT YOU'RE TALKING ABOUT ... I'LL PLAY THE PIANO-GUITAR.
YOU MEAN A KEYTAR?
NO, THE PIANO-GUITAR ...
AND OUR SHOWS WILL BE SO UNDERGROUND YOU'D LIKE HAVE TO SOLVE A SERIES OF RIDDLES JUST TO FIND THE VENUE. ONLY A SMALL ELITE GROUP OF SUPERFANS WOULD MAKE IT. AND THEY'D USUALLY ONLY FIGURE IT OUT IN TIME FOR THE ENCORE...
C'MON SCOOBY. FIND THE HALL!
HMMPHH!
...BUT SINCE WE WOULDN'T DO ENCORES, WE'D ALREADY BE GONE.
BEAT THAT, MUSIC SNOB!
HEY!

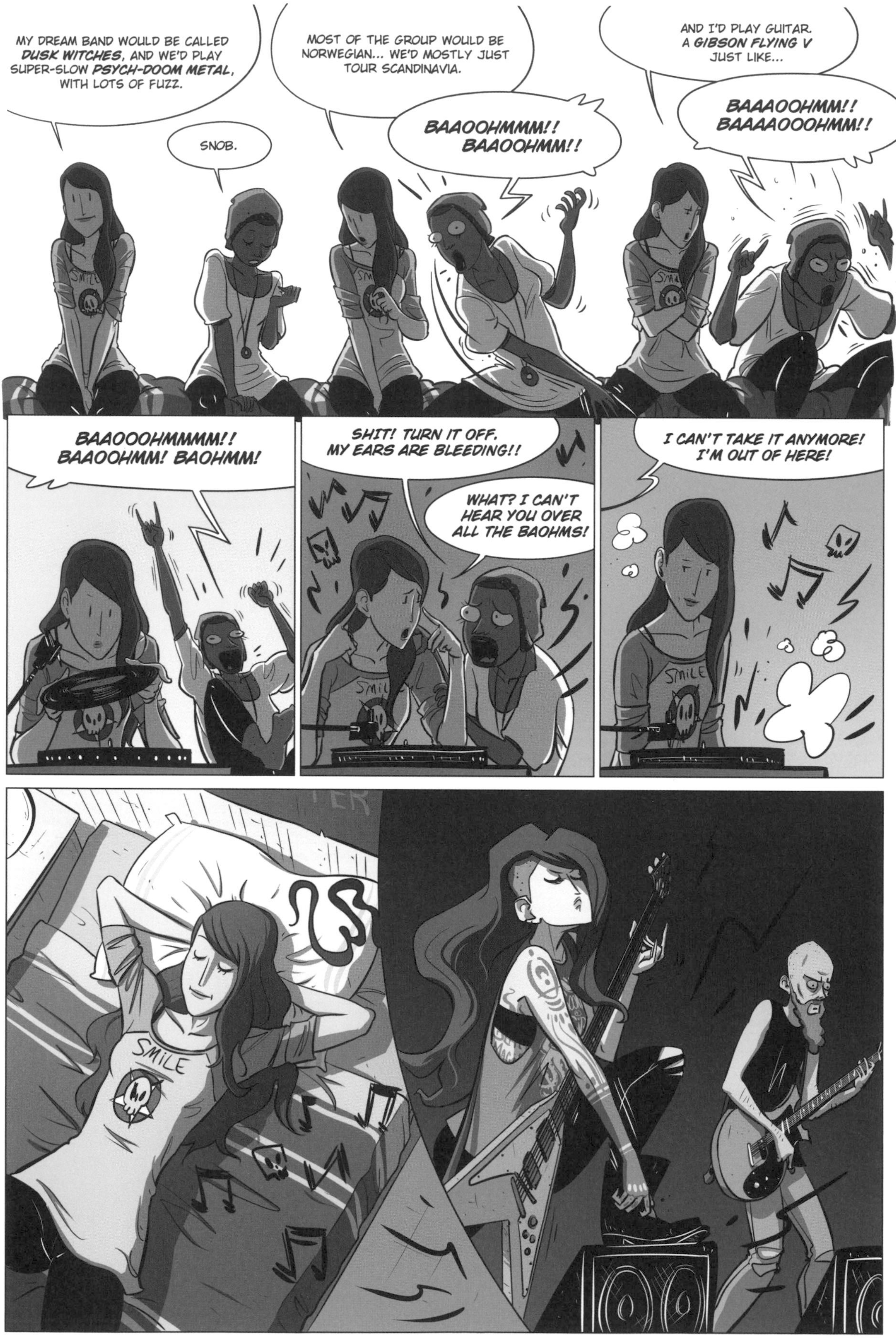
MY DREAM BAND WOULD BE CALLED DUSK WITCHES, AND WE'D PLAY SUPER-SLOW PSYCH-DOOM METAL, WITH LOTS OF FUZZ.
SNOB.
MOST OF THE GROUP WOULD BE NORWEGIAN... WE'D MOSTLY JUST TOUR SCANDINAVIA.
BAAOOHMMM!! BAAOOHMM!!
AND I'D PLAY GUITAR. A GIBSON FLYING V JUST LIKE...
BAAAOOHMM!! BAAAAOOOHMM!!
BAAOOOHMMMM!! BAAOOHMM! BAOHMM!
SHIT! TURN IT OFF. MY EARS ARE BLEEDING!!
WHAT? I CAN'T HEAR YOU OVER ALL THE BAOHMS!
I CAN'T TAKE IT ANYMORE! I'M OUT OF HERE!
SMILE

WHAT IF WE WERE... MANGA CHARACTERS

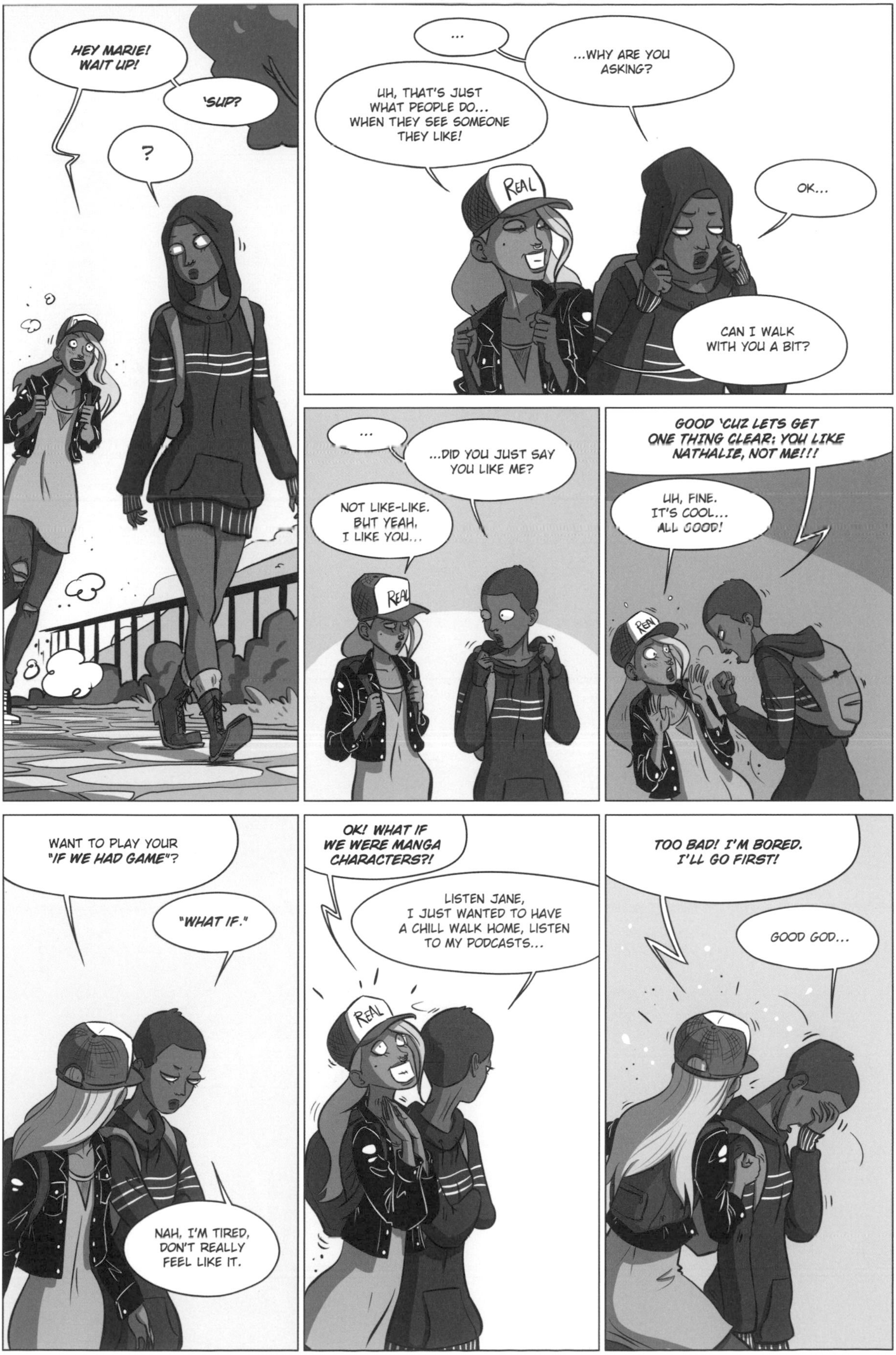
HEY MARIE! WAIT UP!
'SUP?
?
...
...WHY ARE YOU ASKING?
UH, THAT'S JUST WHAT PEOPLE DO... WHEN THEY SEE SOMEONE THEY LIKE!
OK...
CAN I WALK WITH YOU A BIT?
...
...DID YOU JUST SAY YOU LIKE ME?
NOT LIKE-LIKE. BUT YEAH, I LIKE YOU...
GOOD 'CUZ LETS GET ONE THING CLEAR: YOU LIKE NATHALIE, NOT ME!!!
UH, FINE. IT'S COOL... ALL GOOD!
WANT TO PLAY YOUR "IF WE HAD GAME"?
"WHAT IF."
NAH, I'M TIRED, DON'T REALLY FEEL LIKE IT.
OK! WHAT IF WE WERE MANGA CHARACTERS?!
LISTEN JANE, I JUST WANTED TO HAVE A CHILL WALK HOME, LISTEN TO MY PODCASTS...
TOO BAD! I'M BORED. I'LL GO FIRST!
GOOD GOD...

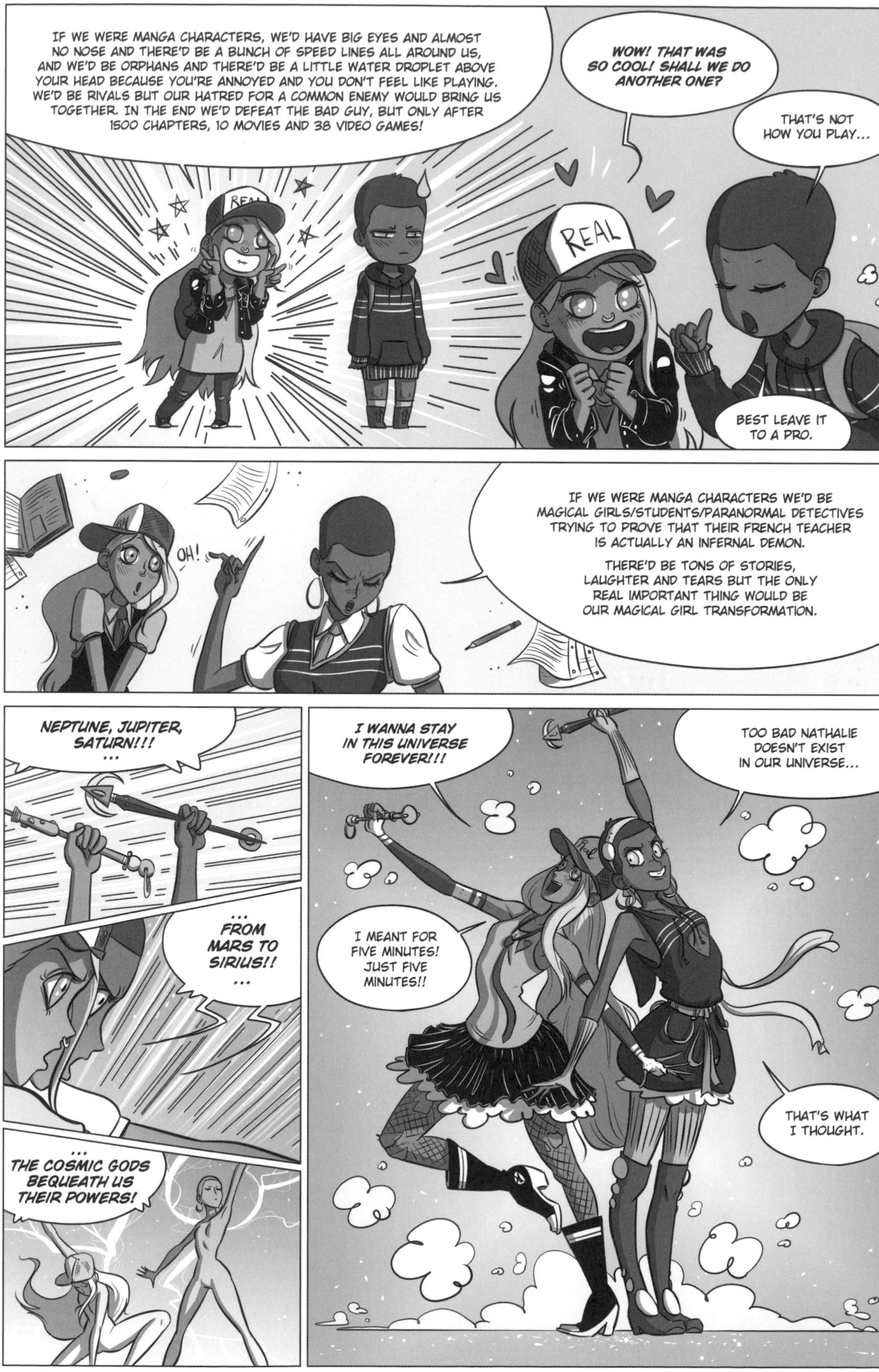
IF WE WERE MANGA CHARACTERS, WE'D HAVE BIG EYES AND ALMOST NO NOSE AND THERE'D BE A BUNCH OF SPEED LINES ALL AROUND US, AND WE'D BE ORPHANS AND THERE'D BE A LITTLE WATER DROPLET ABOVE YOUR HEAD BECAUSE YOU'RE ANNOYED AND YOU DON'T FEEL LIKE PLAYING. WE'D BE RIVALS BUT OUR HATRED FOR A COMMON ENEMY WOULD BRING US TOGETHER. IN THE END WE'D DEFEAT THE BAD GUY, BUT ONLY AFTER 1500 CHAPTERS, 10 MOVIES AND 38 VIDEO GAMES!
REAL
WOW! THAT WAS SO COOL! SHALL WE DO ANOTHER ONE?
THAT'S NOT HOW YOU PLAY...
REAL
BEST LEAVE IT TO A PRO.
OH!
IF WE WERE MANGA CHARACTERS WE'D BE MAGICAL GIRLS/STUDENTS/PARANORMAL DETECTIVES TRYING TO PROVE THAT THEIR FRENCH TEACHER IS ACTUALLY AN INFERNAL DEMON.
THERE'D BE TONS OF STORIES, LAUGHTER AND TEARS BUT THE ONLY REAL IMPORTANT THING WOULD BE OUR MAGICAL GIRL TRANSFORMATION.
NEPTUNE, JUPITER, SATURN!!! ...
... FROM MARS TO SIRIUS!! ...
... THE COSMIC GODS BEQUEATH US THEIR POWERS!
I WANNA STAY IN THIS UNIVERSE FOREVER!!!
TOO BAD NATHALIE DOESN'T EXIST IN OUR UNIVERSE...
I MEANT FOR FIVE MINUTES! JUST FIVE MINUTES!!
THAT'S WHAT I THOUGHT.

THAT MANGA EPISODE WAS A BIT REDUCTIONIST. SO LET ME CLEAR A FEW THINGS UP FOR YOU RIGHT NOW.

1: THE WORD "MANGA" JUST MEANS "COMIC." SO IF SOMEONE TELLS YOU THEY DON'T LIKE COMICS BUT THEY LOVE MANGA, YOU GET TO MOCK THEM MERCILESSLY TILL THE END OF TIME.

FUCK YOU ALL

2: THE READING ORDER IS REVERSED. WE READ FROM RIGHT TO LEFT, DOWNWARDS. SAME GOES FOR THE ORDER OF THE BUBBLES. IF THAT SEEMS LIKE TOO MUCH TO ASK, THEN I GUESS THERE ARE A LOT OF THINGS IN LIFE THAT WILL BE A STRETCH FOR YOU.

3: GIANT EYES...
TRUE, MANGA CHARACTERS OFTEN HAVE BIG EYES. GET OVER IT! IT'S NOT SOME MYSTERIOUS JAPANESE HANG-UP. IT'S JUST AN EASY WAY TO ACCENTUATE THE CHARACTER'S EXPRESSIVITY. AND PLENTY OF AMERICAN AND EUROPEAN COMICS HAVE CHARACTERS WITH BIG EYES, TOO.

LIFE'S TOO HARD... TO LEARN SIMPLE NEW THINGS... PFF...

I GIVE UP.

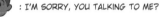

: HEY, YOU LOOK PISSED. IS IT 'CUZ YOU HAVE TINY EYES?

: I DO NOT HAVE TINY EYES! THEY'RE JUST UNREADABLE. ALSO, GET OUT OF MY EXPLANATION!

: I'M SORRY, YOU TALKING TO ME?

 : *YES!!*

: OK. BECAUSE WITH THOSE TINY LITTLE EYES I CAN'T TELL IF YOU'RE LOOKING AT ME OR SOMEONE ELSE.

4: THINK OF THE MOST UNLIKELY SUBJECT AND YOU CAN BE SURE THERE'S A MANGA ABOUT IT. THERE'S A MANGA ABOUT ABSOLUTELY EVERYTHING.

5: THERE ARE DIFFERENT GENRES OF MANGA, THAT ARE NOTHING LIKE WHAT WE'RE USED TO IN THE WEST. FOR EXAMPLE, *MAHO SHOJO* IS A FANTASY SUBGENRE THAT FEATURES YOUNG GIRLS WHO DO MAGIC...

: A WARRIOR THAT BATTLES WITH HIS NOSE HAIRS!

: ALREADY DONE. IT'S CALLED *BOBOBO-BO BO-BOBO.*

: *WOAH...*

: YESSS! MAGICAL GIRLS! LOVE IT!!

: ... WHILE SHONEN FEATURES YOUNG INNOCENT AND NAIVE ORPHAN BOYS WHO GO OFF ON QUESTS TO ACHIEVE THEIR OBJECTIVE, NO MATTER WHAT.

: ARE THERE ANY WITH YOUNG ORPHAN GIRLS?

: DUNNO.

: *YOU SAID THERE'S A MANGA ON ABSOLUTELY EVERYTHING!*

: OK, OK, YEAH IT'S A THING.

WHAT IF WE WERE... OUT IN THE WOODS

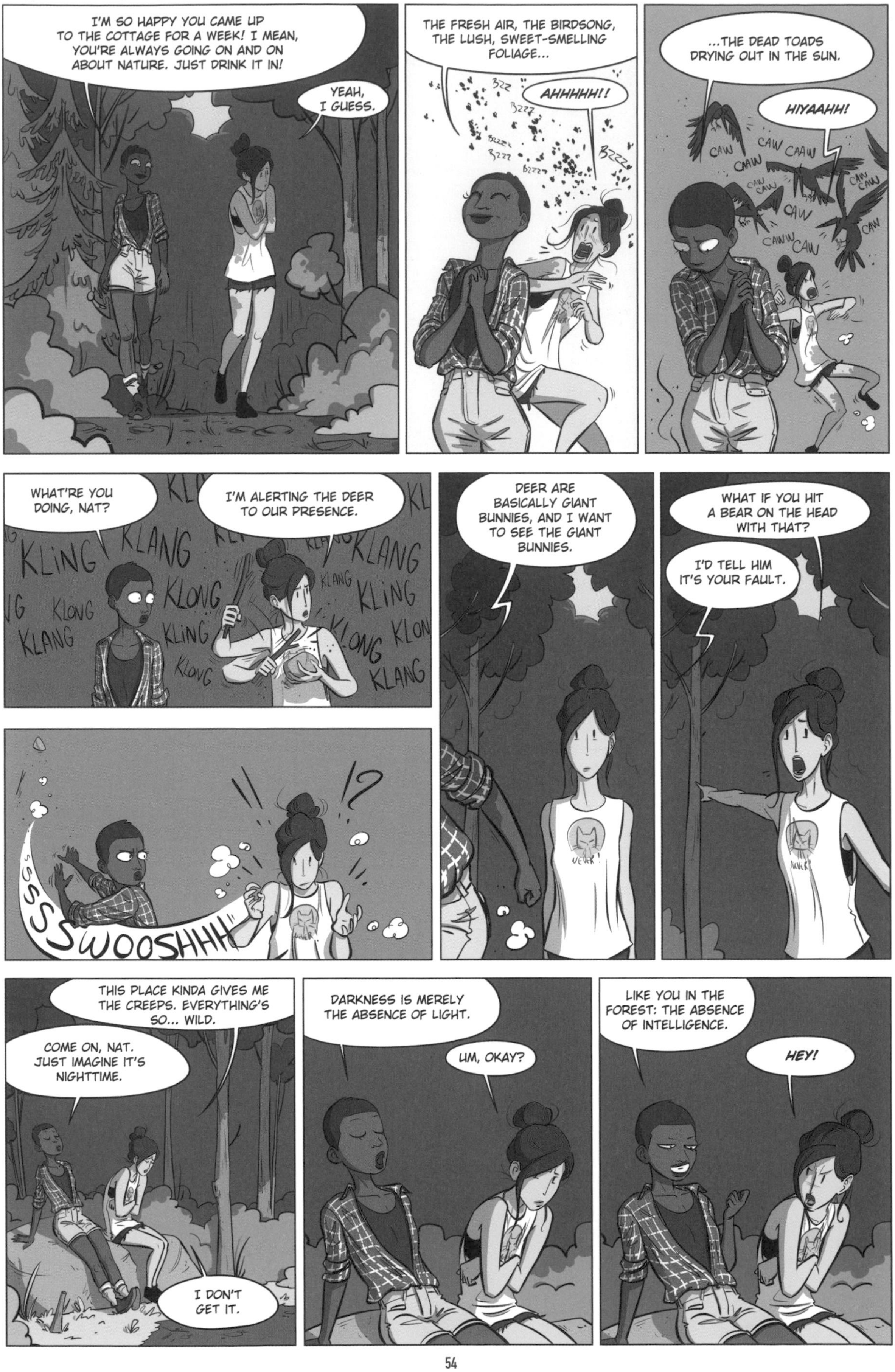

I'M SO HAPPY YOU CAME UP TO THE COTTAGE FOR A WEEK! I MEAN, YOU'RE ALWAYS GOING ON AND ON ABOUT NATURE. JUST DRINK IT IN!
YEAH, I GUESS.
THE FRESH AIR, THE BIRDSONG, THE LUSH, SWEET-SMELLING FOLIAGE...
AHHHHH!!
BZZZ
...THE DEAD TOADS DRYING OUT IN THE SUN.
HIYAAHH!
CAW CAW CAW CAW CAW CAW CAW CAW CAW
WHAT'RE YOU DOING, NAT?
I'M ALERTING THE DEER TO OUR PRESENCE.
KLING KLANG KLONG KLANG KLING KLONG KLANG KLING KLONG KLANG
SSSWOOSHHH
!?
DEER ARE BASICALLY GIANT BUNNIES, AND I WANT TO SEE THE GIANT BUNNIES.
WHAT IF YOU HIT A BEAR ON THE HEAD WITH THAT?
I'D TELL HIM IT'S YOUR FAULT.
THIS PLACE KINDA GIVES ME THE CREEPS. EVERYTHING'S SO... WILD.
COME ON, NAT. JUST IMAGINE IT'S NIGHTTIME.
I DON'T GET IT.
DARKNESS IS MERELY THE ABSENCE OF LIGHT.
UM, OKAY?
LIKE YOU IN THE FOREST: THE ABSENCE OF INTELLIGENCE.
HEY!

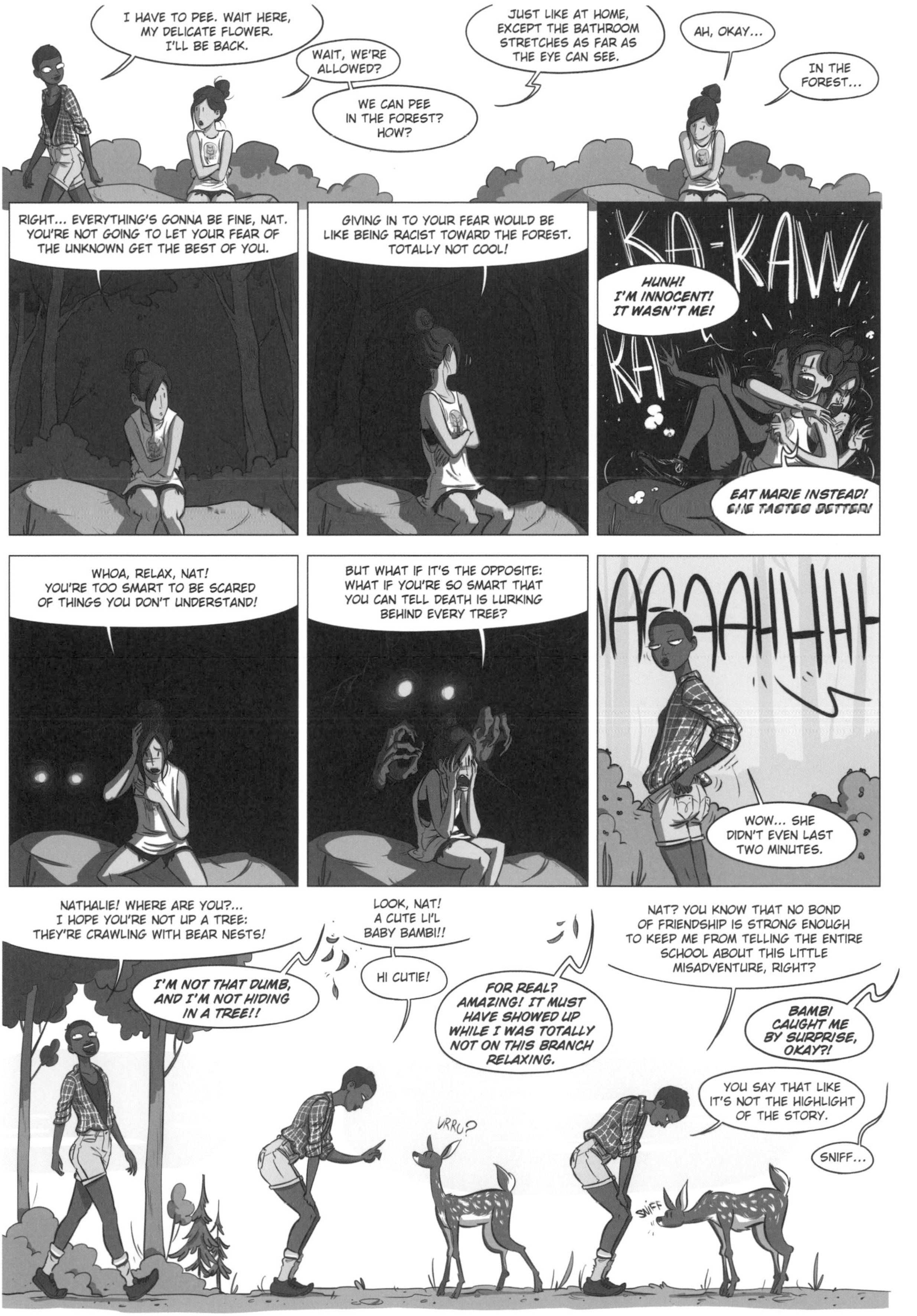
I HAVE TO PEE. WAIT HERE, MY DELICATE FLOWER. I'LL BE BACK.
WAIT, WE'RE ALLOWED?
WE CAN PEE IN THE FOREST? HOW?
JUST LIKE AT HOME, EXCEPT THE BATHROOM STRETCHES AS FAR AS THE EYE CAN SEE.
AH, OKAY...
IN THE FOREST...
RIGHT... EVERYTHING'S GONNA BE FINE, NAT. YOU'RE NOT GOING TO LET YOUR FEAR OF THE UNKNOWN GET THE BEST OF YOU.
GIVING IN TO YOUR FEAR WOULD BE LIKE BEING RACIST TOWARD THE FOREST. TOTALLY NOT COOL!
KA-KAW
HUNH! I'M INNOCENT! IT WASN'T ME!
KA
EAT MARIE INSTEAD! SHE TASTES BETTER!
WHOA, RELAX, NAT! YOU'RE TOO SMART TO BE SCARED OF THINGS YOU DON'T UNDERSTAND!
BUT WHAT IF IT'S THE OPPOSITE: WHAT IF YOU'RE SO SMART THAT YOU CAN TELL DEATH IS LURKING BEHIND EVERY TREE?
AAAAHHHHH
WOW... SHE DIDN'T EVEN LAST TWO MINUTES.
NATHALIE! WHERE ARE YOU?... I HOPE YOU'RE NOT UP A TREE: THEY'RE CRAWLING WITH BEAR NESTS!
I'M NOT THAT DUMB, AND I'M NOT HIDING IN A TREE!!
LOOK, NAT! A CUTE LI'L BABY BAMBI!!
HI CUTIE!
URRU?
FOR REAL? AMAZING! IT MUST HAVE SHOWED UP WHILE I WAS TOTALLY NOT ON THIS BRANCH RELAXING.
NAT? YOU KNOW THAT NO BOND OF FRIENDSHIP IS STRONG ENOUGH TO KEEP ME FROM TELLING THE ENTIRE SCHOOL ABOUT THIS LITTLE MISADVENTURE, RIGHT?
BAMBI CAUGHT ME BY SURPRISE, OKAY?!
YOU SAY THAT LIKE IT'S NOT THE HIGHLIGHT OF THE STORY.
SNIFF...
SNIFF

PERSONALITY TEST: ARE YOU A NATURE GIRL?
(DON'T WORRY, BOYS: YOU CAN BE NATURE GIRLS TOO!)

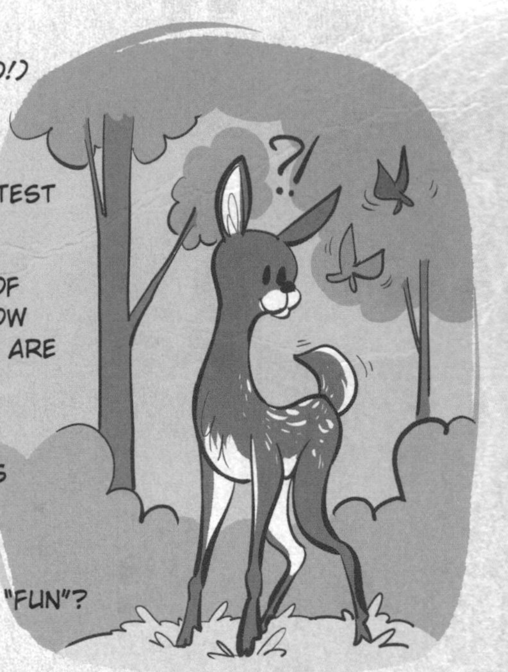
?!

QUESTION 1: ARE YOU AFRAID OF FAWNS?

1. WHY WOULD I POSSIBLY BE AFRAID? THEY'RE THE CUTEST CRITTERS IN THE UNIVERSE! I WANT TO ADOPT 10!

2. NO, BECAUSE I KNOW HOW TO REACT IN THE EVENT OF AN ATTACK. NEVER LOOK THEM IN THE EYE, AND THROW THEM RAW BLOODY STEAKS AS A DIVERSION. (FAWNS ARE BLOODTHIRSTY CREATURES WHO ARE WILD ABOUT RED MEAT).

3. THE ONLY FOUR-LEGGED THING I TRUST THAT COMES FROM THE FOREST IS A TABLE. (GET IT? TABLES COME FROM TREES. DUH!)

4. WHAT'S A FAWN? IS THAT A COOL NEW WAY TO SAY "FUN"?

QUESTION 2: BAMBI IS A MOVIE ABOUT...

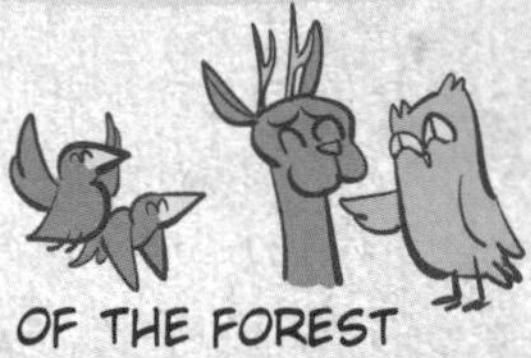

1. ...THE PRETTIEST FAWN IN THE WORLD WHO DISCOVERS THE MEANING OF LIFE BY MAKING LOTS OF ANIMAL FRIENDS!

2. ...A FAWN WHO IS TAUGHT FROM A YOUNG AGE THAT HE'S PRINCE OF THE FOREST (DEER PRIVILEGE). HIS FATHER SHOWS UP FOR THE FIRST TIME WHEN HIS MOTHER GETS SHOT BY HUMANS (ABSENT FATHER). THE STORY THEN ALTERNATES BETWEEN GRATUITOUSLY ADORABLE ANIMALS AND HUMANS SHOOTING AT ANYTHING THAT MOVES AND SETTING FIRE TO THE FOREST. MORAL OF THE STORY? BAMBI IS DOOMED TO REPRODUCE HIS FATHER'S TOXIC BEHAVIOR BY BECOMING AN ABSENT FATHER TOO, BECAUSE HE'S THE NEW GREAT PRINCE OF THE FOREST.

3. I DON'T WATCH HORROR MOVIES.

4. ***"BAMBI-FAWN"***... THAT COULD BE MY NEW RAP NAME...

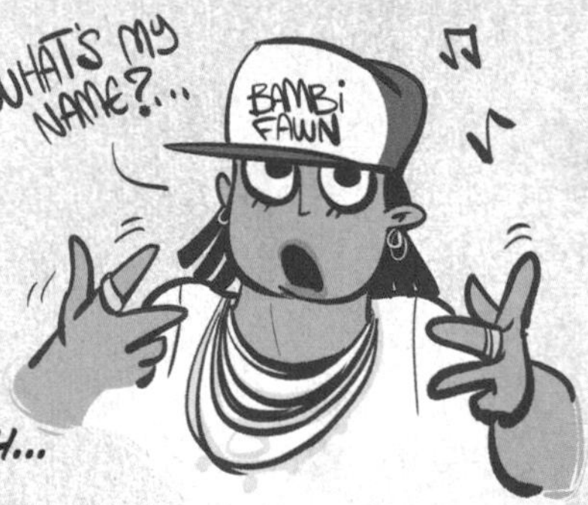
WHAT'S MY NAME?...
BAMBi FAWN

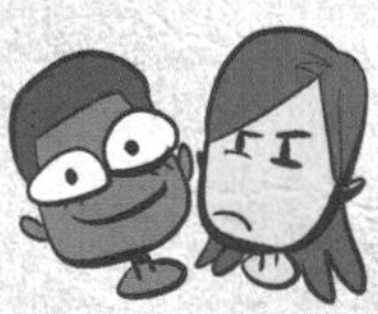

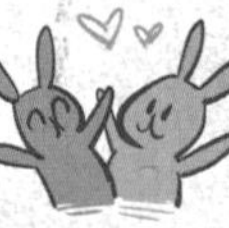

QUESTION 3: IF I HAD TO GO OUT INTO THE WOODS, I'D FEEL SAFE WITH...

1. I DON'T NEED ANYONE ELSE TO FEEL SAFE. BUT IF I HAD TO CHOOSE, I'D GO WITH MARIE. THAT WAY WE COULD HANG OUT.

2. MARIE. BY POOLING OUR EXPERT WILDERNESS KNOWLEDGE AND SKILLS, WE COULD SURVIVE IN THE WILDERNESS FOR YEARS. THOUGH I'D HAVE OBVIOUSLY TO KEEP HER ON TASK SOMETIMES.

3. NATHALIE. THAT WAY, AFTER 15 MINUTES, WE'D GO BACK TO THE CABIN TO TAKE SHELTER FROM THE WILD ANIMALS, AND SPEND THE REST OF THE STAY PLAYING ***ANIMAL CROSSING***. AND YES WE'D REVEL IN THE IRONY. #VIRTUALFORESTFOREVER #POLYGONSDONTHURT

4. TOO MANY QUESTIONS, DUDE...

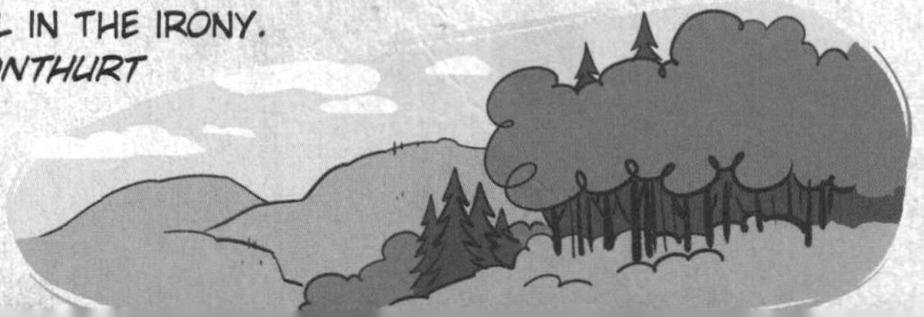

QUESTION 4: CAN YOU NAME FIVE SPECIES OF WILDLIFE LIVING IN YOUR AREA?

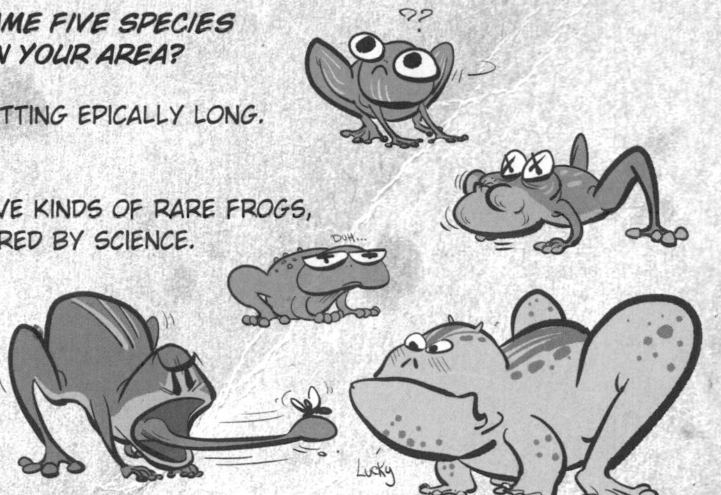
??
DUH...
LUCKY

1. I TOTALLY CAN, BUT THIS TEST IS GETTING EPICALLY LONG. AND THESE QUESTIONS SUCK.

2. EASY... I MEAN, I CAN EVEN NAME FIVE KINDS OF RARE FROGS, TWO OF WHICH ARE STILL UNDISCOVERED BY SCIENCE.

3. DO FARM ANIMALS COUNT?

4. SAME AS ANSWER 3. COWS AND PIGS COUNT TOO, RIGHT?

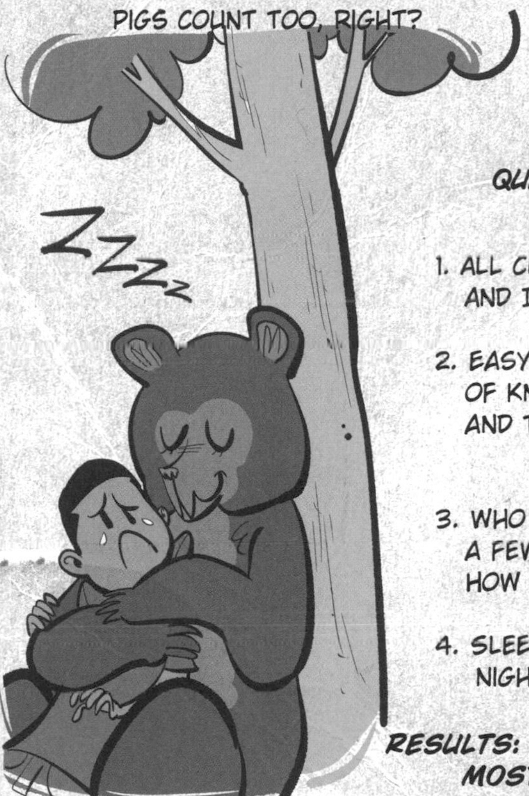
ZZZZZ

QUESTION 5: YOU HAVE TO SPEND THE NIGHT IN THE WOODS. WHERE DO YOU SLEEP?

1. ALL CURLED UP WITH MY NEW FAMILY OF FAWNS. AND I REALLY HOPE THIS IS THE LAST QUESTION...

2. EASY-PEASY. AS A MASTER IN THE VENERABLE ART OF KNOT-TYING, I FIRST TAKE MY TRUSTY HATCHET AND THEN–

(NARRATOR: THIS ANSWER HAS BEEN REDACTED BECAUSE, HONESTLY, NO ONE CARES.)

3. WHO COULD POSSIBLY SLEEP KNOWING THEY ONLY HAVE A FEW HOURS TO LIVE? MAYBE EVEN LESS! STUPID TEST! HOW IS THAT EVEN A QUESTION?

4. SLEEP? WHO SLEEPS AT NIGHT? NIGHTTIME IS FOR PARTYING!

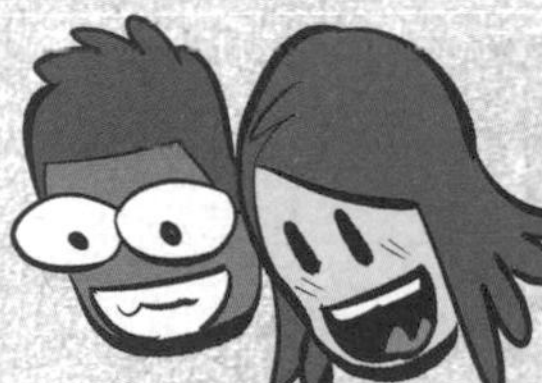

RESULTS: IF YOU ANSWERED MOSTLY NUMBER:

1. YOU'RE NOT JUST A NATURE GIRL: YOU'RE A NATURE GIRL WE ACTUALLY WANT TO HANG WITH! YOU KNOW HOW TO SEE THE BRIGHT SIDE OF EVERY SITUATION, WHETHER IT'S A SWARM OF INSECTS, A RIVER OF MOLTEN LAVA, OR A GANG OF GRIZZLIES RIDING A PACK OF GIANT WOLVES! NICE ONE!

2. YOU'RE OFFICIALLY THE ULTIMATE NATURE GIRL, BUT AT WHAT COST? YOUR LACK OF FLEXIBILITY AND SHOW-OFFY KNOW-IT-ALL BEHAVIOR DRIVES AWAY ANYONE WHO MIGHT WANT TO SHARE THE WOODS WITH YOU (INCLUDING DANGEROUS ANIMALS). YOU HAVE THE SKILLS TO SURVIVE OVER A CENTURY AS A HERMIT IN A CAVE ON A MOUNTAINTOP, BUT NO. ONE. CARES. WAY TO GO!

3. YOU JUST AREN'T A NATURE GIRL, AND YOU KNOW IT. YOU ALSO KNOW THAT AS SOON AS YOU TURN THIRTY, YOU'LL REALIZE THERE WAS NO REASON TO BE SCARED OF THE WOODS, AND YOU'LL IMMEDIATELY BECOME OBSESSED WITH WILDERNESS CAMPING. BUT FOR NOW, PLAYING VIDEO GAMES WITH NATHALIE ALL NIGHT IS ALL YOU NEED, AND THAT'S JUST FINE.

4. WTF DUDE? I DON'T CARE IF YOU'RE IN THE FOREST OR THE CITY: I GIVE YOU A LIFE EXPECTANCY OF 36 HOURS, TOPS.

WHAT IF WE WERE... SICK

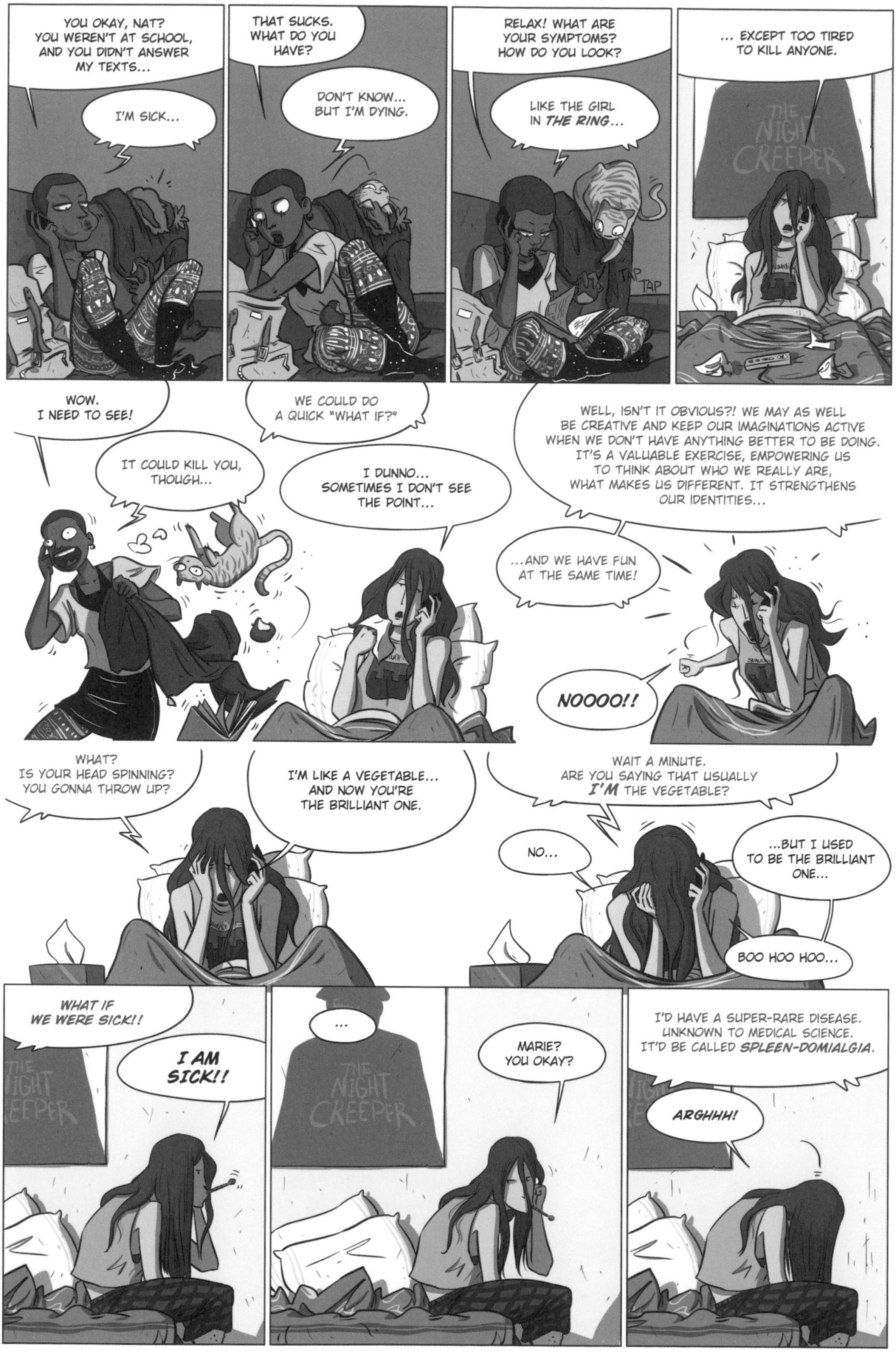
YOU OKAY, NAT? YOU WEREN'T AT SCHOOL, AND YOU DIDN'T ANSWER MY TEXTS...
I'M SICK...
THAT SUCKS. WHAT DO YOU HAVE?
DON'T KNOW... BUT I'M DYING.
RELAX! WHAT ARE YOUR SYMPTOMS? HOW DO YOU LOOK?
LIKE THE GIRL IN *THE RING*...
TAP TAP
... EXCEPT TOO TIRED TO KILL ANYONE.
THE NIGHT CREEPER
WOW. I NEED TO SEE!
IT COULD KILL YOU, THOUGH...
WE COULD DO A QUICK "WHAT IF?"
I DUNNO... SOMETIMES I DON'T SEE THE POINT...
WELL, ISN'T IT OBVIOUS?! WE MAY AS WELL BE CREATIVE AND KEEP OUR IMAGINATIONS ACTIVE WHEN WE DON'T HAVE ANYTHING BETTER TO BE DOING. IT'S A VALUABLE EXERCISE, EMPOWERING US TO THINK ABOUT WHO WE REALLY ARE, WHAT MAKES US DIFFERENT. IT STRENGTHENS OUR IDENTITIES...
...AND WE HAVE FUN AT THE SAME TIME!
NOOOO!!
WHAT? IS YOUR HEAD SPINNING? YOU GONNA THROW UP?
I'M LIKE A VEGETABLE... AND NOW YOU'RE THE BRILLIANT ONE.
WAIT A MINUTE. ARE YOU SAYING THAT USUALLY *I'M* THE VEGETABLE?
NO...
...BUT I USED TO BE THE BRILLIANT ONE...
BOO HOO HOO...
WHAT IF WE WERE SICK!!
I AM SICK!!
...
THE NIGHT CREEPER
MARIE? YOU OKAY?
I'D HAVE A SUPER-RARE DISEASE. UNKNOWN TO MEDICAL SCIENCE. IT'D BE CALLED *SPLEEN-DOMIALGIA*.
ARGHHH!

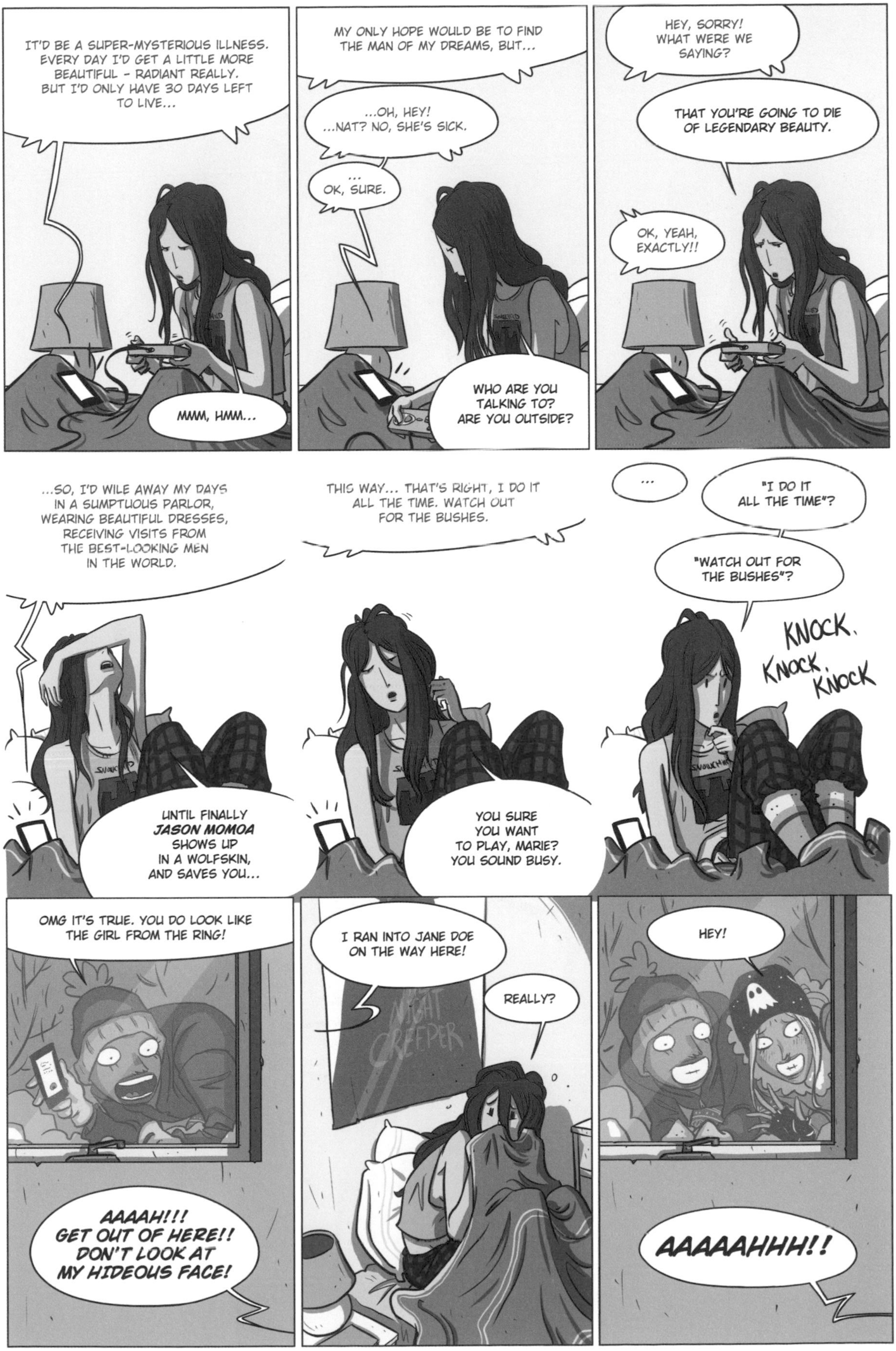
IT'D BE A SUPER-MYSTERIOUS ILLNESS. EVERY DAY I'D GET A LITTLE MORE BEAUTIFUL - RADIANT REALLY. BUT I'D ONLY HAVE 30 DAYS LEFT TO LIVE...
MMM, HMM...
MY ONLY HOPE WOULD BE TO FIND THE MAN OF MY DREAMS, BUT...
...OH, HEY! ...NAT? NO, SHE'S SICK.
... OK, SURE.
WHO ARE YOU TALKING TO? ARE YOU OUTSIDE?
HEY, SORRY! WHAT WERE WE SAYING?
THAT YOU'RE GOING TO DIE OF LEGENDARY BEAUTY.
OK, YEAH, EXACTLY!!
...SO, I'D WILE AWAY MY DAYS IN A SUMPTUOUS PARLOR, WEARING BEAUTIFUL DRESSES, RECEIVING VISITS FROM THE BEST-LOOKING MEN IN THE WORLD.
UNTIL FINALLY JASON MOMOA SHOWS UP IN A WOLFSKIN, AND SAVES YOU...
THIS WAY... THAT'S RIGHT, I DO IT ALL THE TIME. WATCH OUT FOR THE BUSHES.
YOU SURE YOU WANT TO PLAY, MARIE? YOU SOUND BUSY.
...
"I DO IT ALL THE TIME"?
"WATCH OUT FOR THE BUSHES"?
KNOCK. KNOCK. KNOCK
OMG IT'S TRUE. YOU DO LOOK LIKE THE GIRL FROM THE RING!
AAAAH!!! GET OUT OF HERE!! DON'T LOOK AT MY HIDEOUS FACE!
I RAN INTO JANE DOE ON THE WAY HERE!
REALLY?
NIGHT CREEPER
HEY!
AAAAAHHH!!

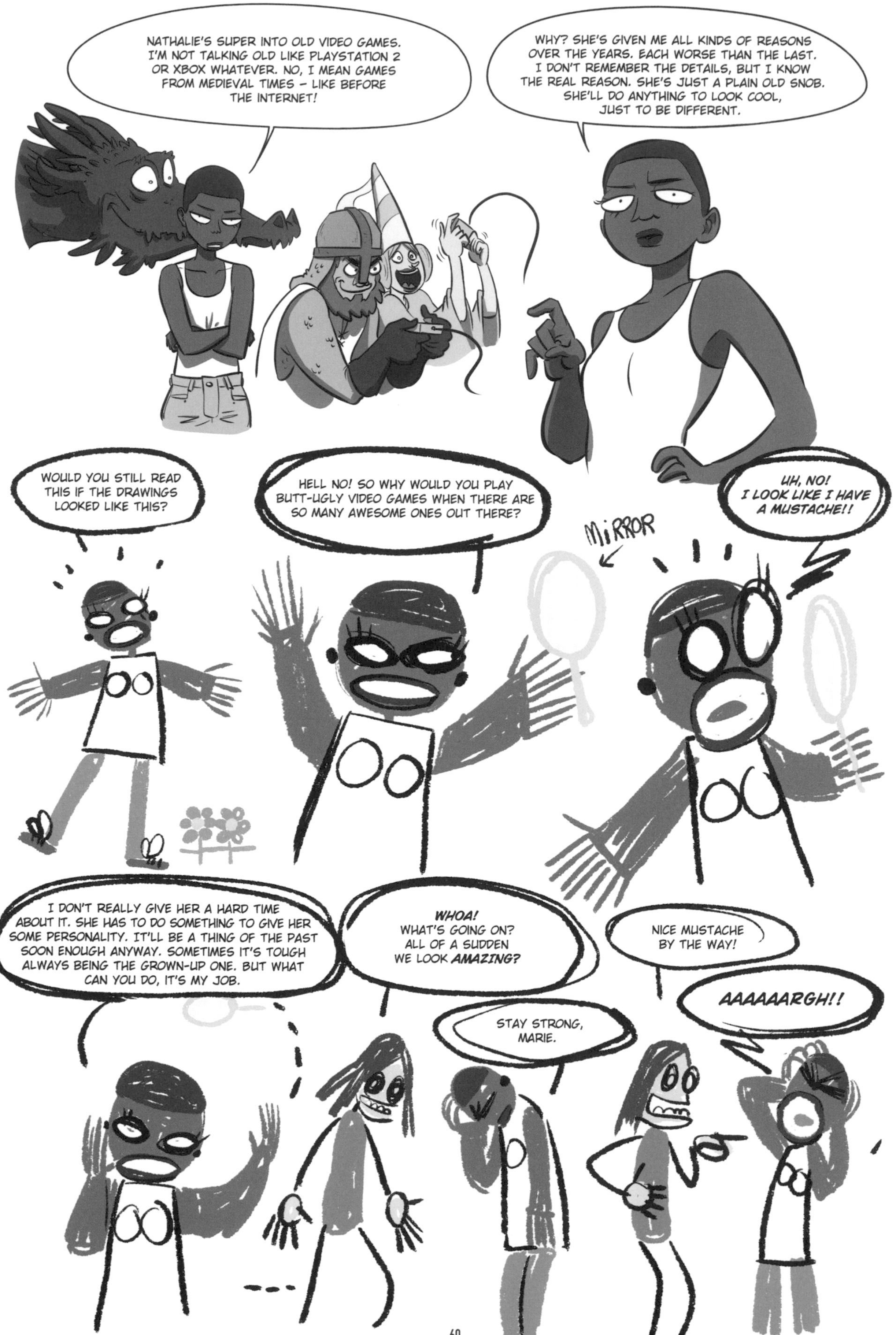
NATHALIE'S SUPER INTO OLD VIDEO GAMES. I'M NOT TALKING OLD LIKE PLAYSTATION 2 OR XBOX WHATEVER. NO, I MEAN GAMES FROM MEDIEVAL TIMES – LIKE BEFORE THE INTERNET!
WHY? SHE'S GIVEN ME ALL KINDS OF REASONS OVER THE YEARS. EACH WORSE THAN THE LAST. I DON'T REMEMBER THE DETAILS, BUT I KNOW THE REAL REASON. SHE'S JUST A PLAIN OLD SNOB. SHE'LL DO ANYTHING TO LOOK COOL, JUST TO BE DIFFERENT.
WOULD YOU STILL READ THIS IF THE DRAWINGS LOOKED LIKE THIS?
HELL NO! SO WHY WOULD YOU PLAY BUTT-UGLY VIDEO GAMES WHEN THERE ARE SO MANY AWESOME ONES OUT THERE?
MIRROR
UH, NO! I LOOK LIKE I HAVE A MUSTACHE!!
I DON'T REALLY GIVE HER A HARD TIME ABOUT IT. SHE HAS TO DO SOMETHING TO GIVE HER SOME PERSONALITY. IT'LL BE A THING OF THE PAST SOON ENOUGH ANYWAY. SOMETIMES IT'S TOUGH ALWAYS BEING THE GROWN-UP ONE. BUT WHAT CAN YOU DO, IT'S MY JOB.
WHOA! WHAT'S GOING ON? ALL OF A SUDDEN WE LOOK AMAZING?
STAY STRONG, MARIE.
NICE MUSTACHE BY THE WAY!
AAAAAARGH!!

WHAT IF WE WERE... PARENTS

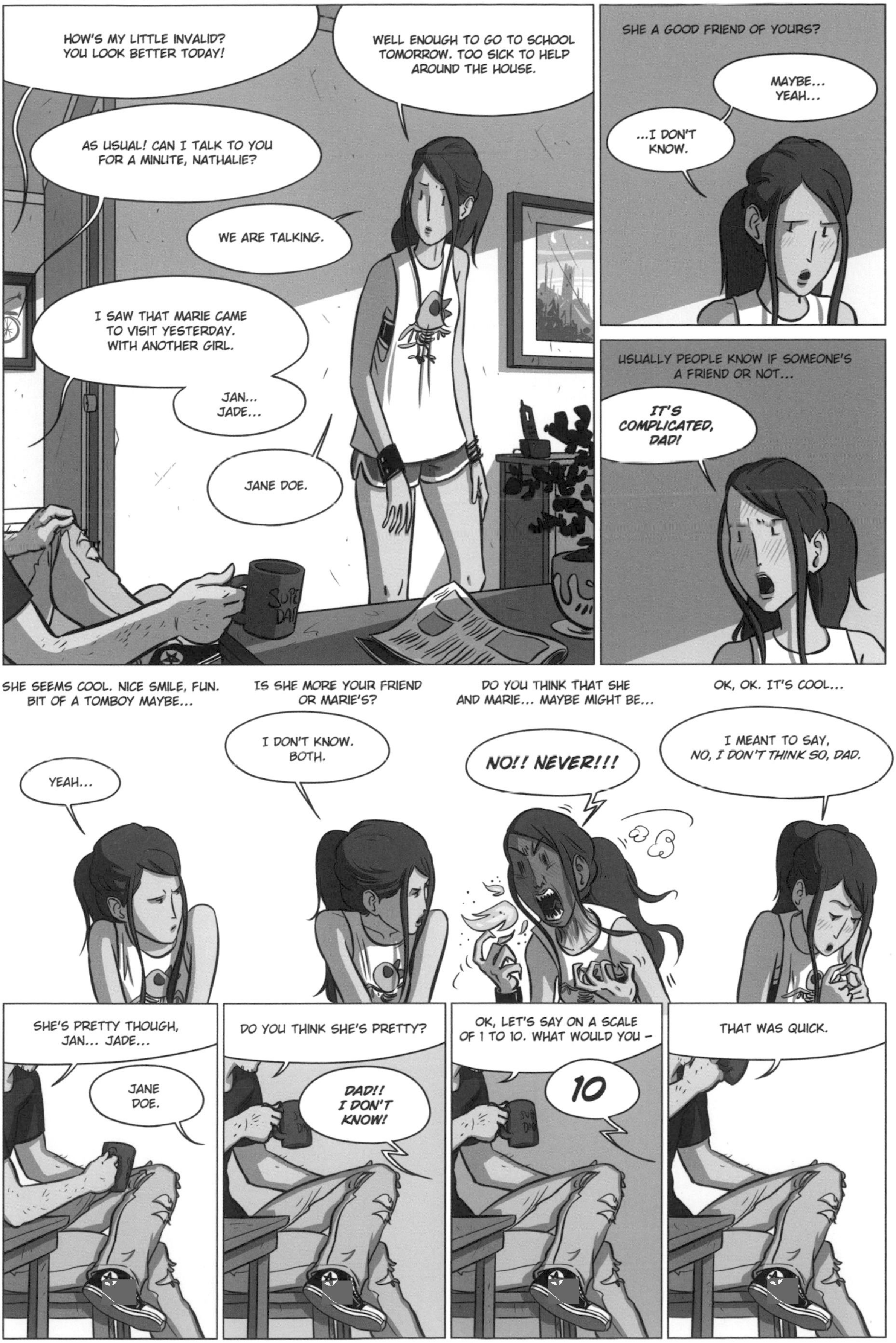
HOW'S MY LITTLE INVALID? YOU LOOK BETTER TODAY!
WELL ENOUGH TO GO TO SCHOOL TOMORROW. TOO SICK TO HELP AROUND THE HOUSE.
AS USUAL! CAN I TALK TO YOU FOR A MINUTE, NATHALIE?
WE ARE TALKING.
I SAW THAT MARIE CAME TO VISIT YESTERDAY. WITH ANOTHER GIRL.
JAN... JADE...
JANE DOE.
SUPER DAD
SHE A GOOD FRIEND OF YOURS?
MAYBE... YEAH...
...I DON'T KNOW.
USUALLY PEOPLE KNOW IF SOMEONE'S A FRIEND OR NOT...
IT'S COMPLICATED, DAD!
SHE SEEMS COOL. NICE SMILE, FUN. BIT OF A TOMBOY MAYBE...
YEAH...
IS SHE MORE YOUR FRIEND OR MARIE'S?
I DON'T KNOW. BOTH.
DO YOU THINK THAT SHE AND MARIE... MAYBE MIGHT BE...
NO!! NEVER!!!
OK, OK. IT'S COOL...
I MEANT TO SAY, NO, I DON'T THINK SO, DAD.
SHE'S PRETTY THOUGH, JAN... JADE...
JANE DOE.
DO YOU THINK SHE'S PRETTY?
DAD!! I DON'T KNOW!
OK, LET'S SAY ON A SCALE OF 1 TO 10. WHAT WOULD YOU –
10
THAT WAS QUICK.

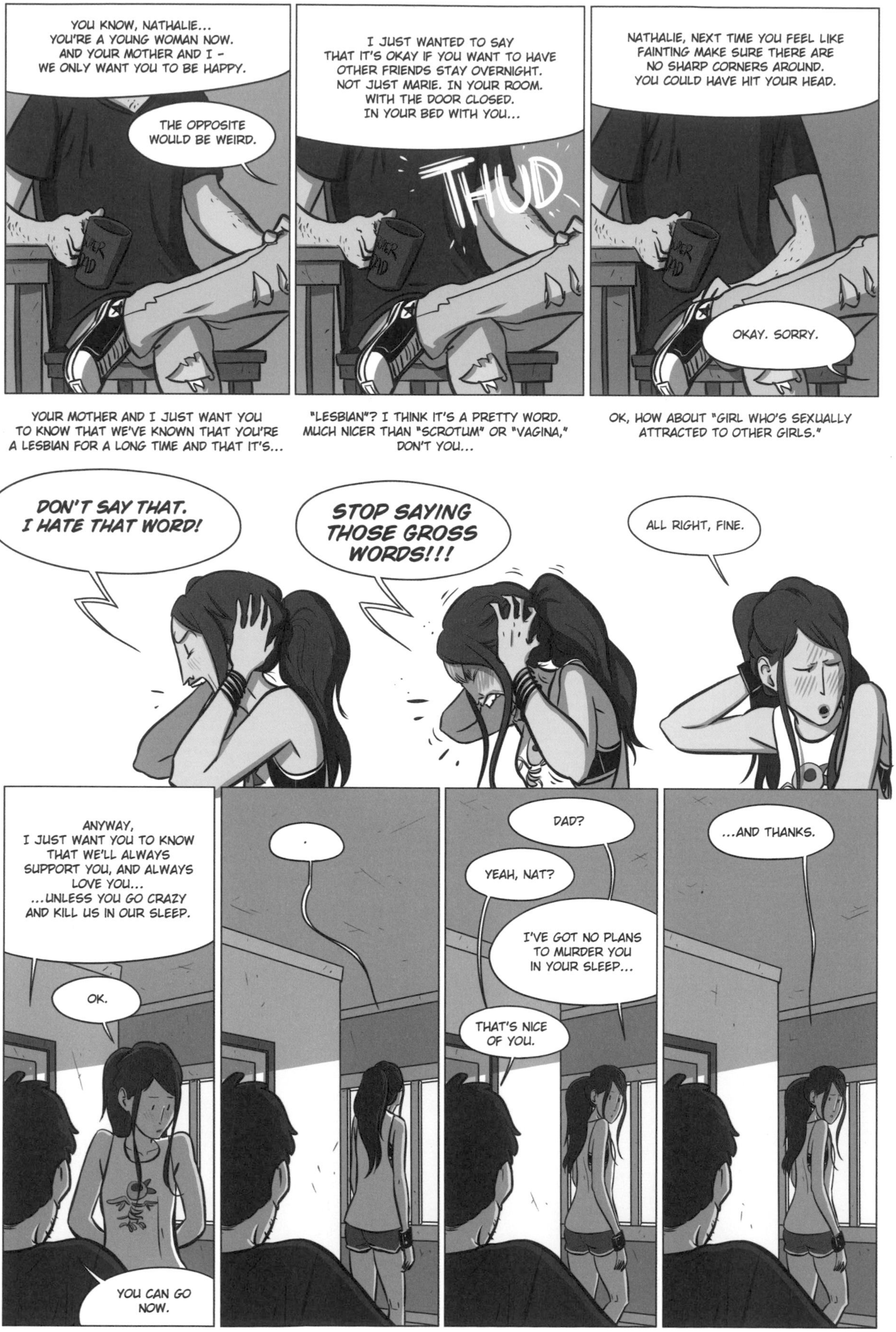
YOU KNOW, NATHALIE... YOU'RE A YOUNG WOMAN NOW. AND YOUR MOTHER AND I - WE ONLY WANT YOU TO BE HAPPY.
THE OPPOSITE WOULD BE WEIRD.
I JUST WANTED TO SAY THAT IT'S OKAY IF YOU WANT TO HAVE OTHER FRIENDS STAY OVERNIGHT. NOT JUST MARIE. IN YOUR ROOM. WITH THE DOOR CLOSED. IN YOUR BED WITH YOU...
THUD
NATHALIE, NEXT TIME YOU FEEL LIKE FAINTING MAKE SURE THERE ARE NO SHARP CORNERS AROUND. YOU COULD HAVE HIT YOUR HEAD.
OKAY. SORRY.
YOUR MOTHER AND I JUST WANT YOU TO KNOW THAT WE'VE KNOWN THAT YOU'RE A LESBIAN FOR A LONG TIME AND THAT IT'S...
"LESBIAN"? I THINK IT'S A PRETTY WORD. MUCH NICER THAN "SCROTUM" OR "VAGINA," DON'T YOU...
OK, HOW ABOUT "GIRL WHO'S SEXUALLY ATTRACTED TO OTHER GIRLS."
DON'T SAY THAT. I HATE THAT WORD!
STOP SAYING THOSE GROSS WORDS!!!
ALL RIGHT, FINE.
ANYWAY, I JUST WANT YOU TO KNOW THAT WE'LL ALWAYS SUPPORT YOU, AND ALWAYS LOVE YOU... ...UNLESS YOU GO CRAZY AND KILL US IN OUR SLEEP.
OK.
YOU CAN GO NOW.
.
DAD?
YEAH, NAT?
I'VE GOT NO PLANS TO MURDER YOU IN YOUR SLEEP...
THAT'S NICE OF YOU.
...AND THANKS.

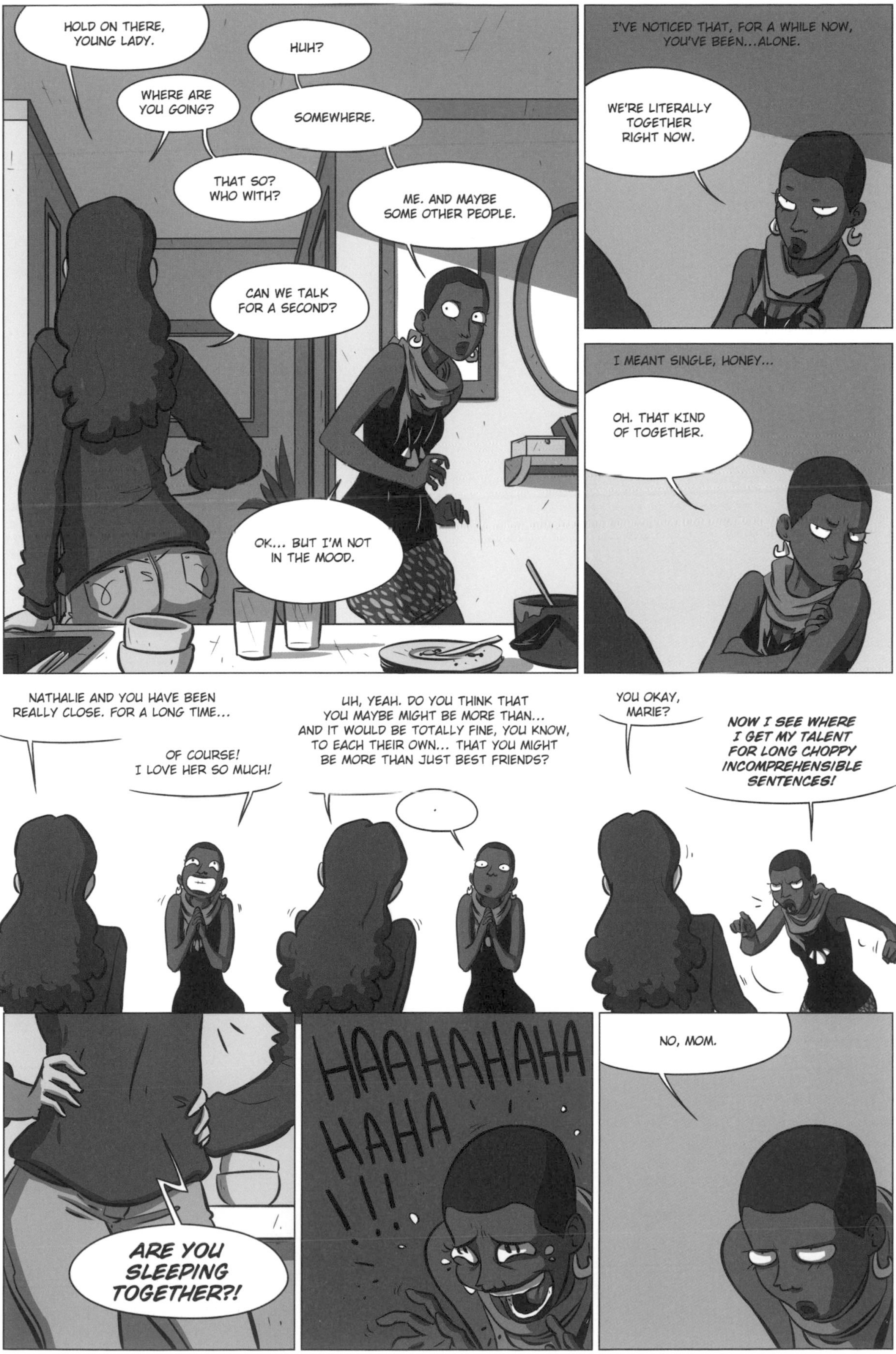
HOLD ON THERE, YOUNG LADY.
HUH?
WHERE ARE YOU GOING?
SOMEWHERE.
THAT SO? WHO WITH?
ME. AND MAYBE SOME OTHER PEOPLE.
CAN WE TALK FOR A SECOND?
OK... BUT I'M NOT IN THE MOOD.
I'VE NOTICED THAT, FOR A WHILE NOW, YOU'VE BEEN...ALONE.
WE'RE LITERALLY TOGETHER RIGHT NOW.
I MEANT SINGLE, HONEY...
OH. THAT KIND OF TOGETHER.
NATHALIE AND YOU HAVE BEEN REALLY CLOSE. FOR A LONG TIME...
OF COURSE! I LOVE HER SO MUCH!
UH, YEAH. DO YOU THINK THAT YOU MAYBE MIGHT BE MORE THAN... AND IT WOULD BE TOTALLY FINE, YOU KNOW, TO EACH THEIR OWN... THAT YOU MIGHT BE MORE THAN JUST BEST FRIENDS?
.
YOU OKAY, MARIE?
NOW I SEE WHERE I GET MY TALENT FOR LONG CHOPPY INCOMPREHENSIBLE SENTENCES!
ARE YOU SLEEPING TOGETHER?!
HAAHAHAHA HAHA !!!
NO, MOM.

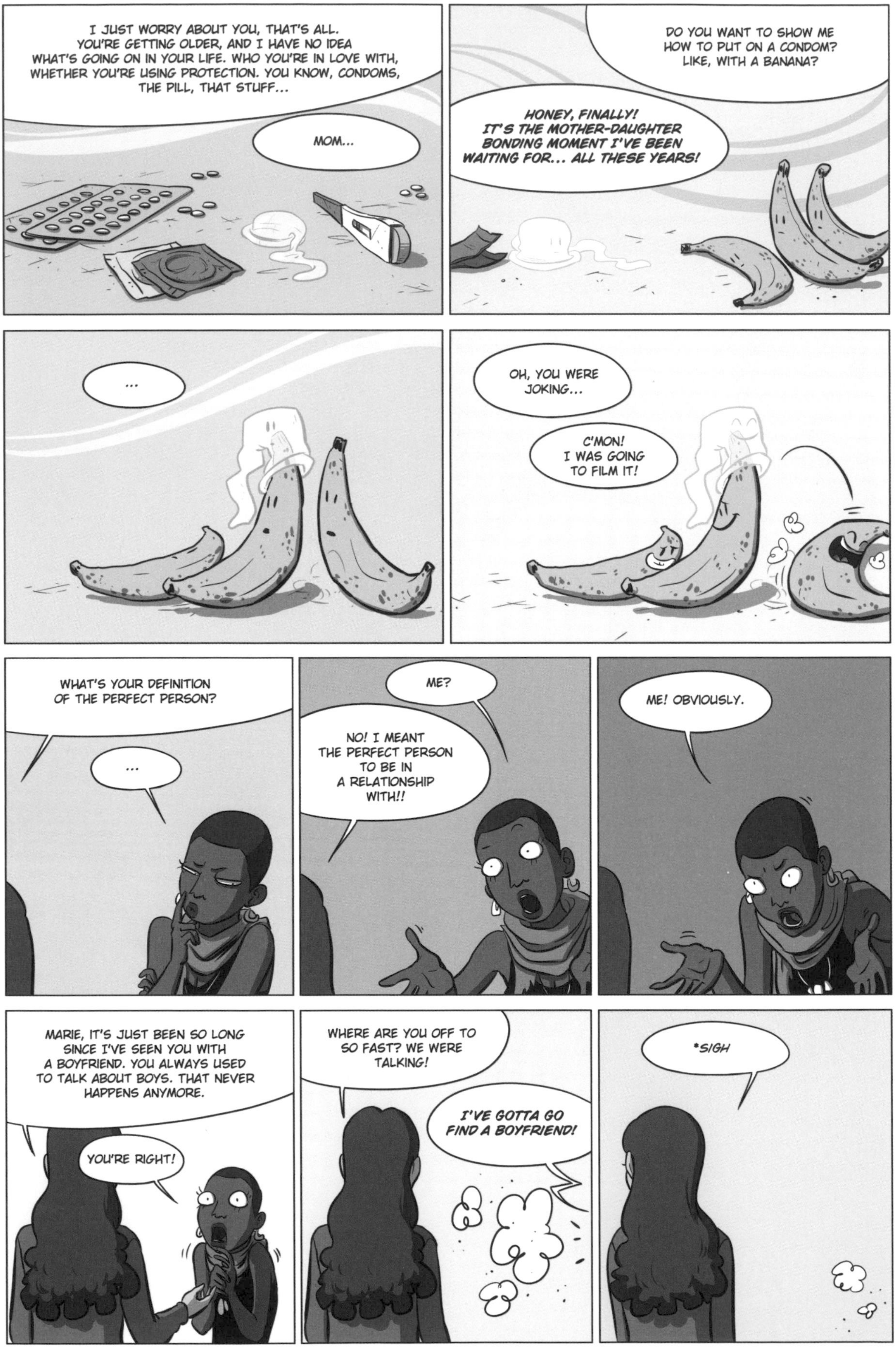
I JUST WORRY ABOUT YOU, THAT'S ALL. YOU'RE GETTING OLDER, AND I HAVE NO IDEA WHAT'S GOING ON IN YOUR LIFE. WHO YOU'RE IN LOVE WITH, WHETHER YOU'RE USING PROTECTION. YOU KNOW, CONDOMS, THE PILL, THAT STUFF...
MOM...
DO YOU WANT TO SHOW ME HOW TO PUT ON A CONDOM? LIKE, WITH A BANANA?
HONEY, FINALLY! IT'S THE MOTHER-DAUGHTER BONDING MOMENT I'VE BEEN WAITING FOR... ALL THESE YEARS!
...
OH, YOU WERE JOKING...
C'MON! I WAS GOING TO FILM IT!
WHAT'S YOUR DEFINITION OF THE PERFECT PERSON?
...
ME?
NO! I MEANT THE PERFECT PERSON TO BE IN A RELATIONSHIP WITH!!
ME! OBVIOUSLY.
MARIE, IT'S JUST BEEN SO LONG SINCE I'VE SEEN YOU WITH A BOYFRIEND. YOU ALWAYS USED TO TALK ABOUT BOYS. THAT NEVER HAPPENS ANYMORE.
YOU'RE RIGHT!
WHERE ARE YOU OFF TO SO FAST? WE WERE TALKING!
I'VE GOTTA GO FIND A BOYFRIEND!
*SIGH

NATHALIE'S DIARY

Hey you.
I'm starting to believe some reptilian must have murdered my father and taken his place. A real father who'd known me for 17 year would know by now that I have no desire to talk about my love life, or sexual preference, or anything else with him. Proof? I can't even write the words without blushing! What's my problem? I'm not ashamed of who I am. You could even say I'm proud to be a ~~lesbian~~.

(Here is written ~~lesbian~~...)

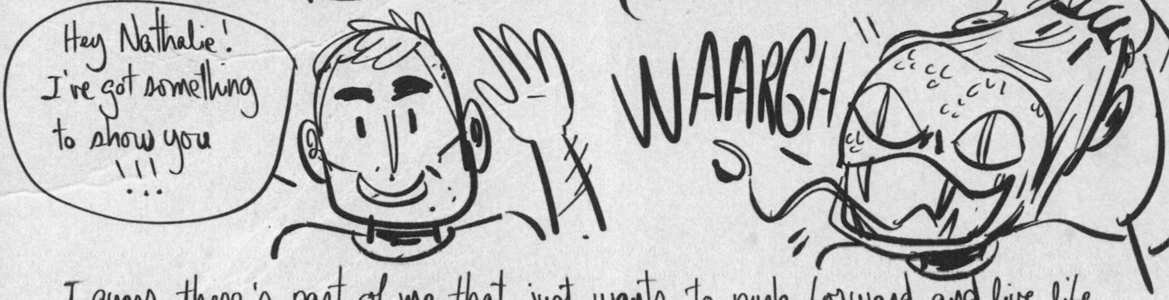
Hey Nathalie! I've got something to show you !!! ...
WAARGH

I guess there's part of me that just wants to push forward and live life to the fullest (love!) And then there's another part of me that wants to stay home where it's safe and play video games and watch cartoons. Why can't I just stay a kid forever? Pretty please? Everything was just so much easier until stupid puberty came along and wrecked everything! Marie just spends all her time dreaming of boys. Seems to work for her. Seriously, her ability to adapt and fit in anywhere boggles my mind. I'm sure that if they just shot her into space and put her in charge of the international space station she'd figure out a way to 1) not be surprised at all and 2) run her team like a well-oiled machine. Even without the first notion of astrophysics.

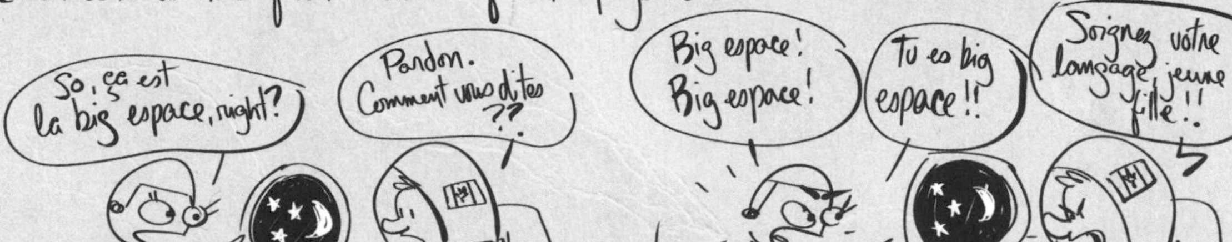
So, ça est la big espace, right?
Pardon. Comment vous dites ??
Big espace! Big espace!
Tu es big espace!!
Soignez votre langage jeune fille!!

Bottom line: reptilian dad, stop talking about ~~lesbians~~. I'll get comfortable with the whole thing when I get there. I know that you love me as only a boa constrictor dad can (bad reptile joke I know). But putting more pressure on me won't get me walking any faster (or crawling!... okay, that's quite enough with the awful reptile jokes).

PS: OK, I have to admit that all I can think of now is Jane Doe sleeping over, in my bed... take care of some business... Be right back...

PSS: ARRGH. I can't help it. I'm thinking about it again! GRRRRR!

DEAR DIARY,

TODAY MOM TRIED SHOWING ME HOW TO PUT A CONDOM ON A BANANA.
I'M GLAD SHE DID, SO I CAN TEASE HER ABOUT IT FOR THE NEXT TWENTY YEARS.
I'M LOOKING FORWARD TO TELLING THE WHOLE FAMILY THE STORY AT CHRISTMAS;
SHE'S GOING TO LOSE IT! MY ONLY REGRET IS THAT I DIDN'T FILM IT. I COULD HAVE
MADE A FORTUNE ON YOUTUBE AND NEVER HAVE TO GO TO SCHOOL EVER AGAIN.

ON A MORE WORRISOME NOTE: MOM WAS CONVINCED ME AND NATHALIE WERE LESBIANS
AND THAT WE'RE DATING! NOT COOL! FIRST OFF, JUST GROSS! I'D TAKE A BULLET
FOR NATHALIE, NO QUESTION. BUT IN A WEIRD SCENARIO WHERE A MURDERER SAYS:
HEY YOU! YOU HAVE TO SLEEP WITH THAT TALL REDHEAD OR I'LL KILL YOU." WELL,
SORRY NAT, THAT'S JUST NEVER GOING TO HAPPEN.

BUT WHAT REALLY WORRIES ME, IS THAT MY OWN MOTHER SHOULD KNOW I'M NOT
INTO GIRLS! SHE'S KNOWN ME FOREVER!

MAYBE SHE'S HAVING A BREAKDOWN? OR WORSE, MAYBE A REPTILIAN HAS TAKEN OVER
HER BODY ON HER APPEARANCE!! GONNA CHECK. BACK IN 5.

...

OKAY SO, SHE'S NOT A REPTILIAN.
NO FAKE MOM COULD EVER IMITATE THE EXPRESSION OF A MOTHER WHO REGRETS
HAVING CHILDREN.
PHEW! WHAT A RELIEF.
THERE'S ONE PROBLEM SOLVED.

IN THE END SHE JUST REMINDED ME THAT IT'S BEEN A LONG TIME SINCE I HAD
A BOYFRIEND. AND I REALIZED SHE'S RIGHT, I HAVEN'T HAD A CRUSH ON A GUY
AT SCHOOL FOR A LONG TIME. I'VE ALREADY GONE OUT WITH ALL THE HALF-DECENT ONES
AND I'VE HAD MY FILL OF ALL OF THEM. HALF-DECENT ISN'T EXACTLY A GLOWING REVIEW.
I'LL KEEP ANNOYING NATHALIE ABOUT HER BROTHER FOR A WHILE LONGER.
SHE LOSES IT EVERY TIME, AND IT MAKES ME LAUGH. LIKE, MAYBE IN ANOTHER LIFE
I'D WANT TO MARRY HIM. BUT I'M NOT AN IDIOT. HE'S OLD AND HE HAS KIDS!
I'M NOT GONNA START BREASTFEEDING AT 17!....

I WONDER: DOES THE MILK IN YOUR BOOBS, LIKE, ACTIVATE WHEN YOU COME INTO
CONTACT WITH CHILDREN? I HOPE NOT BECAUSE I WAS SITTING PRETTY CLOSE
TO A MOM AND HER BABY IN THE BUS YESTERDAY.

SHIT! I DON'T WANT MILK IN MY BOOBS!

WHAT IF WE WERE.... NINJAS

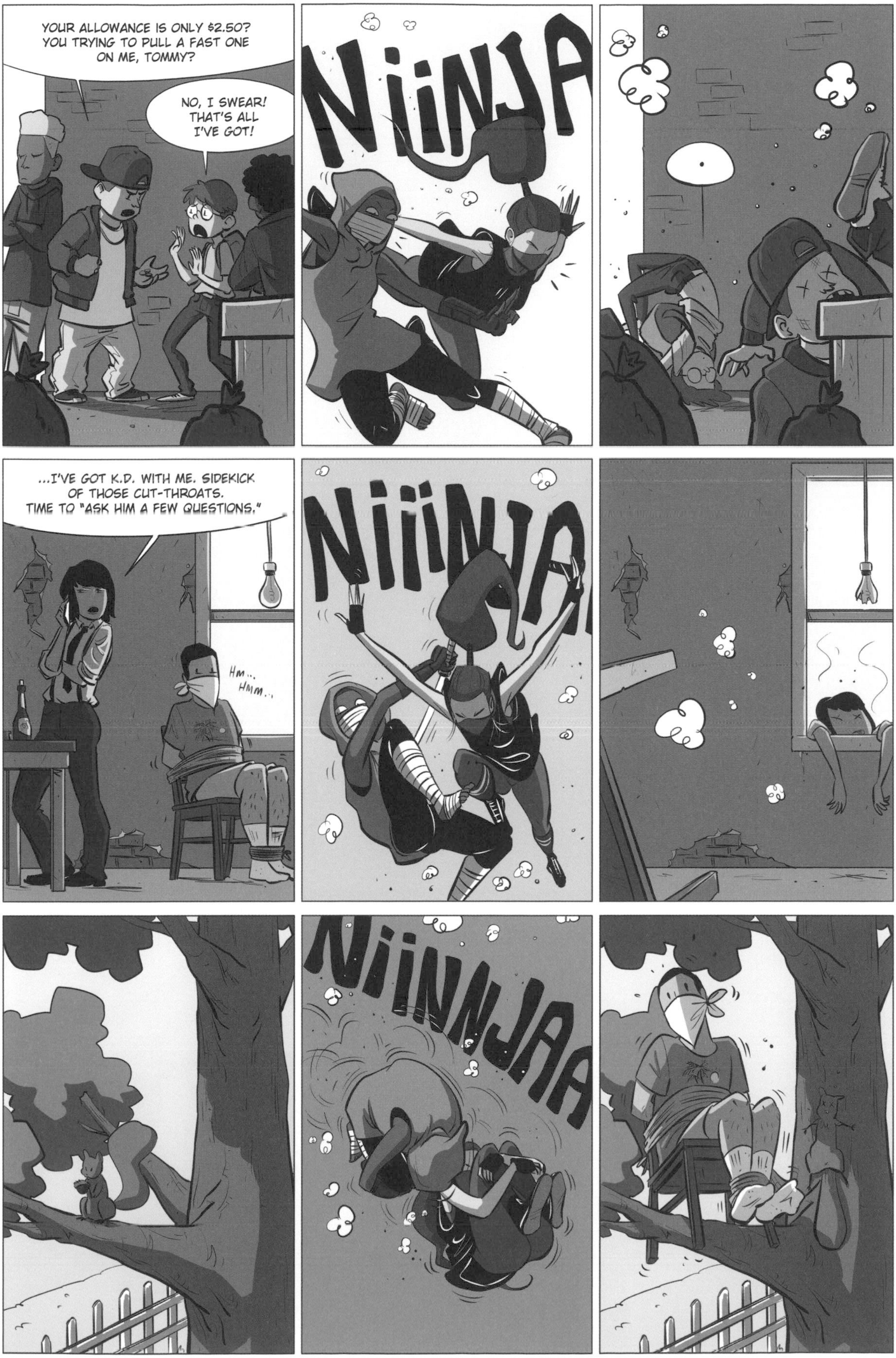

YOUR ALLOWANCE IS ONLY $2.50? YOU TRYING TO PULL A FAST ONE ON ME, TOMMY?
NO, I SWEAR! THAT'S ALL I'VE GOT!
NIINJA
...I'VE GOT K.D. WITH ME. SIDEKICK OF THOSE CUT-THROATS. TIME TO "ASK HIM A FEW QUESTIONS."
HM... HMM...
NIIINJAA
NIINNJAA

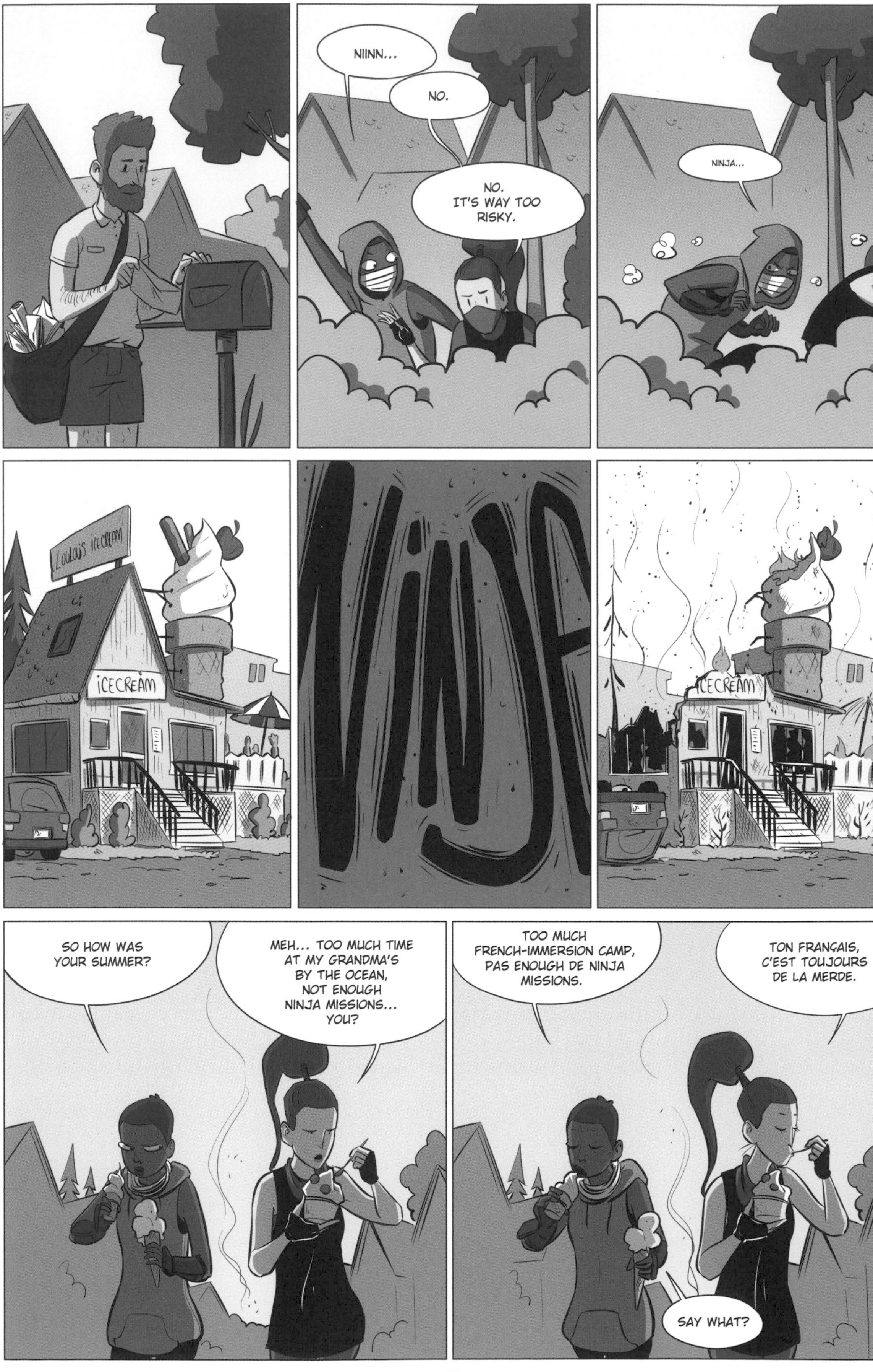
NIINN...
NO.
NO. IT'S WAY TOO RISKY.
NINJA...
Loulou's icecream
icecream
NINJA
ICECREAM
SO HOW WAS YOUR SUMMER?
MEH... TOO MUCH TIME AT MY GRANDMA'S BY THE OCEAN, NOT ENOUGH NINJA MISSIONS... YOU?
TOO MUCH FRENCH-IMMERSION CAMP, PAS ENOUGH DE NINJA MISSIONS.
TON FRANÇAIS, C'EST TOUJOURS DE LA MERDE.
SAY WHAT?

WHAT IF... WE MADE FACES

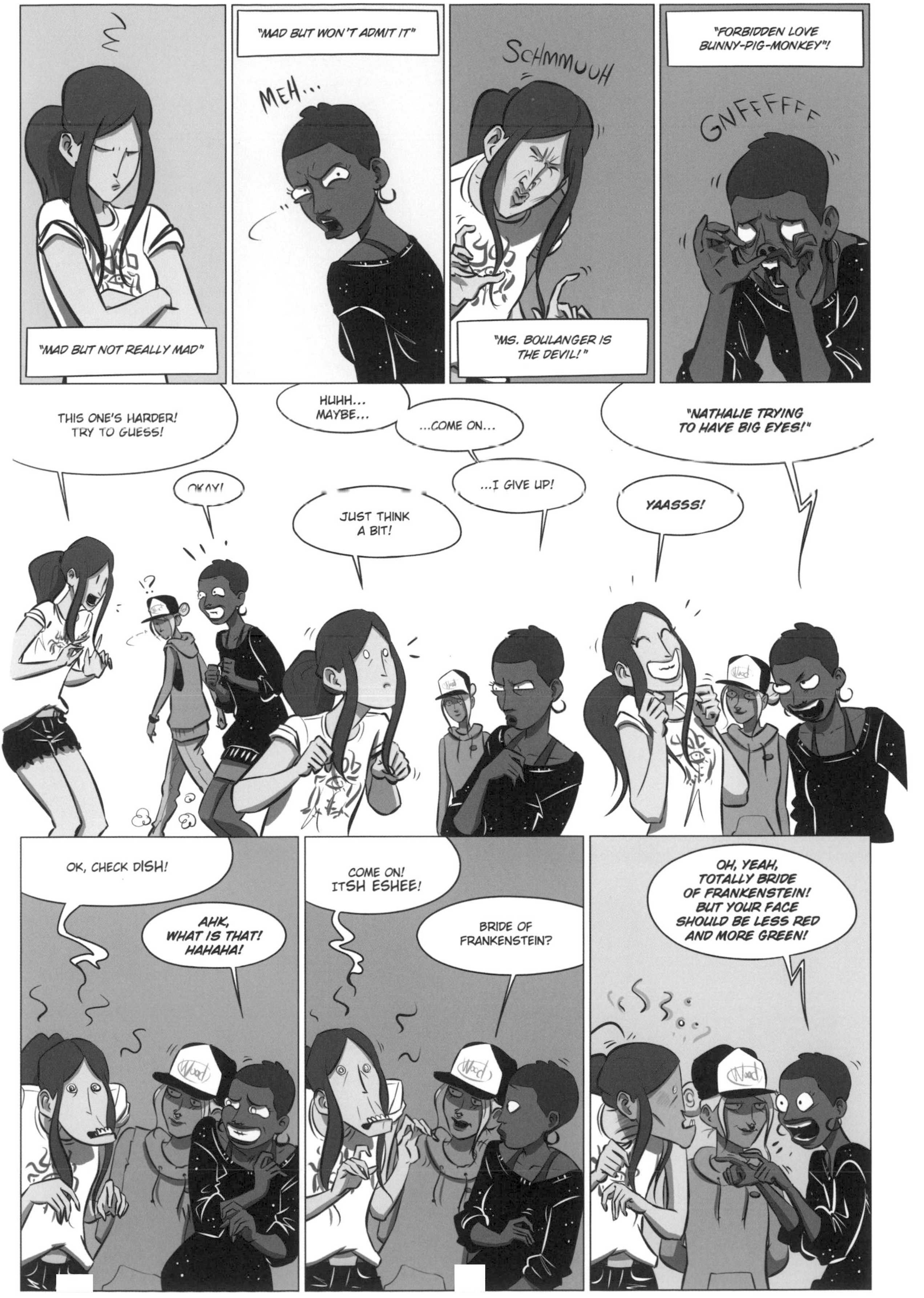
"MAD BUT NOT REALLY MAD"
"MAD BUT WON'T ADMIT IT"
MEH...
SCHMMUUH
"MS. BOULANGER IS THE DEVIL!"
"FORBIDDEN LOVE BUNNY-PIG-MONKEY"!
GNFFFFFF
THIS ONE'S HARDER! TRY TO GUESS!
OKAY!
HUHH... MAYBE...
...COME ON...
JUST THINK A BIT!
...I GIVE UP!
"NATHALIE TRYING TO HAVE BIG EYES!"
YAASSS!
OK, CHECK DISH!
AHK, WHAT IS THAT! HAHAHA!
COME ON! ITSH ESHEE!
BRIDE OF FRANKENSTEIN?
OH, YEAH, TOTALLY BRIDE OF FRANKENSTEIN! BUT YOUR FACE SHOULD BE LESS RED AND MORE GREEN!

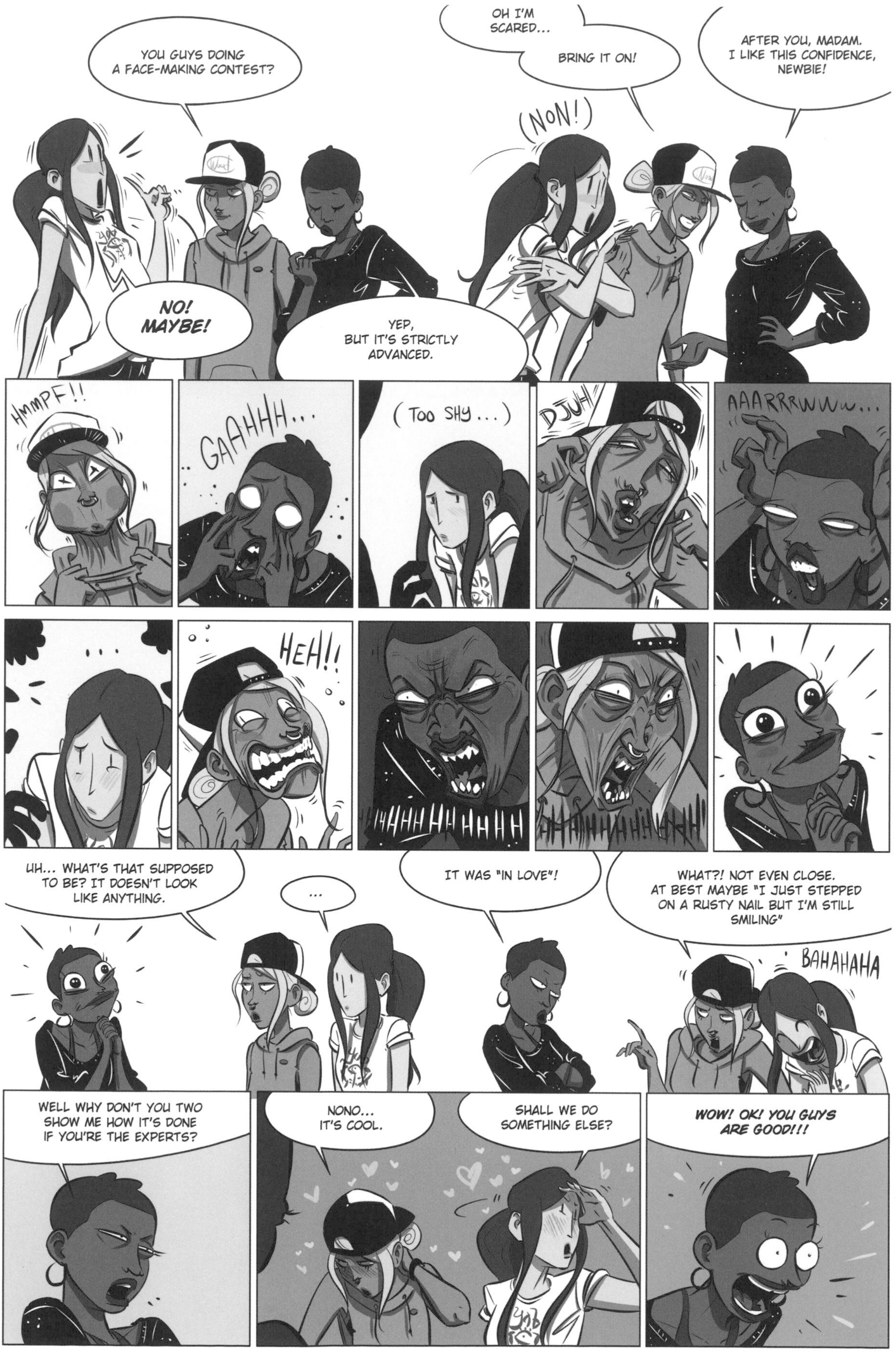

YOU GUYS DOING A FACE-MAKING CONTEST?
NO! MAYBE!
YEP, BUT IT'S STRICTLY ADVANCED.
(NON!)
OH I'M SCARED...
BRING IT ON!
AFTER YOU, MADAM. I LIKE THIS CONFIDENCE, NEWBIE!
HMMPF!!
GAHHH...
(TOO SHY ...)
DJUH
AAARRRWWW...
...
HEH!!
HHHHHHHHHHH
HHHHHHHHHHH
UH... WHAT'S THAT SUPPOSED TO BE? IT DOESN'T LOOK LIKE ANYTHING.
...
IT WAS "IN LOVE"!
WHAT?! NOT EVEN CLOSE. AT BEST MAYBE "I JUST STEPPED ON A RUSTY NAIL BUT I'M STILL SMILING"
BAHAHAHA
WELL WHY DON'T YOU TWO SHOW ME HOW IT'S DONE IF YOU'RE THE EXPERTS?
NONO... IT'S COOL.
SHALL WE DO SOMETHING ELSE?
WOW! OK! YOU GUYS ARE GOOD!!!

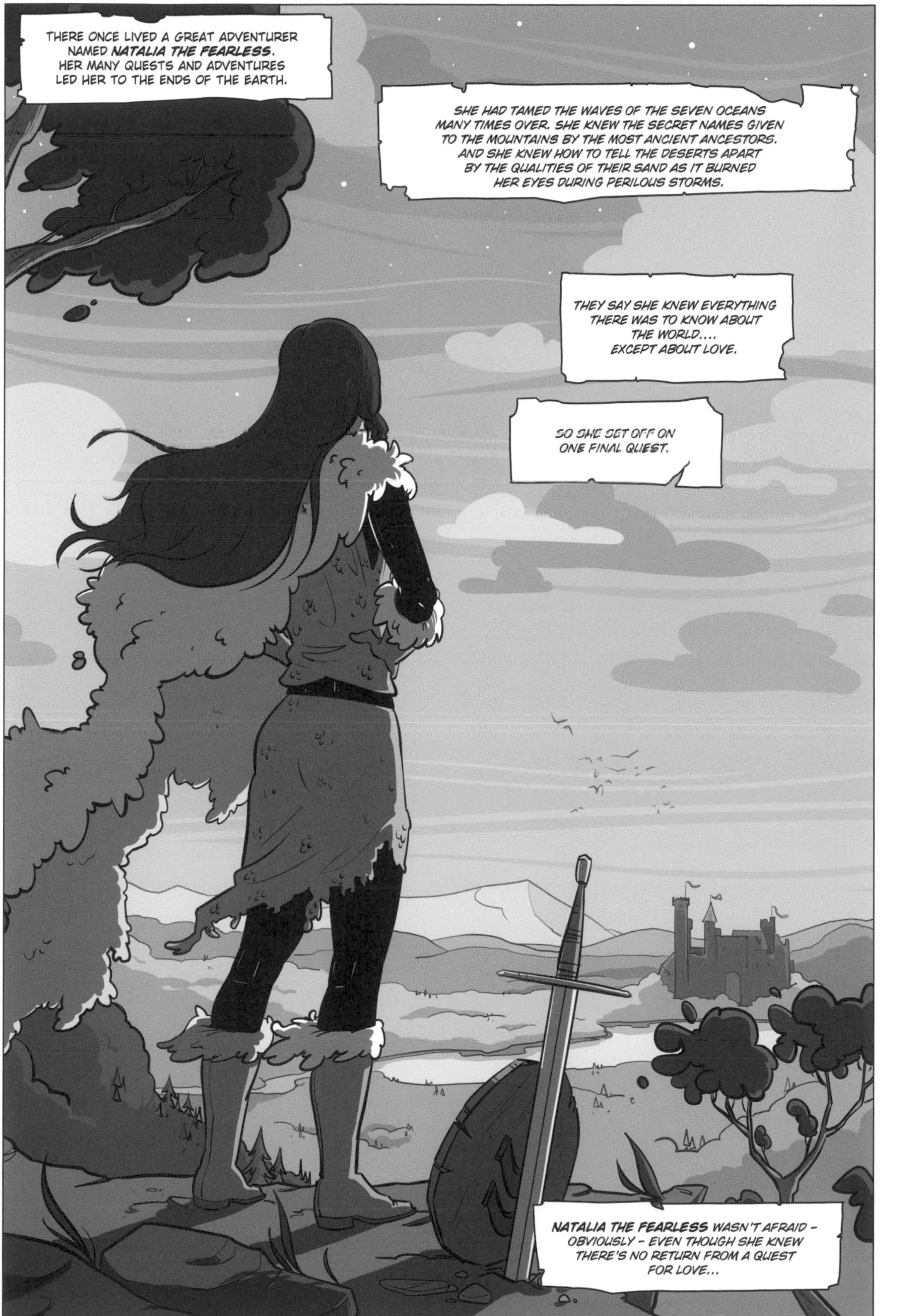
THERE ONCE LIVED A GREAT ADVENTURER NAMED **NATALIA THE FEARLESS**. HER MANY QUESTS AND ADVENTURES LED HER TO THE ENDS OF THE EARTH.
SHE HAD TAMED THE WAVES OF THE SEVEN OCEANS MANY TIMES OVER. SHE KNEW THE SECRET NAMES GIVEN TO THE MOUNTAINS BY THE MOST ANCIENT ANCESTORS. AND SHE KNEW HOW TO TELL THE DESERTS APART BY THE QUALITIES OF THEIR SAND AS IT BURNED HER EYES DURING PERILOUS STORMS.
THEY SAY SHE KNEW EVERYTHING THERE WAS TO KNOW ABOUT THE WORLD.... EXCEPT ABOUT LOVE.
SO SHE SET OFF ON ONE FINAL QUEST.
NATALIA THE FEARLESS WASN'T AFRAID – OBVIOUSLY – EVEN THOUGH SHE KNEW THERE'S NO RETURN FROM A QUEST FOR LOVE...

WHAT IF WE WERE... BRAVE

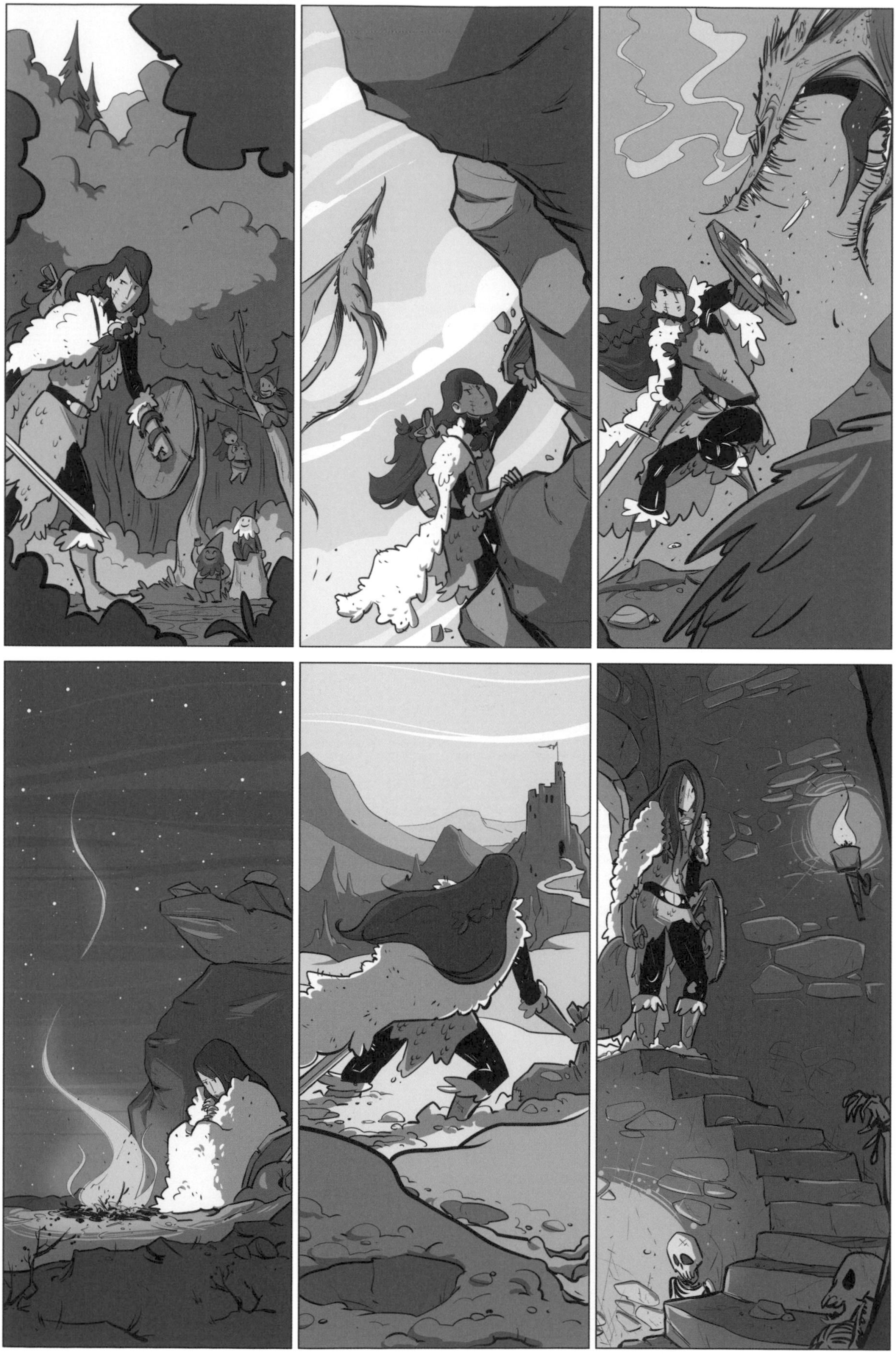

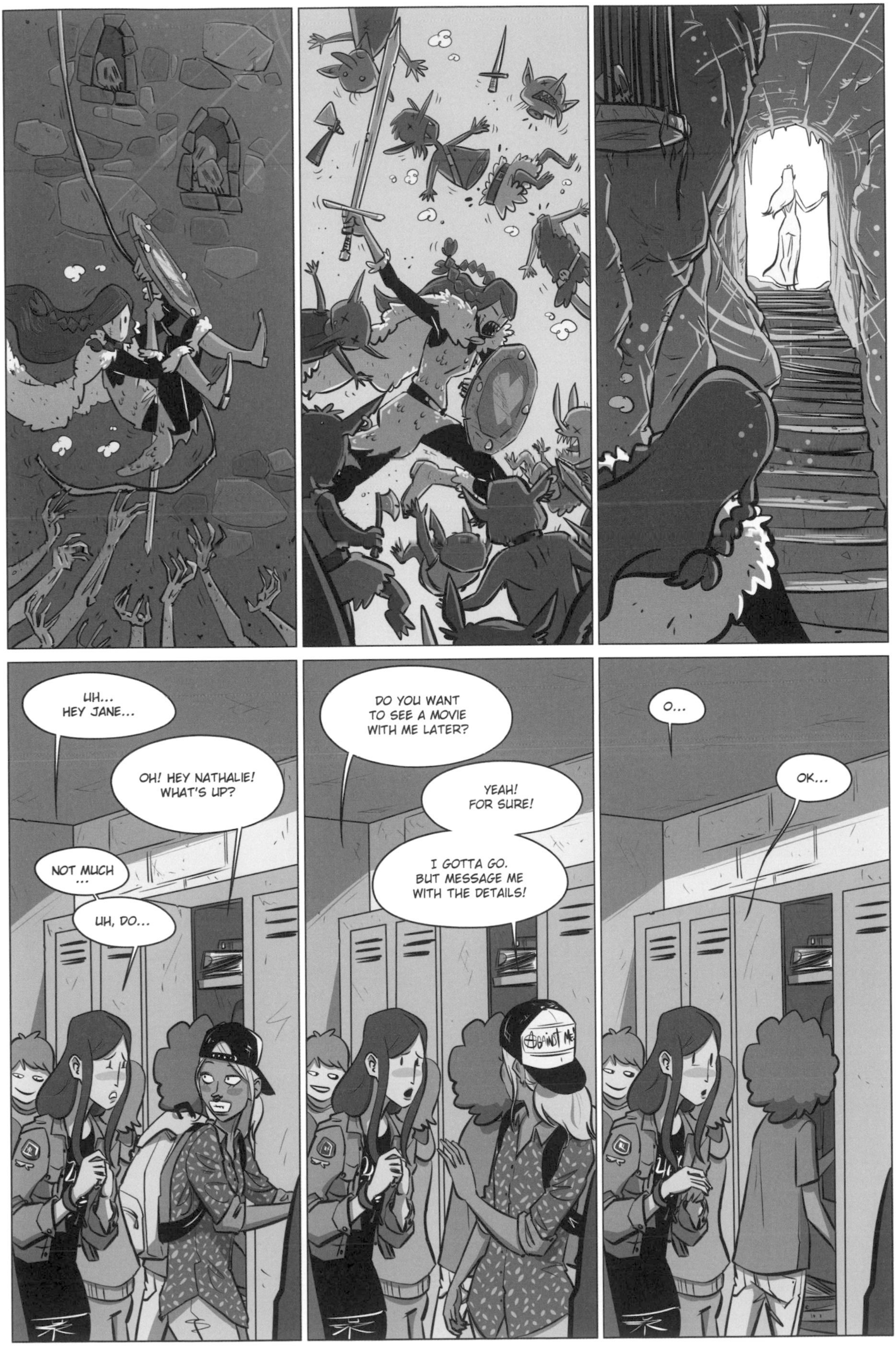
UH...
HEY JANE...
OH! HEY NATHALIE!
WHAT'S UP?
NOT MUCH
...
UH, DO...
DO YOU WANT
TO SEE A MOVIE
WITH ME LATER?
YEAH!
FOR SURE!
I GOTTA GO.
BUT MESSAGE ME
WITH THE DETAILS!
AGAINST ME
O...
OK...

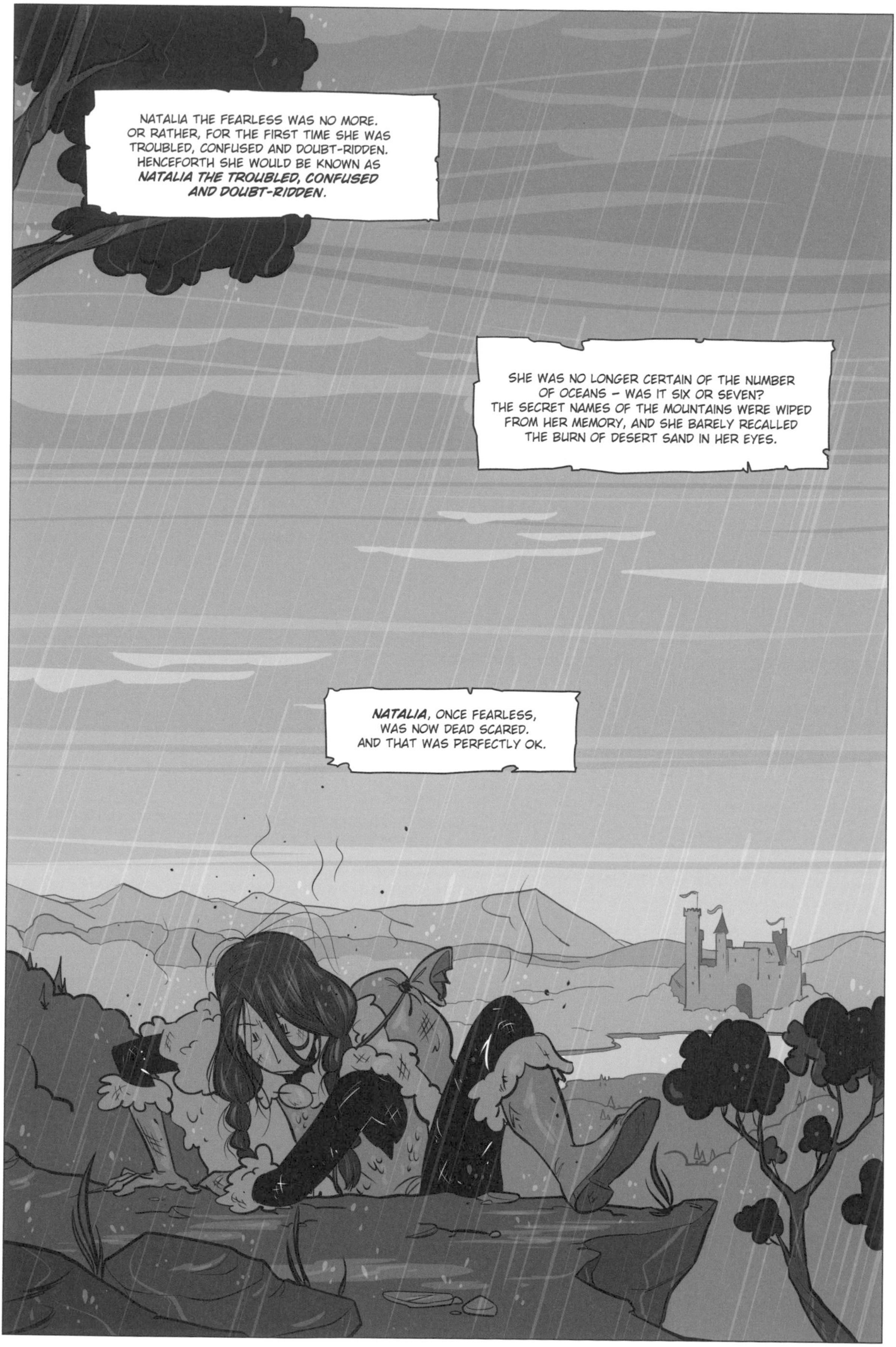
NATALIA THE FEARLESS WAS NO MORE. OR RATHER, FOR THE FIRST TIME SHE WAS TROUBLED, CONFUSED AND DOUBT-RIDDEN. HENCEFORTH SHE WOULD BE KNOWN AS ***NATALIA THE TROUBLED, CONFUSED AND DOUBT-RIDDEN***.
SHE WAS NO LONGER CERTAIN OF THE NUMBER OF OCEANS – WAS IT SIX OR SEVEN? THE SECRET NAMES OF THE MOUNTAINS WERE WIPED FROM HER MEMORY, AND SHE BARELY RECALLED THE BURN OF DESERT SAND IN HER EYES.
NATALIA, ONCE FEARLESS, WAS NOW DEAD SCARED. AND THAT WAS PERFECTLY OK.

- ***NAME:*** SASUKE, CAT OR STUPID CAT.

- ***AGE:*** NINTH YEAR OF HIS NINTH LIFE, BUT STILL NO WISER THAN A MAYFLY.

- ***HEIGHT:*** CAT HEIGHT.

- ***WEIGHT:*** A BIT MORE THAN IT SHOULD BE, BUT STILL FINE.

- ***ZODIAC SIGN:*** NO ONE CARES ABOUT ZODIAC SIGNS, BUT IF YOU REALLY NEED TO KNOW, HE'S A GEMINI.

- ***FAVORITE ANIMAL:*** THE ONLY LIVING CREATURE BIG OR SMALL THAT SASUKE LIKES IS MARIE. HE SHARES HIS TIME EQUALLY BETWEEN HATE AND RELAXATION.

- ***FAVORITE ACTIVITIES:*** GLARING HATEFULLY AT SQUIRRELS AND BIRDS THROUGH THE WINDOW, SLEEPING, PESTERING MARIE AND PLANNING TO ATTACK HIS ENEMIES (SO BASICALLY EVERYTHING AND EVERYONE).

- ***SPECIAL MOVE:*** WARRIOR BERSERK RAGE (USED 99% OF THE TIME AGAINST HIS CAT FOOD BAG).

- ***OTHER:*** THIS CAT IS DUMB, AND IS NAMED AFTER A NINJA FROM THE NARUTO SERIES, WHO IS JUST AS DUMB.

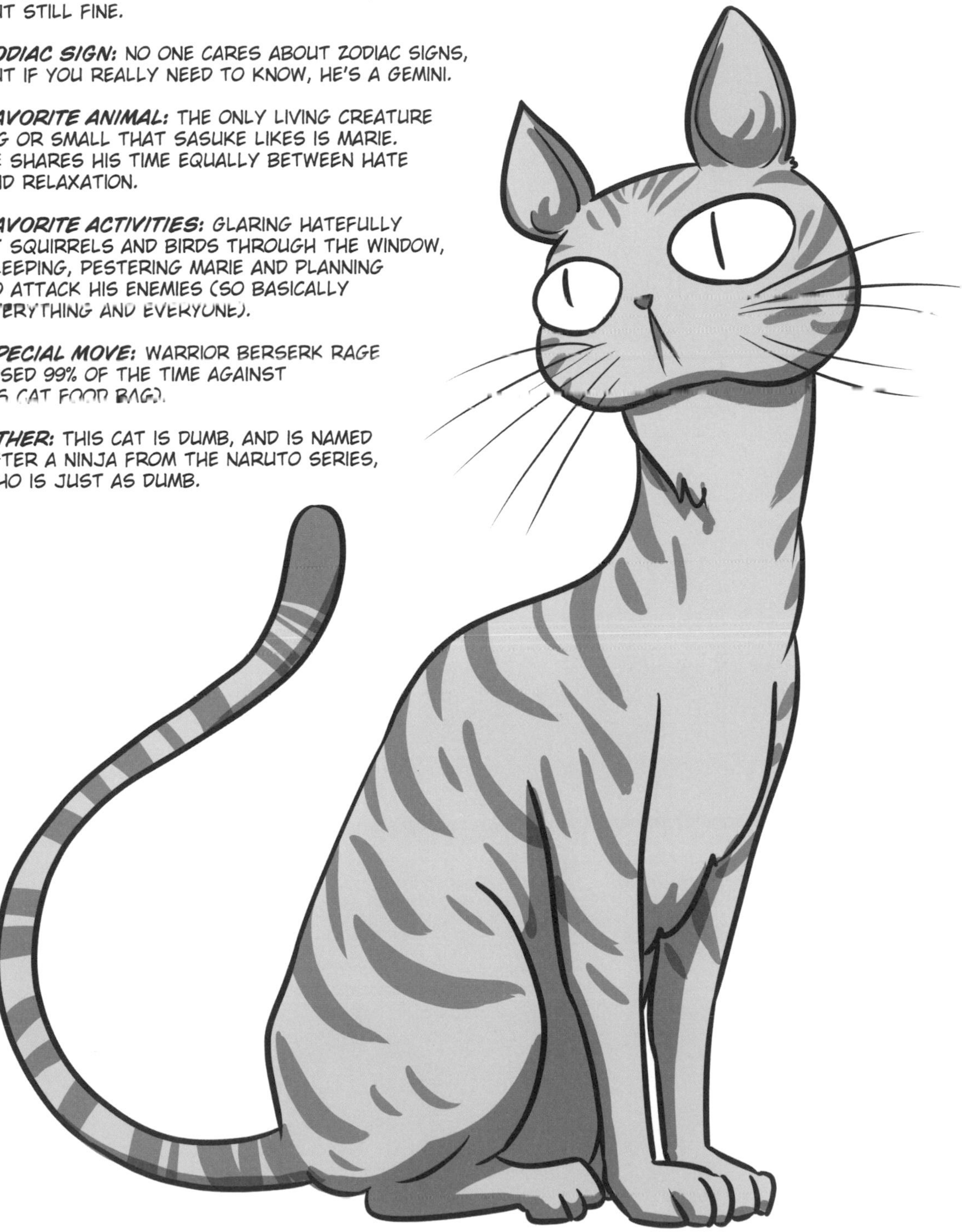

WHAT IF WE WERE... ROMANCE COLUMNISTS

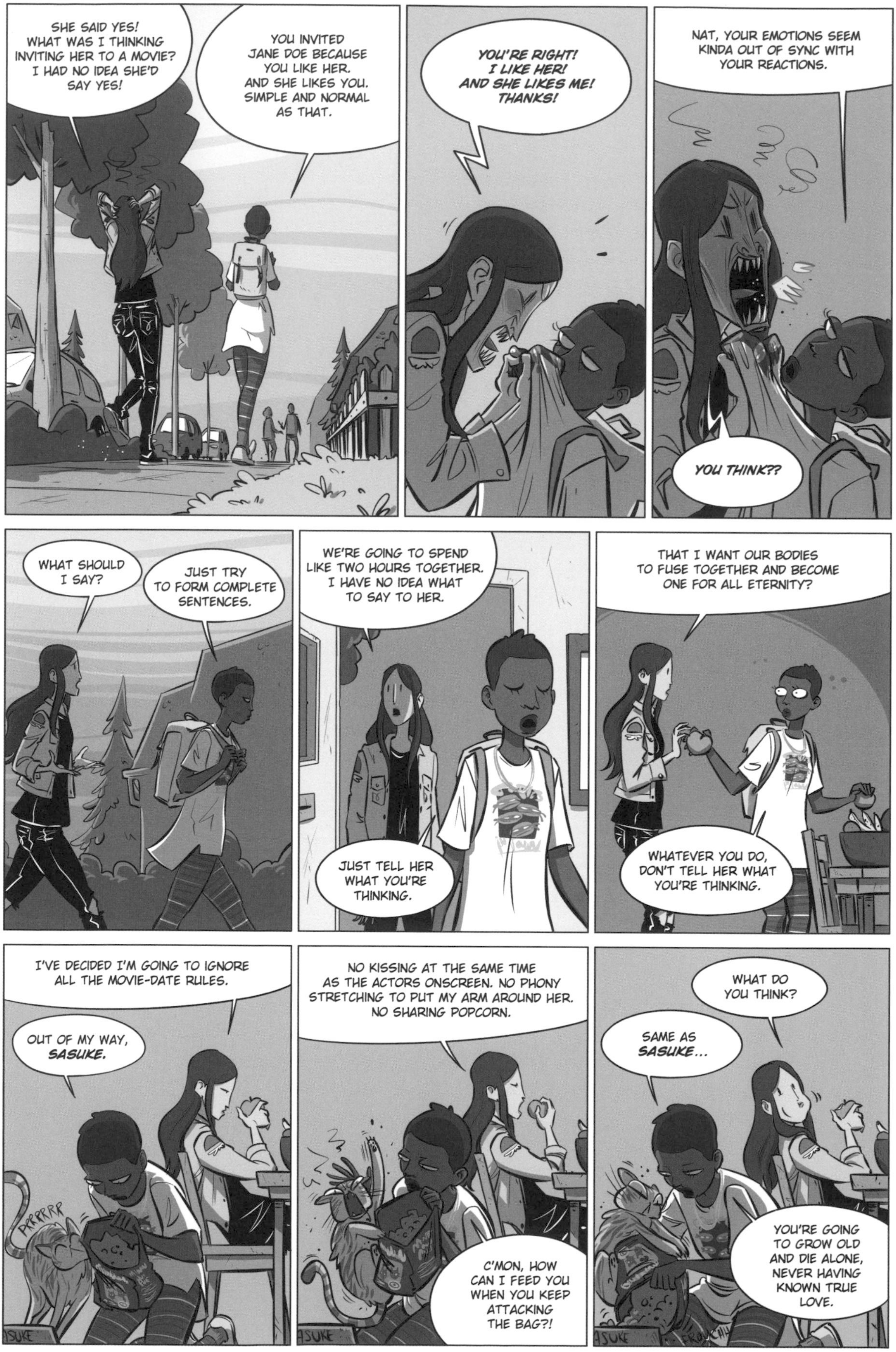
SHE SAID YES! WHAT WAS I THINKING INVITING HER TO A MOVIE? I HAD NO IDEA SHE'D SAY YES!
YOU INVITED JANE DOE BECAUSE YOU LIKE HER. AND SHE LIKES YOU. SIMPLE AND NORMAL AS THAT.
YOU'RE RIGHT! I LIKE HER! AND SHE LIKES ME! THANKS!
NAT, YOUR EMOTIONS SEEM KINDA OUT OF SYNC WITH YOUR REACTIONS.
YOU THINK??
WHAT SHOULD I SAY?
JUST TRY TO FORM COMPLETE SENTENCES.
WE'RE GOING TO SPEND LIKE TWO HOURS TOGETHER. I HAVE NO IDEA WHAT TO SAY TO HER.
JUST TELL HER WHAT YOU'RE THINKING.
THAT I WANT OUR BODIES TO FUSE TOGETHER AND BECOME ONE FOR ALL ETERNITY?
WHATEVER YOU DO, DON'T TELL HER WHAT YOU'RE THINKING.
I'VE DECIDED I'M GOING TO IGNORE ALL THE MOVIE-DATE RULES.
OUT OF MY WAY, SASUKE.
PRRRRRR
NO KISSING AT THE SAME TIME AS THE ACTORS ONSCREEN. NO PHONY STRETCHING TO PUT MY ARM AROUND HER. NO SHARING POPCORN.
C'MON, HOW CAN I FEED YOU WHEN YOU KEEP ATTACKING THE BAG?!
WHAT DO YOU THINK?
SAME AS SASUKE...
YOU'RE GOING TO GROW OLD AND DIE ALONE, NEVER HAVING KNOWN TRUE LOVE.

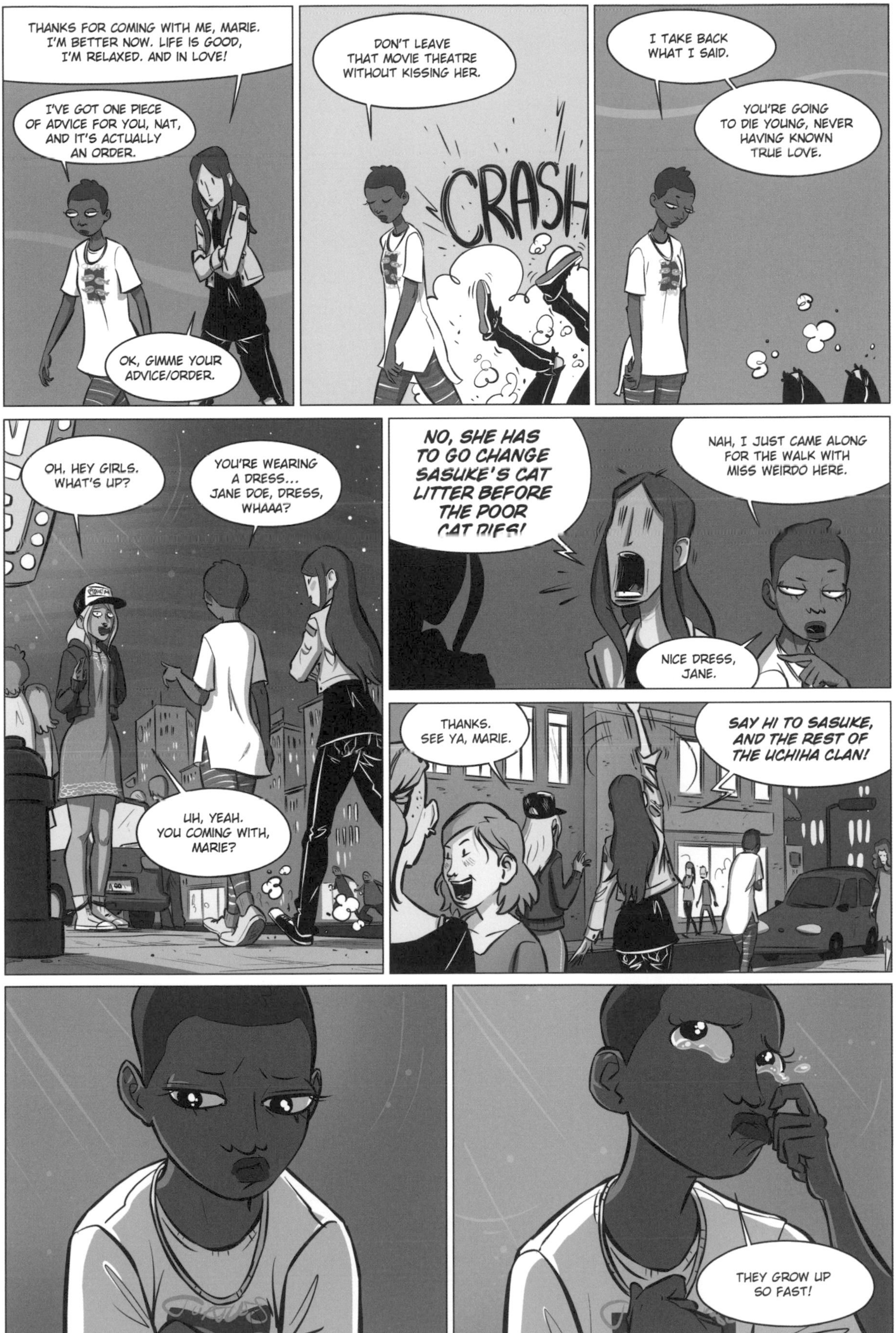
THANKS FOR COMING WITH ME, MARIE. I'M BETTER NOW. LIFE IS GOOD, I'M RELAXED. AND IN LOVE!
I'VE GOT ONE PIECE OF ADVICE FOR YOU, NAT, AND IT'S ACTUALLY AN ORDER.
OK, GIMME YOUR ADVICE/ORDER.
DON'T LEAVE THAT MOVIE THEATRE WITHOUT KISSING HER.
CRASH
I TAKE BACK WHAT I SAID.
YOU'RE GOING TO DIE YOUNG, NEVER HAVING KNOWN TRUE LOVE.
OH, HEY GIRLS. WHAT'S UP?
YOU'RE WEARING A DRESS... JANE DOE, DRESS, WHAAA?
UH, YEAH. YOU COMING WITH, MARIE?
NO, SHE HAS TO GO CHANGE SASUKE'S CAT LITTER BEFORE THE POOR CAT DIES!
NAH, I JUST CAME ALONG FOR THE WALK WITH MISS WEIRDO HERE.
NICE DRESS, JANE.
THANKS. SEE YA, MARIE.
SAY HI TO SASUKE, AND THE REST OF THE UCHIHA CLAN!
THEY GROW UP SO FAST!

WHAT IF WE WERE... ALL ALONE

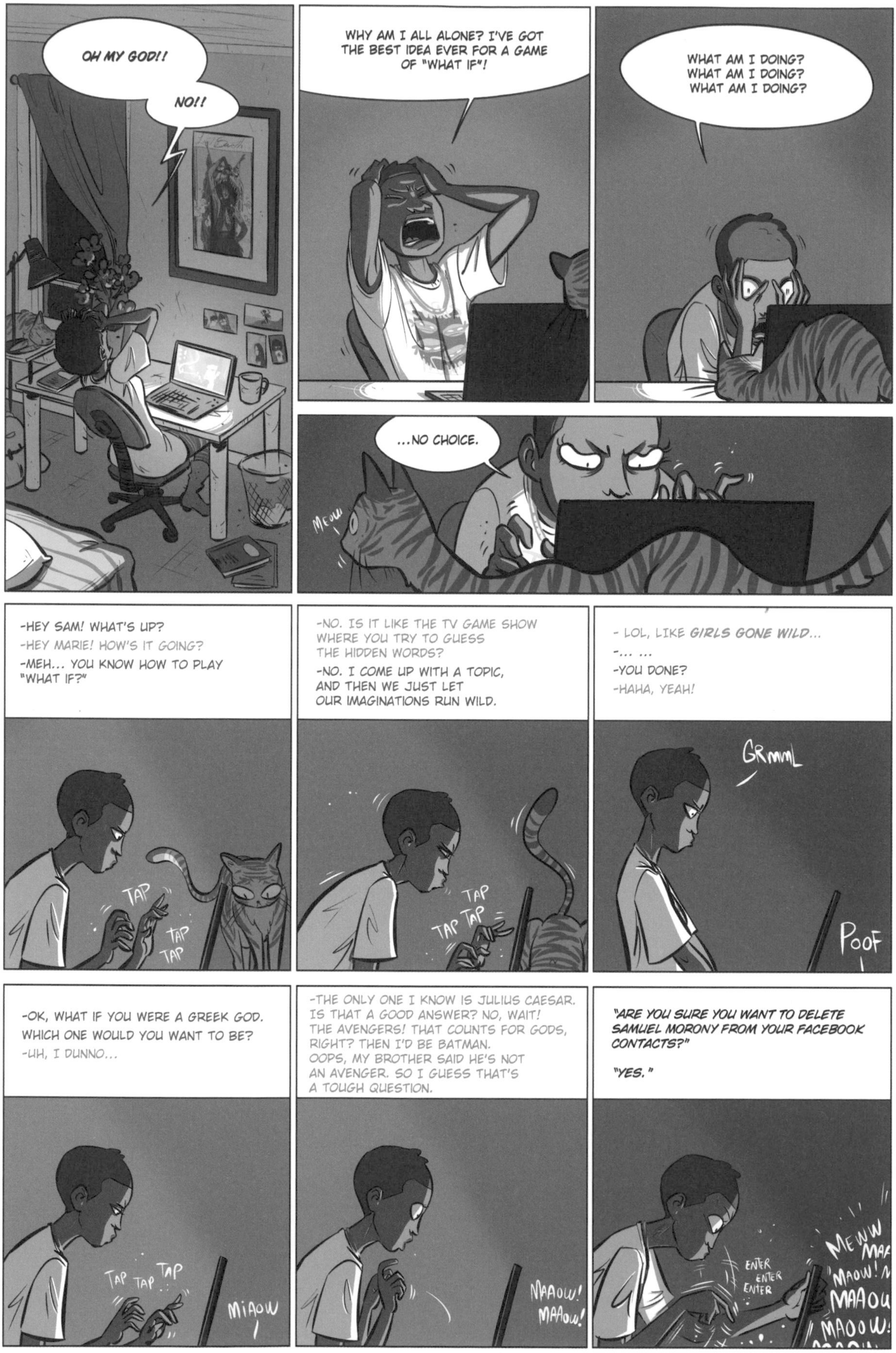
OH MY GOD!!
NO!!
WHY AM I ALL ALONE? I'VE GOT THE BEST IDEA EVER FOR A GAME OF "WHAT IF"!
WHAT AM I DOING? WHAT AM I DOING? WHAT AM I DOING?
...NO CHOICE.
MEOW
-HEY SAM! WHAT'S UP?
-HEY MARIE! HOW'S IT GOING?
-MEH... YOU KNOW HOW TO PLAY "WHAT IF?"
TAP TAP TAP
-NO. IS IT LIKE THE TV GAME SHOW WHERE YOU TRY TO GUESS THE HIDDEN WORDS?
-NO. I COME UP WITH A TOPIC, AND THEN WE JUST LET OUR IMAGINATIONS RUN WILD.
TAP TAP TAP
- LOL, LIKE GIRLS GONE WILD...
-... ...
-YOU DONE?
-HAHA, YEAH!
GRMML
POOF
-OK, WHAT IF YOU WERE A GREEK GOD. WHICH ONE WOULD YOU WANT TO BE?
-UH, I DUNNO...
TAP TAP TAP
MIAOW
-THE ONLY ONE I KNOW IS JULIUS CAESAR. IS THAT A GOOD ANSWER? NO, WAIT! THE AVENGERS! THAT COUNTS FOR GODS, RIGHT? THEN I'D BE BATMAN. OOPS, MY BROTHER SAID HE'S NOT AN AVENGER. SO I GUESS THAT'S A TOUGH QUESTION.
MAAOW! MAAOW!
"ARE YOU SURE YOU WANT TO DELETE SAMUEL MORONY FROM YOUR FACEBOOK CONTACTS?"
"YES."
ENTER ENTER ENTER
MEWW
MAOW!
MAAOU
MAOOW!

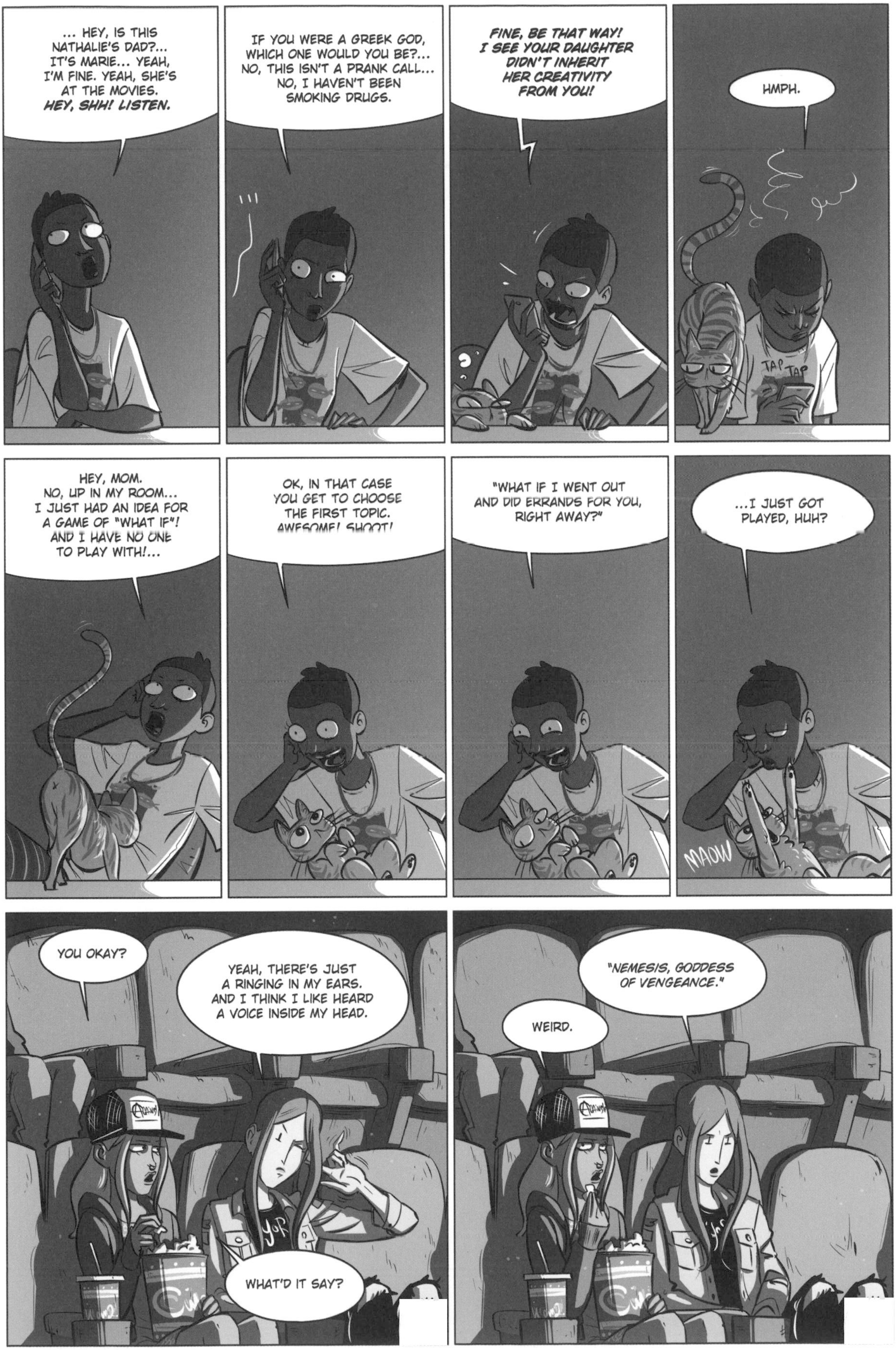
... HEY, IS THIS NATHALIE'S DAD?... IT'S MARIE... YEAH, I'M FINE. YEAH, SHE'S AT THE MOVIES. HEY, SHH! LISTEN.
IF YOU WERE A GREEK GOD, WHICH ONE WOULD YOU BE?... NO, THIS ISN'T A PRANK CALL... NO, I HAVEN'T BEEN SMOKING DRUGS.
FINE, BE THAT WAY! I SEE YOUR DAUGHTER DIDN'T INHERIT HER CREATIVITY FROM YOU!
HMPH.
TAP TAP
HEY, MOM. NO, UP IN MY ROOM... I JUST HAD AN IDEA FOR A GAME OF "WHAT IF"! AND I HAVE NO ONE TO PLAY WITH!...
OK, IN THAT CASE YOU GET TO CHOOSE THE FIRST TOPIC. AWESOME! SHOOT!
"WHAT IF I WENT OUT AND DID ERRANDS FOR YOU, RIGHT AWAY?"
...I JUST GOT PLAYED, HUH?
MAOW
YOU OKAY?
YEAH, THERE'S JUST A RINGING IN MY EARS. AND I THINK I LIKE HEARD A VOICE INSIDE MY HEAD.
WHAT'D IT SAY?
"NEMESIS, GODDESS OF VENGEANCE."
WEIRD.

WHAT IF WE WERE... AT THE MOVIES

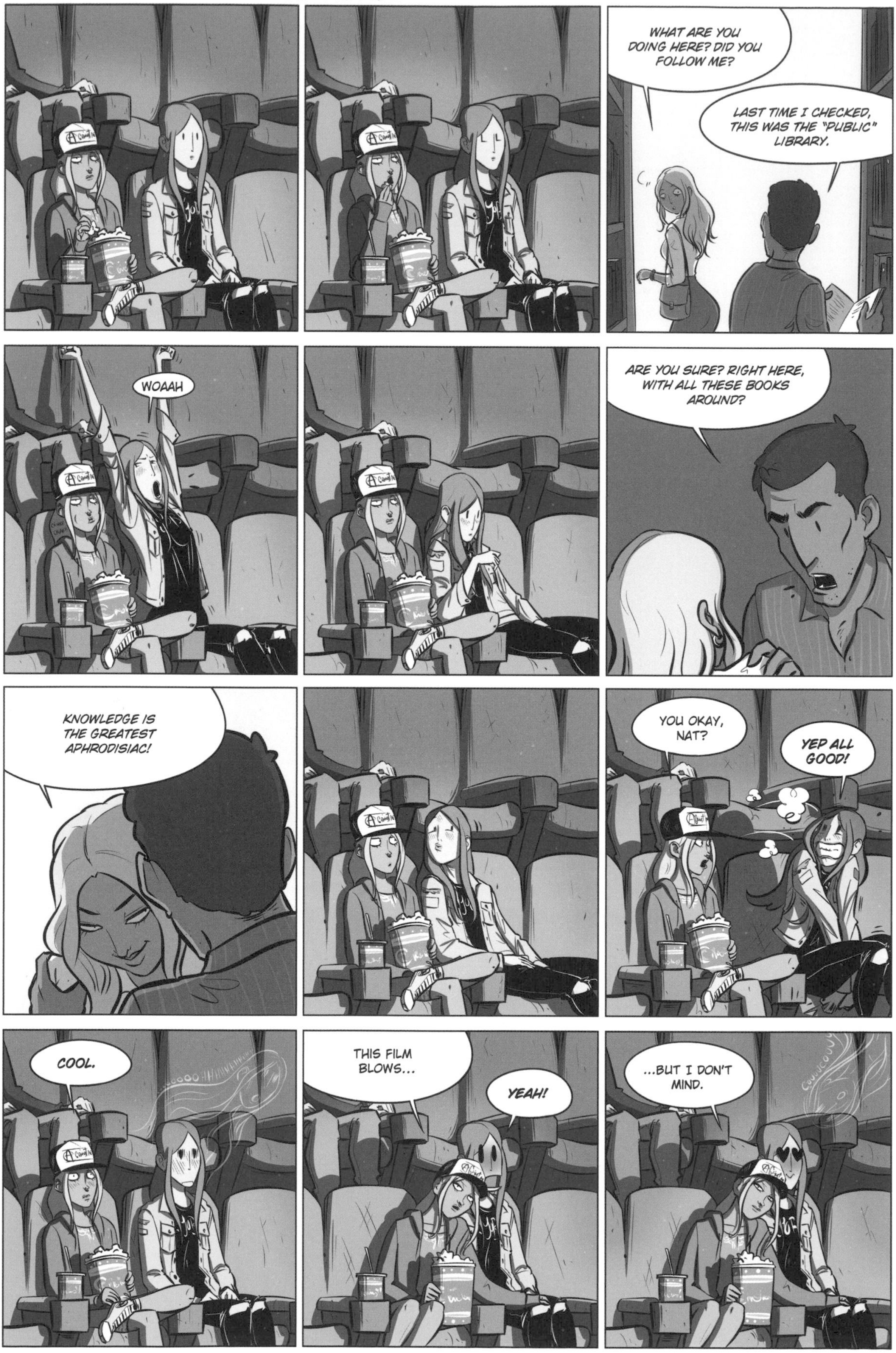
WHAT ARE YOU DOING HERE? DID YOU FOLLOW ME?
LAST TIME I CHECKED, THIS WAS THE "PUBLIC" LIBRARY.
WOAAH
ARE YOU SURE? RIGHT HERE, WITH ALL THESE BOOKS AROUND?
KNOWLEDGE IS THE GREATEST APHRODISIAC!
YOU OKAY, NAT?
YEP ALL GOOD!
COOL.
THIS FILM BLOWS...
YEAH!
...BUT I DON'T MIND.

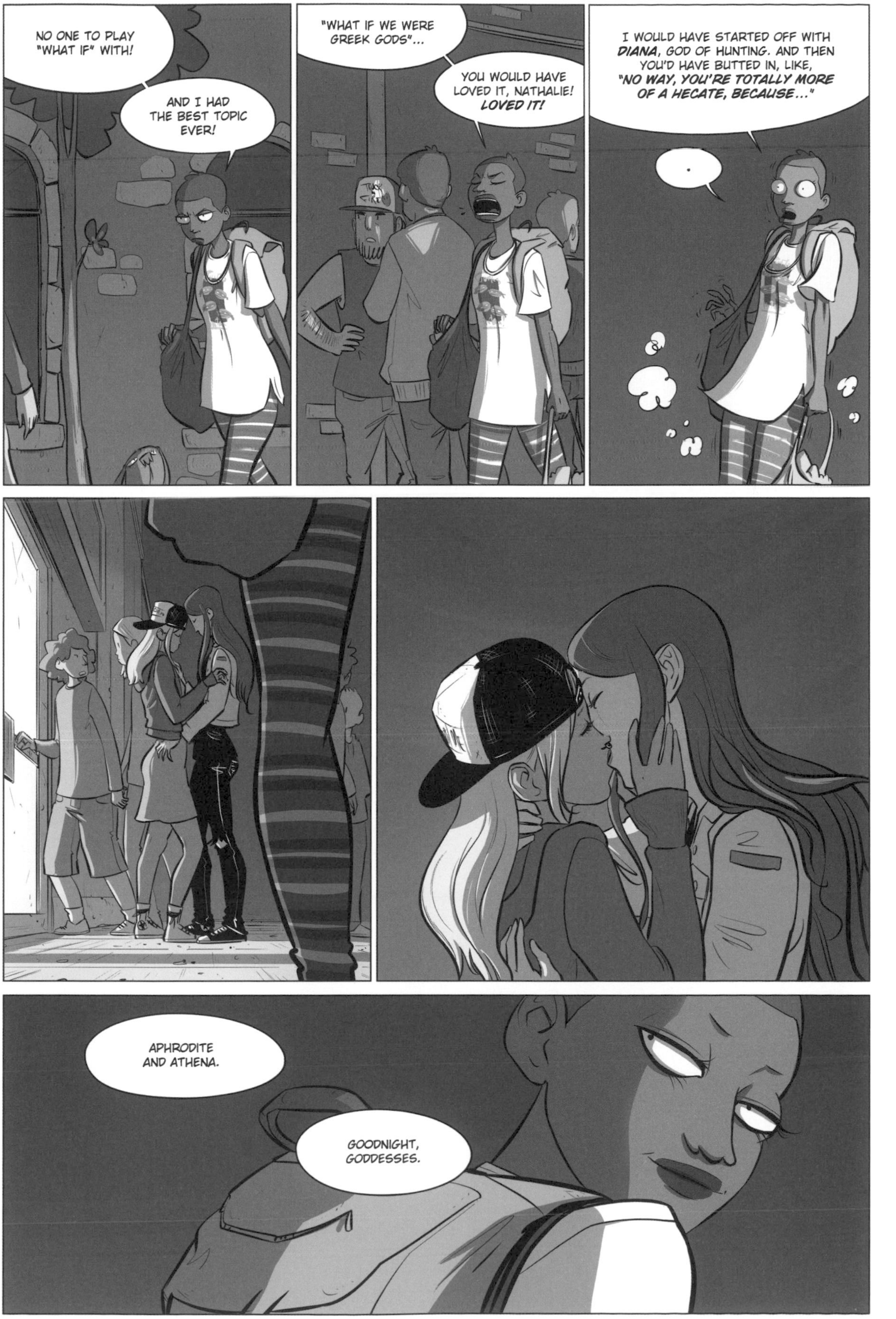

NO ONE TO PLAY "WHAT IF" WITH!
AND I HAD THE BEST TOPIC EVER!
"WHAT IF WE WERE GREEK GODS"...
YOU WOULD HAVE LOVED IT, NATHALIE! ***LOVED IT!***
I WOULD HAVE STARTED OFF WITH ***DIANA***, GOD OF HUNTING. AND THEN YOU'D HAVE BUTTED IN, LIKE, ***"NO WAY, YOU'RE TOTALLY MORE OF A HECATE, BECAUSE..."***
.
APHRODITE AND ATHENA.
GOODNIGHT, GODDESSES.

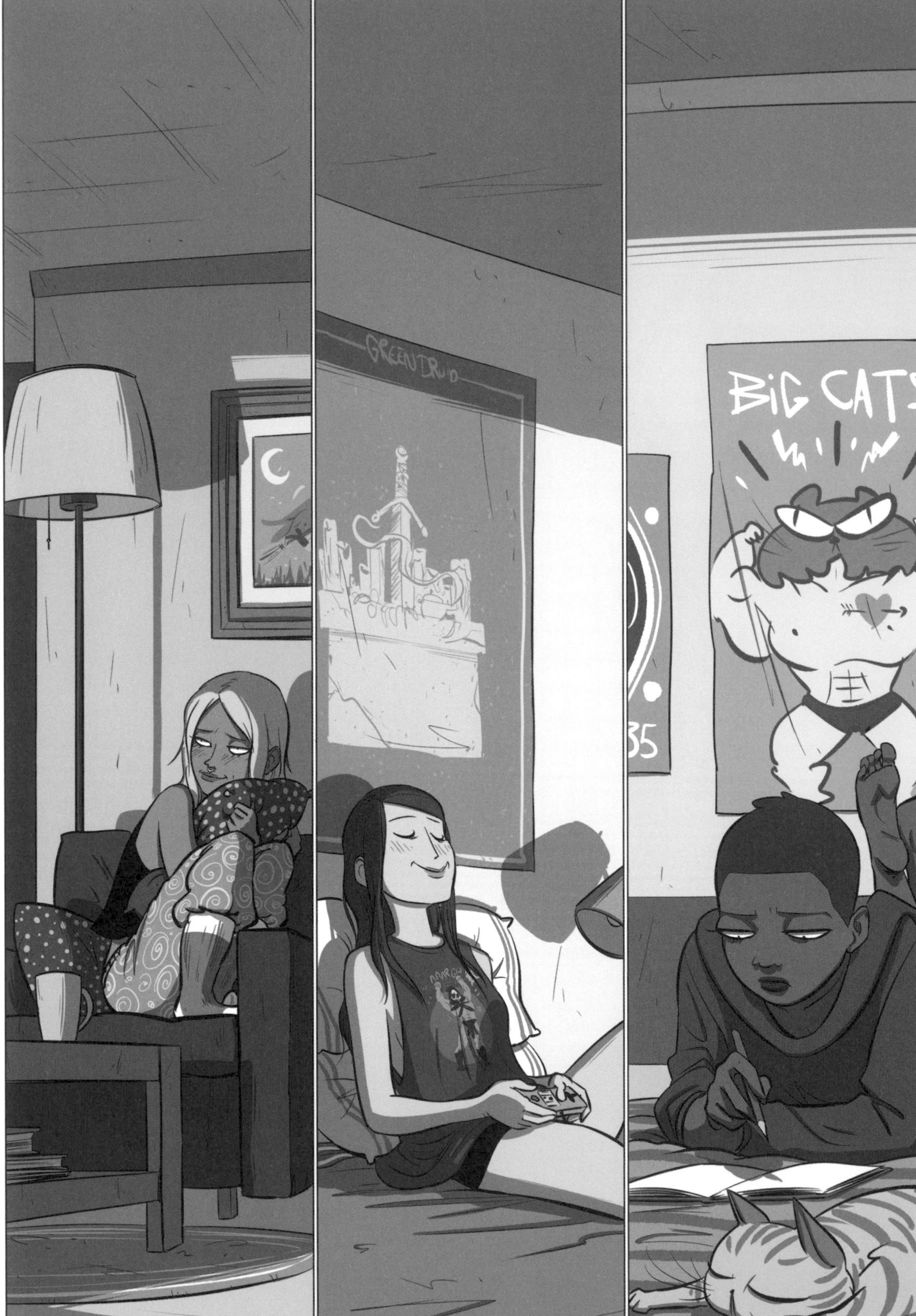
BiG CATS

DEAR DIARY,

IT FINALLY HAPPENED. NATHALIE AND JANE. I'M SO HAPPY FOR THEM, BUT I FEEL WEIRD ABOUT IT AT THE SAME TIME. I CRIED WHEN I GOT HOME. AND THEN I CRIED AGAIN. ONCE BECAUSE THERE WERE NO MORE PEANUT BUTTER COOKIES LEFT, AND ONCE BECAUSE MY MOM ASKED IF I'D SEEN THE REMOTE. THEN I LAUGHED MY HEAD OFF WATCHING A VIDEO OF GOATS PASSING OUT FOR NO REASON. IT WAS LIKE THE 350TH TIME I'VE SEEN IT. I SHOULDN'T HAVE FOUND IT THAT FUNNY. AM I LOSING IT?

AND EVERYTHING WAS GOING SO WELL JUST A FEW HOURS EARLIER. I WAS SURFING THROUGH LIFE LIKE A - LIKE A SURFER RIDING A SURFBOARD OVER THE WAVES. (WOW, MY ENGLISH TEACHER MIGHT NOT BE CRAZY ABOUT THAT SIMILE. ANYWAY...) SO NOW MY BOARD IS BROKEN, THERE ARE NO MORE WAVES LEFT, AND A SHARK BIT OFF HALF MY LEG. (MUCH BETTER, MARIE! EXCELLENT WORK.) (NOTE TO SELF: WRITE POEM ABOUT SURFING.)

I'M NOT JEALOUS!! NOT AT ALL!! I DON'T EVEN KNOW WHAT JEALOUSY WOULD FEEL LIKE. (IS IT COOL?) IT JUST FEELS LIKE THIS MIGHT BE THE END OF AN ERA. NATHALIE'S LIFE IS GOING TO CHANGE A LOT, AND THAT MEANS MINE WILL TOO. AND THAT'S JUST FINE. CHANGE IS GOOD.... IT'S JUST THAT I LIKED THE LIFE WE HAD, SO MUCH! I'M NOT AFRAID JANE IS GOING TO TAKE NATHALIE AWAY FROM ME, EXACTLY; I FEEL LIKE LIFE IS GOING TO TAKE CARE OF THAT. MAYBE IN A MONTH OR TWO SHE'LL GET BORED OF ME? I KNOW, HARD TO IMAGINE ANYONE GETTING BORED OF ME, BUT ANYTHING IS POSSIBLE. I HAVE TO BE MENTALLY PREPARED. HMM... NAH, THAT WON'T HAPPEN.

I HOPE NATHALIE WILL BE HAPPY. I HOPE JANE DOE WILL BE NICE, AND WON'T HURT HER. SHE BETTER NOT, UNLESS SHE WANTS TO SEE ME TRANSFORM FROM THE SURFER WITH NO WAVES INTO A NUCLEAR MEGALODON SHARK READY TO EAT HER BEST FRIEND'S NEW GIRLFRIEND! KIDDING! CALM DOWN, MARIE. JANE'S A NICE PERSON. ALSO YOU DON'T KNOW HOW TO SURF.

ALRIGHT, I'M GOING TO GO CRY ONE MORE TIME, FORCE SASUKE TO CONSOLE ME, AND THEN GO TO BED. TOMORROW WILL BE A NICE DAY, THE BIRDS WILL BE CHIRPING AGAIN, AND I'LL BE READY TO CONQUER THE WORLD AGAIN.

PEACE

SHIT, IT'S SUPPOSED TO RAIN TOMORROW... AND WE HAVE BORING-ASS MATH CLASS... HEY DIARY, WE'VE GOT A DISCUSSION TO HAVE ABOUT THE POINTLESSNESS OF MATH CLASS. THERE'S NO POINT HAVING SUCH EASY QUIZZES. I MEAN, WHY ARE PEOPLE EVEN STRESSING ABOUT IT? THE ANSWERS ARE ALL IN THE QUESTIONS. I GUESS IT'S JUST ONE MORE OF LIFE'S MYSTERIES.

I GUESS... BYE.

HEY! HOW THE HELL DO I KNOW WHAT A MEGALODON IS? WHAT'S GOING ON WITH ME? AM I SOMEHOW LEARNING ALL KINDS OF THINGS AGAINST MY WILL? I'M GOING TO HAVE TO FIGURE THIS OUT. AND NOT ONE WORD TO NAT! BEING THE "DEEP" ONE IS HER THING, I DON'T WANT TO STE L HER PERSONALITY. POOR BABY.

OK, BYE FOR REAL NOW.

WHAT'S NEXT FOR MARIE, NATHALIE, JANE DOE AND SASUKE THE CAT?

-PRIMARY SCHOOL FLASHBACKS
-NATHALIE GOES PRINCESS-CRAZY
-THE ORIGIN STORY OF ***WHAT IF***
-MARIE BREAKS THE UNIVERSE
(FOR REAL!)
-SASUKE'S STILL JUST AS DUMB
-AND THE GIRLS' NEW LOOKS

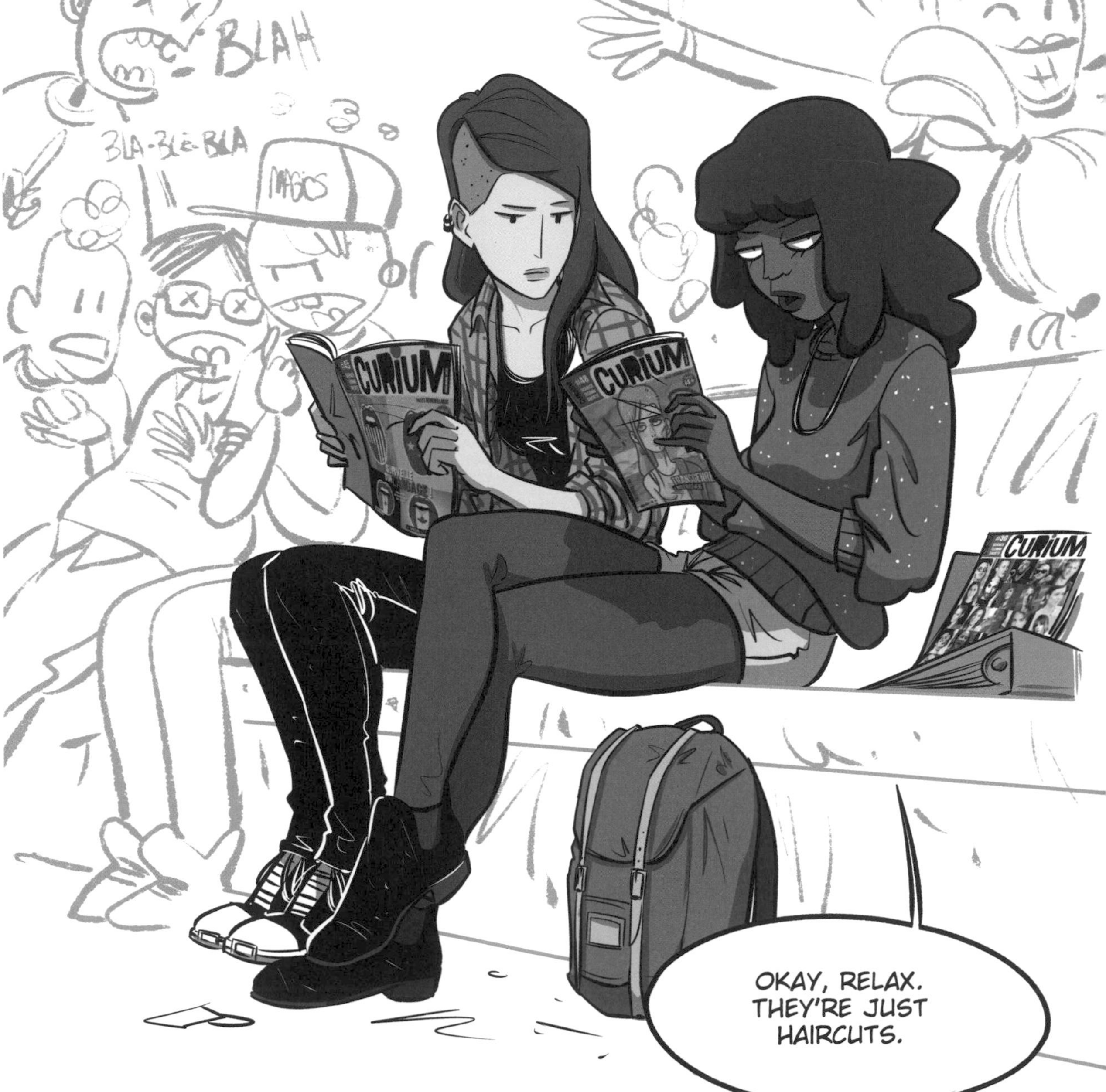
BLAH
BLA-BLE-BLA
CURIUM
CURIUM
CURIUM
OKAY, RELAX. THEY'RE JUST HAIRCUTS.

WEB SITE:
AXELLELENOIR.COM

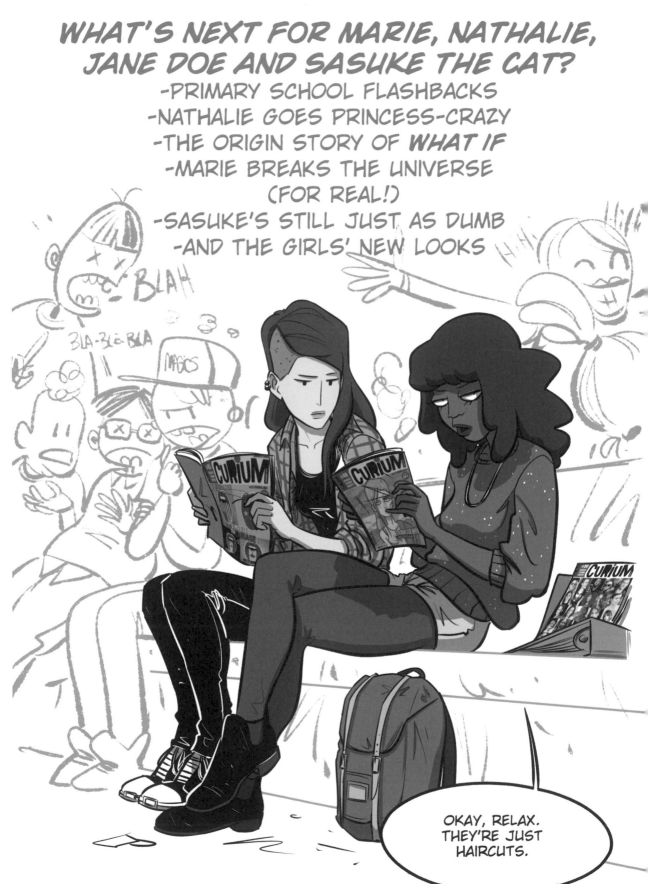

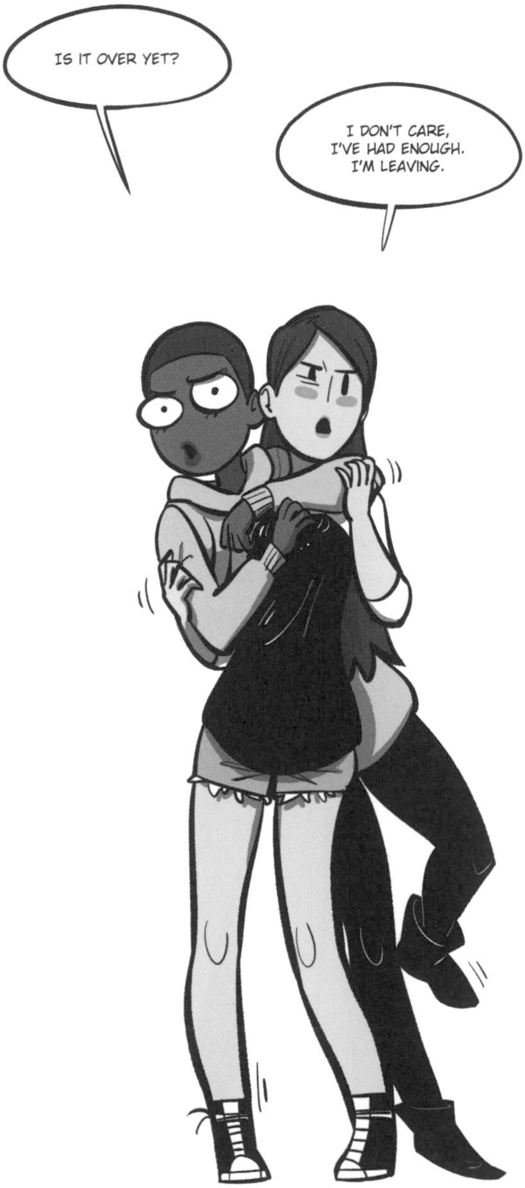
IS IT OVER YET?
I DON'T CARE, I'VE HAD ENOUGH. I'M LEAVING.

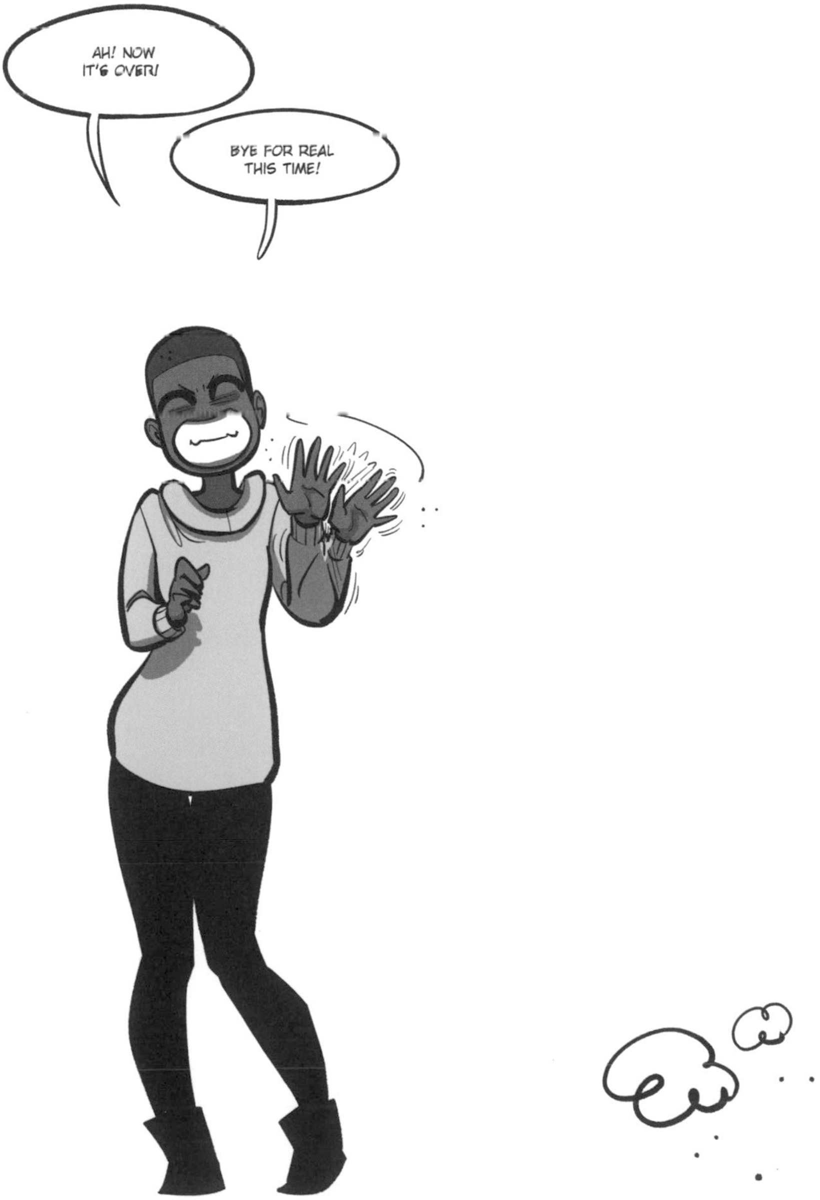
AH! NOW IT'S OVER!
BYE FOR REAL THIS TIME!

WHAT IF
WE WERE
...